COME TRAILING BLOOD

Paul Smith was born and raised in Dublin. His education has been rather do-it-yourself. He left school when he was eight. His first job was driving a donkey and coal cart, his last regular job was teaching English at Uppsala in Sweden.

This, his first novel published in the United States in 1959 (now published in Great Britain for the first time), was hailed immediately by the critics.

Reviewing the original American edition of this novel, Dorothy Parker wrote in *Esquire*: 'Paul Smith can combine black terror with riotous hilarity - rather in the same way that O'Casey can do it. I realize that to put a writer's name on the same page with that of Sean O'Casey is giddily high praise. But now, I think, is the time for it. And so, ladies and gentlemen, Mr Paul Smith . . .'

COME TRAILING BLOOD

Ω————————————————————————

PAUL SMITH

QUARTET BOOKS   LONDON, MELBOURNE, NEW YORK

This book was first published under the title
Esther's Altar
by Abelard-Schuman, New York, 1959

First published in Great Britain,
in an edition revised and retitled by the author,
by Quartet Books Limited 1977
A member of the Namara Group
27 Goodge Street, London W1P 1FD

ISBN 0 7043 2138 6

Typesetting by Bedford Typesetters Limited

Printed in Great Britain by litho at The Anchor Press Ltd
and bound by Wm Brendon & Son Ltd
both of Tiptree, Essex

For Vanessa Redgrave

Earth does not understand her child,
  Who from the loud gregarious town
Returns depleted and defiled,
  To the still woods, to fling him down.

Earth cannot count the sons she bore:
  The wounded lynx, the wounded man
Come trailing blood unto her door;
  She shelters both as best she can.

EDNA ST VINCENT MILLAY
from *The Return*

ONE

EASTER MONDAY

1

As if in search of miracles or martyrdom a single solitary swan in revived assurance slid over the sullen waters of the Grand Canal. Along the banks trees in their ritual celebration of renewal shook in a noise that had begun in the dark and was distant, but now, in the glaze of morning, was coming closer and sharper. Across from the trees on the left bank and separated from them by a narrow cobbled road, a line of four-storey tenements with rail-fenced basements stood stunned in the glare of an unmerciful sun, their windows still darkened into black as if death had flown through them and left the shadows of its wings. Through the hall of Number Twelve a damp wind keened its way from the clothes-line-strung backyard and out the door which Janey Reilly left swinging open behind her as she came venting her fury at the sham hypocrisy of the world into which she had awakened that morning.

"Ah! Put a sock in it, ya tea-guzzler!" Janey screamed back into the empty hall and stood listening as her voice accurately aimed rocketed up through the quiet house before her attention was caught and held by the knob on the door of the parlor on her right. She stood with eyes unflinching watching the brazen glitter of brass caught in the sun, then turned and the hall door swung to behind her. Suspecting the morning she paused to test it, then she began to swing the empty milk can she carried against the railings of the basement. A curtain was lifted on the window of the room on her right and a hand motioned her off and away.

"Ah, keep your hair on!" she cried, "I'm going." But she didn't. Instead and with demoniac exuberance she clattered the can off the railings again, then sat down where she was on the top step. Her eyes blue and clear-cut went with annihilating mockery on a streel of the houses and the deserted canal that would later, when the day was well aired, tumble into life: with the kids first, spurting out the doors; followed by the men, out in tight only-worn-on-Sunday suits, moving with foxy caution and hidden grins of expectancy towards the pubs and the hair of the dog which today would have to be chalked up, their reserved-for-Mass-going pious faces watched anxiously from the windows by their wives who would see them out of sight before they began to scream at the kids, the screams assaulting the red hair-tipped ears of Protestant shopkeepers with the mouths of governesses – out with their scrubbed woollen-stockinged children, to take with spinsterly precision the soft air of the canal, their cold expression-less expressions contrasting with the almost moronic everything-in-the-garden's-lovely ease of their Catholic customers, and tenants ever ready to nod a greeting from the windows or dip a head or bend a knee at the sight of their betters or at the approaching footfall of a priest. In the afternoon, when the men came back from the pubs the women would leave the windows and the kids be locked out and the mothers and fathers take to their beds, for fathers and mothers were always sick on Sundays; and Bank Holidays were no better.

A burst of strange internal anger tore itself loose from Janey's mouth as she urged her eyes to the bridge and the corner of the street that went to meet it, encountering in their journey a young man who held himself with military erectness despite his crutch and who was heading towards her from the direction of Rock Street. She named him, and dismissed him, but kept him in sight as he drew alongside her and began climbing the steps.

"And how are you, Janey?" he asked as he went past and through the door, but she didn't answer for she had long ago measured Ba Fay's worth to her. Then muttering her feelings only

2

when she heard an inner door open and close she said, "A lot the better at meeting you, you oul' ram." She spoke over a woman's laugh which she could hear in the house behind her and over the loud roar of the water churning in the locks at the bridge and which now took her attention for the first time, leaving her deaf to the other, sharper sounds coming from the heart of the city on which her pinafored back was turned. She thought about the water. Listened to its roar as it rushed through the lock gates to the dark green depths below and saw its floundering as it crashed in foaming impotence at the granite walls which were just about able to confine it. The watery inferno of the locks had held most, if not all, Janey's real and imagined enemies, beginning with the nun who was her teacher at the convent school and ending with Christina Swords, her latest victim; but this morning, that had begun earlier than most, the dead under-water eyes of Christina Swords failed to hold her attention and she turned away – giving her mind to the other sounds and then she dismissed these also, and once again her glance swept in contempt the deserted canal.

"Nothing ever happens in this place," she said, and her lips hardly moving were thoughtful with bitterness and sun.

But something *was*. Morning was coming with merciless continuity and formal order. Somewhere a bronze cock was screaming the legend of day. A bell chimed in the church in Leeson Park and was echoed by another from the nearer church the Protestants had lifted. In the distance the Dublin mountains, under a scattering of snow, reared up to chalky puffs of tenuous cloud – and along the canal gulls on enormous wings gargled with bland indifference the glazed morning. Through the trees the wind waved, stroking, fingering bones, drawing blood, and the sun which was powerless to melt Janey Reilly's seething discontent was nevertheless warming with a brazen wantonness the birthpangs of a new revolution. Today was Easter Monday, the year was 1916, and in the churches yesterday they were crying joyfully, 'Christ Has Risen!' But today in the sun, in the streets behind her, they were saying Ireland had risen, casting aside after centuries of oppression the shackles of her bondage, stretching her torn limbs in the exulting life-giving sun, bearing her wounds with pride towards the High Altar of freedom promised her by a handful of men unskilled in the art of

3

war, and with only boys for warriors and dreams for ammunition. But it was enough. In war the first success was everything. And the luck of the moment was with them. The auguries were good, for wasn't England with her social, military and political pressures up to her murderous neck in war with Germany? And if Ireland was ever to strike a blow for freedom now was the time. And what matter if in the doing the gutters were to run heavy with the blood of idealists? There were more where they came from. Idealists were born in every generation. Besides God helped those who helped themselves. And in the meantime there was the climax to the first few weeks of hasty planning to get them past the first hurdle of mounting shock.

But for Janey Reilly nothing was happening, and she was sitting hugging her own laborious melancholy to herself when the door opened behind her and a man said softly, "Janey! C'm'ere!"

"Shove off!" she answered without turning to discover whose voice was cutting in.

Then the man stood beside her, and bent, or sagged to examine. She saw the large pores in the large fleshy nose – saw the drink-bleary eyes twitch in cunning and her own unmercifully blue flashed their own white warning. "I hear," Hammy Collins said, "that Christina Swords caught you trying to lift her bit a brass yesterday."

Janey rose to her feet.

"You're light-fingered, Janey," he said and laughed sly. "Need to watch yourself or them fingers of yours could land you in trouble." He paused, and smiling, tilted his head sideways and down. "When I heard you had tried to deprive Christina of her one and only possession, I said to myself, 'That young wan'll be the death of Christina Swords.' " He went on, as Janey stepped back, not listening but watching, wanting to smash the mouth in the slack-jawed face; but she could do nothing but stand and listen until, on a change of mood, he said "Ah, but you're a good child and I said so when Christina was going on about you." He reached out and put his hand as gently as he could on her shoulder but she rid herself of the hand in one quick shrug.

"Anyway, like the rack and the thumbscrew, what happened yesterday is over and done with," he said with a grin. "What

4

I wanted to ask you about is that watch!"

Her glance, which for a fraction of a second had been lowered, lifted and took aim at him. And suddenly a little smile crept onto her pale face.

"Ah, the watch you took off the MacDonalds' mantelpiece. Remember?"

Janey could have nodded.

"Where is it?" he asked quietly. "We could make a bit on that watch you and me." His voice furred and his breath fell in sappy spray onto her pale lips shining from bites and parted over the bony structure of teeth. She raised her head and now her blue eyes were staring at him with a peculiar look. They wore a filmed softness, like eyes that have been washed with milk.

He drew close and she let him until his face was touching hers. He could see the veins of her eyeballs with all their tributaries. Their lashes locked. She made a breathing sound then into his eyes and with quiet venom she hissed, "Rat shit!" She wrenched herself free and saw him stagger back against the railings – then brace to grab, but she sidestepped the raised arm and in one spring was laughing up at him from the pavement.

"Hammy the Hands! Hanseling the day with the few shillings scabbed from his wife's fancy man." She moved a step closer and stared up with pure hatred. "That watch isn't all you'd like, is it Hammy?" She swept back her hair with a solid hand, then turned and walked away, dismissing him as her mind clawed Christina Swords. She hadn't thought the house would hear about the door-knob, though she supposed she should've known Christina Swords wouldn't be able to keep a thing like that to herself. Well, one of these days Christina Swords would be sorry she hadn't. One of these days . . . She turned the corner into the street and from where he stood on the top step Hammy Collins watched her.

"Fuckin little bitch!" he said. He should've left the watch alone. Till after. Was she leggier today? And her tits? Could've sworn they'd been jolted into sudden flesh! Something not shagging right about that young wan! Wasn't frightened of her. Just something . . . Fuckin raging yeah but not frightened! Not him and just to prove it he'd wait till she came back and . . . Intention died at crotch level. 'Fuckin demon she was.' He

5

turned back into the hall, his step jaunty and light when he reached the room.

His wife Maisie looked at him, but there was no pause in what she was saying to the man sitting on the edge of the bed watching her push her hair into place with wide tortoise-shell combs. "And since when, I asked, have you cared about what's going on in the world as long as you can go to your four Masses a day!" Maisie paused and Ba Fay grinned. He hadn't looked at Hammy. "What I want to know is," Maisie went on, "does that woman think I've reached the age of forty being lightminded?"

"All right. Quit that now and give us a clean collar!" Hammy said.

"Of course I will," she answered over her shoulder. "It's on the pianner."

"Don't tell me you haven't one?"

Maisie drew her gaze from the depths of the looking glass over the mantelpiece, and under the force of it Hammy shifted uneasy. "I wouldn't dream of telling you any such thing," she said. "The wonder is I talk to you at all." She surveyed her husband's face, sprouting a sandy growth of beard that he removed only on Sundays.

His glance fell. He fussed with the belt holding up his trousers and moved away to the door where his coat hung.

"Jasus! you're the cool customer."

She watched his near-grin mask an anger he didn't dare loose on her with Ba Fay in the room. "And what, if you don't mind my asking, did you use for a collar yesterday?"

He held up a red muffler and turned to the man on the bed. "A collar a week is all I ask. One lousy collar to go to Mass in."

Maisie laughed. "Go wan now, you saint-hunter! If they hung you for the number of times you've been to Mass you'd die innocent." She fixed a last straying strand of hair into place – the gesture lifting breasts under a white silk blouse that failed to disguise. "Will you listen," she asked, "to the Litany he's carrying on with over a shagging oul' collar?" She turned to Ba Fay whose narrowed eyes had kept her in focus all the time she was talking to Hammy. Withdrawing his mind from where it had taken him he eased back on the bed, and from the money in his trousers pocket

6

selected a half-dollar ready to slip it to Hammy at the first break in what was now a one-sided debate, for Hammy had had more than enough of Maisie's tongue and was shifting round the room making himself busy, while his mind's eye lined up the bottles of Beamish Ba Fay's half-dollar would buy, for under the lash of Maisie's anger he had heard the grind of the bedsprings and from the corner of his eye had seen the familiar search going on in the blue serge pocket.

"Innocent men, women and children are being gunned down in their tracks by British soldiers all over this city this very morning, and all he can do is stand there nagging heaven over a shagging oul' collar!" Maisie turned to Ba. "Wouldn't you think if he'd an ounce of manhood left in him he'd be out there on them streets shouldering a gun!"

Ba didn't answer, because he didn't agree with her. He himself had no intention of shouldering a gun, and saw no reason why Hammy should. He was looking for a safer occupation. It was all very well for the mitered and lozenged-suited to worry about the state of the nation since they were the ones with something to lose. But he wasn't doing any quick and shady deals in rat-infested tenements or household goods. And when had he ever had more than a semi-circular stare and a slight bend of the head, and that only in apprehension, from anyone in this fuckin city in his life. What difference did it make what color the flag was or who flew it? The stars and stripes, or the tricolor! Who cared? Revolutions! They had bollix all to do with a man like him who was dependent on nothing or nobody but himself. Furthermore, he had just come back from the Real War, the war to end all wars – and had done all the fighting he was ever going to do at 'Wipers' and might still be there if some bollix of a Kraut hadn't shot the leg off him.

Ba was only twenty-eight then and he was only thirty now and the loss of the leg wasn't any hindrance. He made out. Weren't many men walking the streets of this kip who could do the job on one woman that he did on three, and signs on . . . Thank Jasus it was the leg and not his balls, that would've . . . He paused in his thoughts to hear Hammy speaking.

"When my country calls I'll be ready." He tied the muffler

round his neck and tucked the ends into the waistcoat that didn't match the jacket.

"For what?" Maisie flung the question.

Hammy didn't answer, but moved lightfootedly and straightened up the black army-issue crutch standing against the foot of the bed and said, "There y'are, Ba. Oul' reliable."

Ba nodded and slipped the half-crown into Hammy's open hand.

"Enjoy yourselves." Hammy eased himself across the room to the door.

Maisie half turned to look at him – her eyes filled with wintery scorn. "Ah, there he goes. All boyish beauty under the grime of years. Mr Robert Emmet himself!"

Hammy held himself erect. "When Ireland calls . . ." He saluted her and the door closed behind him.

"Where are we going?" Maisie shattered the silence.

"Howth." Ba's hands closed on his crutch as he drew himself up off the bed.

Maisie shot him a side glance. Howth was for knackers and miles from anywhere. Nothing but sea-gulls and cliffs and sea. Silences. Nettles. Roads and lanes of flint stones that cut the feet off you. Protestants. Homespun, square-faced, beaked feeble and ferocious Protestants – all passing judgement on souls when they weren't gallivanting among the rocks and bracken like animals with lung trouble. And all Protestant reproach and silent sullenness and looking as if you owed them something – and as if it was towards them alone the sins of the world were scurrying on fast feet. Or you were. Made you feel as unwanted as the last discolored stump in the gum of a pauper. Which was a bit shagging much when you thought. After all it was the Protestants who were the invaders, the settlers and the unwanted. They were the grabbers with the best land and the best jobs and the best houses. They were the ones who didn't belong in the country and never would. It was no wonder the Republicans had taken to the gun and the streets. And not a minute before their time. She just wished to Jasus she had the strength of will to join them. Howth! A miserable cold Protestant kip. And certainly neither a fitting place or assembly for the first day of the week herself and Ba were to spend together; and then she remembered . . .

8

"You can forget Howth!" she said looking up at him and trying to fight his hands off while at the same time rejecting with a movement of her hips the offer his body was making. "There's a war on or have you forgotten?"

"That'll be over before the day's out." Ba's eyes were slits, knowing clever slits.

"There are four or five hundred rebels out there and twenty or thirty *thousand* British soldiers?" He bent to kiss and into her mouth he poured a mumbled animal sound. He took hold of her breasts; they lay heavy and firm in his hollowed hands; he could feel the nipples through her blouse; her breasts were like birds, great big, warm, wild birds, they throbbed in his hands, waited. "Christ!" He pulled her to him: he was tall, big, strong. A stallion. He could have lifted her sky high on the thing that glowed and bumped against her and the money in his trousers pocket.

"Come on . . . !"

She shook her head.

"Quick!"

"No!"

"Look!"

"I know!"

But today he could not tempt her: whereas always before she had been so hungry on his arrival he had hardly closed the door before she fell on him ravenously, propelling him with her need towards the bed and somewhere that he deliberately left unlocated till that exact point where he was infected with her appetite, and took over. But now from his tongue trying to drag from her throat resistance to his thirst she tore herself free, sidestepping on legs trembling and knocking the reach he made for her.

"We've time," he said.

"We haven't!"

"Why not?" His lips barely moving.

She didn't answer. She took her coat from behind the door and then from a hook on the dresser a moss-green straw hat that someone had made festive with a single red rose of gauze.

"We are taking Esther Quinn out with us today," she said or gulped. And waited.

9

If she had children they would have come now and grouped and waited with her for something to happen, some event to which they themselves might or might not have contributed. The children like herself stood in the silences of expectation. But nothing happened. Just a shout of confused exasperation. The room shuddered. The children turned to look, not at the man, but at their mother, as if what was coming would come from her. It didn't.

"Christ tonight!" She saw him draw back his lips from his teeth as if something inside him was making intolerable demands. Something was.

"Ah, Ba, it's Easter Monday! And God help her, Esther hasn't a soul in the world to care whether she lives or dies. And yesterday she waited all day for Billy Boy Beausang to turn up and he didn't and . . ."

"And because he didn't?"

"Of course if I'd known you would make a calamity out of it I'd never have asked her."

"Why did you?" He was having a business finding a cigarette and lighting it.

"I had to!"

"What do you mean you *had* to?"

"I had to stop her covering up the statue of the Virgin."

"Who cares?" It wasn't quite disbelief, but almost.

"I care," she said quietly. "I care very much. And so does everybody else in this house." But she more than most, and with more reason, was afraid of any interruption in the Novena she had begun to the statue of the Virgin four days ago. For the getting of what the others were wanting did in the heel of the hunt rest upon themselves and the might of the needs that drove them whereas what she wanted must come from God.

"And so to prevent any catastrophe falling on this priest and statue ridden kip, I'm to be lumbered with that piece of mouse meat!"

"You don't understand." And never will. He took the world for granted. And she could not even begin to explain her own, and the nagging unease that fell upon the house the times Esther Quinn covered up the blue, white and gold statue of the Virgin, for unlike herself and her neighbours Ba Fay had no faith in prayer

10

or statues and being a man who went to neither church, chapel nor meeting house, couldn't be expected to. She looked at Ba. He stood tall and dark and handsome. He had fathered sixteen children on three other women.

"It's the things we want," she said, and into the inquiring silence began to express her shame. "The things we pray for. Children. Getting you back from France. Something that will stop the titters, the pity that isn't pity. The jeers that I'm barren. The name-calling that I know goes on behind my back, and in drunken or rowdy moods to my face. 'Empty Arms! Empty . . .'" She stopped speaking. Voices came at them from other rooms, other houses.

Prominent voices, finding something at which to complain, and because every morning is the first.

"Christ and you've great faith in the powers of Esther's Totem Pole!" Ba had begun to ease out.

"Apart from you I've never known anybody else who could get through the day without faith in something."

Achievement through magic! Ba shrugged and reached for his crutch because he did not know what else to do. With a twist round the table Maisie was beside him. "It's only for this one day that's all. And tonight when we get back . . ."

"Sure!"

Groaning aloud for what had been withheld from him Ba reached down and spread his right hand across what he had to hide. He had a violent erection. It stood in his tight trousers muscular and rigid and exposed for all the world to see. 'Fuck it anyway' he thought. "We better go so," he growled.

On the landing ahead of Maisie as she climbed to Esther Quinn's, the door of the Gosses opened and closed behind Liam Martin. From where she stood at the scrubbed topped table in the middle of the room, Sarah Goss, dark and icon-faced nodded her greeting at the man she hoped one day to see her daughter Mollo marry, while her husband Jamesie put another chair into place for him.

"Her ladyship," Sarah said, "will be out in a minute."

Jamesie Goss, grey, thin and tall, smiled affection, before he gestured with an un-workmanlike hand towards the long Georgian windows behind him, hung with lace curtains white and stiff with starch. "It's started then?"

Liam Martin nodded. "The Volunteers have taken over most of the houses and buildings around the Green, and I met Hammy Collins in the street and he said they also had the Castle and Jacob's biscuit factory." Liam Martin grinned to make light of the news, for Sarah he saw had paused in her preparations of the meal and was gazing at her husband in anxiety. "Of course you can't believe the Lord's Prayer out of Hammy Collins' mouth . . ."

"But you listen to him just the same." Behind Sarah the curtains to the other room parted, and Mollo Goss stood with them. She went towards Liam who wanted to touch her but was deterred from doing so before her father and mother. He contented himself with looking. There was a soap-and-water freshness about her, and in the morning light her hair had a coppery tinge. For a second her eyes like moths that had escaped out of apple trees met his, then released she swung lightly around the table.

"I'm starving, Ma."

Sarah shrugged off the hug of arms. "Are you ever any other way? Though where you put it I'll never know." Her dark glance skimmed the body of her daughter moving on to her father as if she must touch and be reassured before she could finally rest. She put her face to his. "Come on, Da. Let's start."

"Wait for me!" And Jamesie Goss paused in the very act of sitting, to wait for his son John who came still half asleep towards him.

"You'll be late for your own funeral." Sarah Goss eyed her first born, the dark head, and hair that needed cutting, the fringed eyes directed as usual at his Da as he took his place beside him at the table.

"He's a growing boy," Jamesie said. "He needs his sleep." He seemed to hold his breath when John turned still sleepy eyes on him as though, Sarah thought, he was afraid of missing the least flicker of his son's face.

"Well, come on Jamesie," she said, "we can't wait all day. Pass Liam the bread."

Jamesie did as he was bid, and nobody pretended to notice the hostility blurring his wife's voice. "I didn't hear you come in last night," she said to John passing him a cup of tea and waiting, teapot in hand.

"You were asleep," John said.

"It was midnight before I closed my eyes." She turned to Mollo. "Did you hear him come in last night?"

"I heard," Mollo said. And she had, but only an hour after she heard her Da come in from his work that morning, and only half an hour before her Ma got up to light the fire.

John unseen by Sarah winked his thanks across to Mollo.

But Sarah, unconvinced, was speaking again and now it was concern that showed in the dark eyes that matched her son's. "I hope you're not getting yourself mixed up with the Republicans again," she said, reminding John of the promise she had extracted from him only last week that he would and had quit the Volunteers. "Because you've done your bit for them and the Cause risking arrest with your speeches at street corners. In fact you've done more than enough."

"No man can do enough." John spoke with calm decisiveness.

"Well I know one who has, and I'll not stand by and see you make a martyr of yourself by doing more."

"Martyr?" John raised eyes she had never been able to read.

"Yes, martyr! It's all a woman's expected to rear nowadays. Martyrs! For the British and the Irish. Cannon fodder in the shape of soldiers. Living, breathing, walking, guns, that'll fight and fight until they're killed or left, like Ba Fay below, maimed and fit for nothing."

"Ba Fay would hate that description of himself," Mollo laughed into a mood the very ticking of an eye could explode, and it troubled her, as it always did; the bitterness that crept into her mother's voice whenever conflict arose between her and her son.

"Sarah thinks the whole burden of the country lies solidly and squarely across the broad shoulders of her children." Jamesie's face crinkled into a smile was directed at Sarah and meant to placate.

"You are making too light of this!"

"Sarah! Please wait!"

"For what? For him to give himself over to death?"

"No! But until we find out if there's any justification for the ructions you seem bent on creating." Jamesie turned to his son but all John did was shake his head. "See, Sarah! You're courting blood pressure, and for no reason."

"Maybe!" Sarah spoke out of her conflicting throat. "But if there is a reason then he should be told, and now, that him and the likes of him pitting life and limb against the might of the British Army won't get a grain of thanks for it. The only ones to profit out of this will be the politicians, the place hunters, and the piety painted toughs hankering to be the new Ascendancy. The Eamons, the Jacks and the Williams. They'll pause long enough in their gallop to the big jobs and the fat bank accounts to scribble the 'Rest in Peace' after your names. And like their fathers and grandfathers and the generations that bore them that's *all* they'll do. But you and the fools of men like you won't be around to share the plunder or fatten yourselves on the Remembrance Dinners." Sarah paused and her hands on the table searched but could not find. "Remembrance Dinners! Remember what! Remember that hungry men make good soldiers! Remember the boys and how the plunder is to be divided. Remember the last glass of brandy the Eamons, the Jacks and the Williams swilled down their gullets? And there'll be no Remembering needed to know where the next brandy or the next big job is coming from, for you and the men like you will have seen to that beforehand."

John got to his feet. Life had already sluiced his long muscular body, leaving it smooth. It threw his mother into a shadow. He would have walked but in the confines of the room this wasn't possible. He knew that the eyes had fixed. And saw that on the mantelpiece even the alarm clock had begun to stare. He was isolated in a small room crowded with people who waited. For what? "I don't understand," he said. The room loosened. He turned to Sarah. "I've heard you say over and over again that sooner or later the people would have to fight if they were ever to gain control over their own lives. You said the Rising was inevitable."

"I know," Sarah's gaze flew to her husband. "But in the flurry of years I forgot to give myself warning. I didn't realize that he would grow up so soon, or that the Citizen's army would be needing boys."

"Christ! Mother I'm nineteen!" John exploded beside her.

She turned her head to look up at him. "I know. Old enough for our masters to keep you busy with politics and divert your mind and attention from asking where your next cut of bread is coming from and your next day's work."

At the table Jamesie pushed back his chair and went to the window. Her glance followed him. He was looking tired, even old now that she could see him in the full glare of light. Into her throat came a tight new and sudden terror that she could not swallow. Jamesie was an old man in the sun. An old man. She would have gone and put her arms around him and kissed him. Jamesie Goss. He was also Jamesie Goss, a decent hardworking man, wouldn't harm a hair of your head, and learned, but like his son would

15

never open up or admit much of what was sewn up inside him, and a bit dreamy, ya know, said the people along the canal.

"I'll do the beds," she said suddenly and getting to her feet went about doing so.

Jamesie saw the curtains to the other room close behind her and then beckoned John over to the window.

"You meant it just now. There is nothing for your Ma or me to worry about?"

"No! I didn't." He thought he heard the sickening lurch his father's heart gave. "Please Da! Ma doesn't understand. She agrees we have to fight but she thinks somebody else should do the fighting."

"But why you?" Jamesie could have screamed the question.

And behind them John heard Mollo begin on purpose to raise her voice.

"I should have lied," he said.

"You never have. Not to me." Jamesie could have been denying a charge brought against his son by somebody else.

"About this I should have, for now you'll go fretting and for no reason."

"No reason?"

"Da, listen!" John pushed past the appeal in the eyes raised to his – searching for words that would demolish the fear darkening his Da's face. "It'll be all right I swear. Listen, Da . . ." he paused, for now he was doing what he had never done. He was nailing his Da to the wall with lies. But he had no choice, he thought, sensing the relief his lies gave. And afterwards . . . there would be time to explain, ask forgiveness . . . He heard his father telling him to speak easy . . . slow down . . . not to upset himself – saw the blue-striped shirted chest against which he would now have hidden and felt the hands under his elbows and saw his father's face come back into focus. The loved gentle features of his Da.

He reached and Jamesie stood while his son folded his arms about him and gently and lovingly buried his face and darkly bristling chin into the flesh of his neck. In a silence as solid as a tombstone they stood this way without moving. Their breaths rising and stroking each other. Then Jamesie jerked his head back suddenly and dragged himself away from his son. He stood and stared out the window. Sarah had not seen.

"You won't fret?"

"No!" Jamesie turned his face away as if to hide scars. Against it the sun was warm, and already had the heat of summer in it. And he *would* fret . . . His mind was fretting now, fretting in a blinding panic for this boy standing tall beside him, one arm angled as if to protect resting across his shoulders making clear to the world the subtle link that existed between these two and which was out of place in the abrasive and harsh reality of the tenements, where father–son relationships were nearly always an armed truce and at best an act of toleration. But Jamesie Goss loved his son. Not inordinately, but almost. Loved him with a grave and apprehensive love for which until now, there was no clear reason.

There had been nothing unusual in the circumstances of John's birth. He was born nine months after Jamesie and Sarah's marriage, to the delight of Sarah, who hid her puzzlement at her husband's indifference to his son and came to the conclusion that men weren't natural. They lacked 'nature', and Jamesie whose eyes could read a silence and whose lean face was sometimes quick as conscience and as clear as mirrors was in the heel of the hunt no different from the rest of the men going, for when Sadie Ennis, the midwife, put John into his arms he had done nothing but stand there staring down at the child before handing it back without a word.

But Sarah was wrong. On the shuddering iron bed she could not see or hear the thin thread of the cry the baby gave as Jamesie held him. An unearthly sound it was, and lost. Hardly a sound at all, but it bore through Jamesie as nothing had done before; it froze him; gathered all the queer sensations of the night and reached through all he had ever been, to nerves in cells of tenderness which nothing and nobody had touched before. "Another jewel for the dowdy streets," the midwife said. And took him from him. His son. He bent and kissed Sarah before walking away, leaving the room with a heavy step, aware that the child she held was opening up a virginal unsowed region of his heart as nothing before had had the power to do.

Sarah hadn't. He married her to escape the strangling grip of

17

tight-fisted and gut-greedy parents who prevented him emigrating to America by demanding he acknowledge moral duties imposed by events of the past. They brought his obedience about by appealing to his pity, heedless in their greed and fear of want to the thing they were killing, for they could offer him nothing with which to replace the dream, nor did they try to as their hands shut tight on the few pounds they had come close to losing, for wasn't Jamesie the good chap to stay on in a job out of which he could supply their needs, for he'd settle down now . . . in a country dark with ignorance and torn asunder with unemployment and strife. His father and mother had their way, and in the returning calm after the upheaval of his near escape he met Sarah, who at that time was everything he wasn't.

She was three years younger, laughing, boisterous and assured, taking from the world only what she wanted and infusing into him by degrees some of her own private rebellion at the life around her, when she wasn't mocking his timidity of it. She questioned, and pondered long and thoughtfully on his answers, and rekindled a spark out of the ashes of his vision of that new and vast country across the sea, bringing it by her wide-eyed interest within his grasp again, and thinking possession of her would mean escape to it he married her.

And exchanged one insurmountable summit for another, for Sarah had about as much time for his ambitions as his mother and father had. Sarah wanted a home that boasted a stained-oak china cabinet and children, and she wanted them in that order, and *now* she told him, hushing his suppositions with promises of, "After. After, Jamesie," and so he gave in to her too, turning his back on the distance that he would never explore now, and moving on to the failures that were to become more familiar in his hands than his dreams had ever been. But Sarah didn't only take. She had given him love, a warm generous love, loving him tenderly, constantly and voluptuously, forgiving him the apathy into which he suddenly lapsed after a few months of marriage and his inability to keep a job for more than a week at a time, for he, who had always been steady and hard-working had now no heart for unvaried routine. But she never nagged, or vexed by demanding explanations or by asking where this, that or the other was to

18

come from, but went on loving and accepting all his moods but one. And that, in her ignorance, she killed finally and utterly. But for the death of one dream she gave him another. She gave him John.

His daughter drew him from the window and the fret of panic by asking him to look at the front wheel on the basket cart in the hall, and with which she made her living. "It came off on Saturday," she said edging herself between him and John, "and I'll be needing it again in the morning."

"You hope!" Jamesie said, but his attempt at lightness was she saw feeble.

"People have to eat." Sarah came through from the other room as Jamesie bent to search in the press of the dresser for the few tools he kept there.

"Food, sex and entertainment! All essential commodities," Liam Martin commanded Sarah's attention. Mollo listened, or half listened, and wondered what her Da would say when he discovered there wasn't a thing wrong with the wheels on her cart. And in a flash of sudden anger directed at her mother cursed a situation that was forever making childish invention necessary. And yet she was always having to invent some way of separating Jamesie from John, alerted to the act by the shock of silence that fell on the room and which she found unbearable and was nearly always the prelude to a bitter attack made upon John by his mother and incomprehensible to him, an almost explosive violence for which there was never any known reason and which left him and Jamesie stunned.

"Ah, will you whist?" she heard Sarah airily dismiss Liam's banter and saw her dark brooding glance find and light on Jamesie as he went towards the door. "Will you be back?" Sarah asked, and when Jamesie nodded she stepped back into the other room. For a long time the silence held.

Rough and awkward sounds of motion came up through the whole house. Then they heard a bed being pulled out from the wall and the swish of bedclothes flung aside, and Liam Martin looking at John said: "I thought it was off."

"So did we," John glanced at the faded cretonne curtains on the doorway.

19

"What happened?" Mollo questioned abruptly.

Both men looked at her before John said, "I'm not sure, but I suspect it may have something to do with the sinking of that ship."

"But you don't know," Liam said.

"No! I don't *know*," John replied.

"That's the trouble with this whole damn business," Liam said, "nobody knows anything."

"Except what it is we're fighting for," John said quietly.

"We don't even know that anymore," Liam said. "And how could we when orders are being issued from every lane and backyard in Dublin? And all of them different. And tell me something, what do you fight with, and before you answer I know what you're thinking and what it is you've been told. But you know as well as I do that there isn't enough ammunition in this country to even hinder the British Army."

There might have been, if a ship disguised as a Norwegian timber vessel, and stacked from stern to bow with rifles, machine-guns, rounds of ammunition and gelignite, hadn't come up against a British patrol boat off Tralee . . . where the arms that were to have freed Ireland were to have landed. But it had been stopped, and the ship, scuttled by its own crew, now lay at the bottom of the bloody sea. The loss was still being kept a secret from those who had a right to know. The Irish with their native slyness and obscene lust for secrecy about everything. Even about the time of day.

Well he knew what there was to know and he would tell John Goss . . .

And did, speaking before the decision to do so had formed in his mind. John showed no surprise. He continued to trace his thoughts with a matchstick on the grained face of the scrubbed topped table.

"All the more reason for striking now," he said, and only the rigid set of his mouth showed what he was thinking.

"With what? For Christ's sake!"

"Our fists, if necessary."

Mollo resented Liam's concern. She resented his state of mind which she did not understand. It wasn't as if he was doing the fighting. He expounded, when he talked about it at all, a policy of diplomacy to end the British occupation of Ireland. Talk them out

20

of the country, he said. He was against violence. Against armed force, believing any resistance the country might offer would end in waste of life, and the inevitable destruction of the small footholds already gained on the way to ultimate freedom. The fact that England was already fighting a war with Germany didn't mean you could start another in her own backyard without her knowing – or that she would be too busy, even unable to raze Ireland to the ground. She had done it before over and over. And would do so again. England was still lousy with Cromwells. And as for relying on a German success on the Western Front to smash England's defences and allow Germany to send substantial help before the Rising was crushed – that was a load of balls.

John Goss shot a glance at the inner room, but there was no pause in the sounds coming from it. He reached across and touched the back of Liam's hand. "Stop looking at me as if I was deciding the fate of nations or as if you were."

Liam was slow in rising up from the depths of the near despair into which he had sunk. "You are mad!" he said.

"I know," John said. Suddenly wanting but unable to explain feelings and emotions which had sprung out of depths he could not fathom. How they each felt about Ireland was something they could neither understand. They had known each other in all things except this one thing. Maybe when this was over? Maybe then? But how explain the inexplicable? What could he say that would make Liam understand why he was prepared for defeat and death, believing either to be an honorable necessity, and believing that either must prove successful by rousing the spirit of the nation, by making the Irish cause once more an international question. Maybe he should have tried harder with Liam. But something had always come between him and the things he wanted to say to the people he loved. Was that how it was for everyone? With chances missed? Was that how it was with his Da? He remembered how Jamesie had looked that morning as he crept quietly into the room, stopping even in his dread of finding his Ma awake to look down on him before he hurried to the sanctuary of the little room and Mollo's worried questioning. Lost to the world his Da had been, in his tired sleep, his grey head turned to the new day's sun, whose rays lay like laths across him pinning his frailness down under the white quilt, its white ordinariness taking the harm out of what the sun seemed to be doing. He could have gone down on his knees beside the bed to nudge weeping and crying like a dog nosing a bird that has, for some strange reason, no more movement. His Da. What chances had he missed? A man who never used his tongue except to give utterance to the love in him, and not only for his own family but for the family of the world, a man who sometimes and unaware spoke his dreams aloud, quiet unambitious dreams that he laughed at because the concern in his childrens' and wife's eyes told him they could now never be realized. But were there others? More important, that he John, didn't know about?

And his Ma? Eyeing the world with confidence and seeming to take for granted the logic of growth and continuity. Standing firm and unshakable between them all, isolated in some mysterious way from him, yet sheltering them all in a warmth of love that denied all sense of consciousness of worry or privations, as though in her love for them she had never known either. And yet he could remember seeing her, after one of her senseless attacks on him and when she thought their attention elsewhere looking upon his Da with a pity and tenderness that stripped bare the caution and left exposed her sorrow and her love for him. Catching himself or Mollo watching she would hurry to undo possible damage stirring herself and them into some lighthearted activity, changing the lingering sounds of lament to those of expectation as she set the room to rights and made tea; while all the time, behind the laugh in her eyes, her mouth continued to pour forth inaudible tears.

"You've been pawing that table like a blind man for the last five or ten minutes," and, from the scene he saw or was dreaming, he was brought back by Mollo – bringing him back over the distance he had strayed as she had done all their lives, and laughing now at the habit he shared with Jamesie of stressing with his full dark mouth the expression of his eyes.

"Where were you?" she asked.

"Thinking," he said, his face still lengthened in concentration.

"What about?" She passed him a fresh cup of tea.

"Time! It isn't long enough." He stirred his cup carefully. "Where will you go today?" he asked.

22

"Do we have a choice?" Liam put the question quietly.

"He wants to be sure he doesn't walk into trouble," Mollo said, with malice, "you know Liam!"

"That isn't true!" Sarah coming out upon them lashed. "And you have no right to speak that way, Missy!"

Mollo flamed. "Just the same, he keeps walking away."

"Let her alone." Liam reached a hand but Mollo drew back. "Anyway she's right," he said. "Centuries of poverty and subjection have made the Irish cautious."

"That's still no way to speak to anyone," Sarah said. Her voice and face hiding a deeper anger.

"She doesn't mean half she says," Liam said.

And she didn't and Sarah knew this. Nevertheless she could say things that were scalpel sharp and barbed with malice, and be unaware that they were. Knowing her you forgave her. But if you loved her, the hurt she inflicted was not easy to forget. And Liam did. Had loved the skinny cavernous child. Before Mollo there had only been an aunt or cousin who, when she remembered him at all, only did so to throw him a bit to eat or a rag to cover his nakedness with or the remains of a paillasse to fling in the corner of the room and on which he slept. His relationship to the woman wasn't any clearer to her than it was to him, and as she moved into the street with him, the neighbors' answers to his subsequent questions didn't tell. A silent taciturn woman except in drink and then she wouldn't let him cross the door. She died, secretly, silently, in her bed in the dead of night, and fearing the anger she had familiarized him with if her slumber was disturbed, he lived with her corpse for a week and didn't know it. Made wise to the ways of the world by the street, he survived her going by means that in the street were considered unorthodox only if you were caught. But with first-class examples all around him, he began as a master, and the fruit and vegetables lifted from outside shops, or off the farmers' carts coming over the bridge and into the city, not only kept him fed and put the odd jacket on his back but paid the two-and-sixpence that was needed to rent the room as well. Wanting to *know* school was no effort, and without guidance kept himself at it until he had got all that a handful of teachers were able or prepared to give him. When at twelve, they turned him out

23

of the school, he turned to books, begged, borrowed or robbed from the public libraries, each one breeding in him a hunger for more and yet more knowledge.

Mollo Goss, who couldn't bear to shift her attention from the surge of life around her and who suspected that the pages of a book were in some way a threat to her, was forever prophesying that one day he'd wake up blind from them, he'd see. The fact that he was able to laugh at that juxtaposition of ideas dawned on him, and he knew then the time had come to get out and take from the world his place in the sun.

But in Ireland inequalities do not vanish before the determined will. And where did a man begin in a city like Dublin, nut strung with conventions that hid the inadequacies of those who had it in their power to shift over and make room for another but wouldn't. Safeguarded with crowded cunning and a little knowledge themselves, however stupidly applied, they held the barriers firm, demanded that before another was qualified to take his place beside them his credentials must match theirs. Liam's didn't. He had none of the prerequisites, he was not of the middle classes, the son of a civil servant or a judge, he carried in his pockets no letters of introduction from relatives or friends, and he could not boast of (or even apologize for not) having taken honors in subjects that seemed myriad to him, and with which the whispering academics with their pilfering and rapacity for other people's facts, beguiled themselves, and which in the world and in the dense static confidence of the universities passed for learning. He was a man without a birth certificate and couldn't even prove he had been born. But because he had to live in a world that did everything in its power to prevent him doing so, Liam, like John, became a builder's laborer, for which no reading or writing had been necessary. The knowledge amassed from the countless books thus gave him no more than a philosophy, for the ambition had already been there.

"You're making a calamity out of nothing!" Mollo said coldly. "He won't die of shock!" The sun flashed in her copper-tinged hair and touched the sudden tempest in her face before she said suddenly, "I'm sorry Liam." He drew her hand into his and began to fold her finger into the fist he was making.

24

"I don't know what gets into you," Sarah said, but the glance Liam threw her begged silence.

He knew well the cause of Mollo's barb and the implication of her saying he wouldn't die of shock. And he wouldn't, for his pacifist attitude to the Rising was something he and Mollo had discussed before now and had become the one bone of contention between them. Not that she wanted him to throw in his lot with the Republicans the way her brother had, for she saw and, without understanding why, recognized that Liam was anything but an idealist, and that John was. And being a practical person she agreed with her mother that the fruits of glory, when they did fall, would not land within miles of the men fighting for them. And yet she resented Liam's cynicism about the principles of war and couldn't help feeling that he should do something, but was uncertain what form that something should take.

"You've a tongue like a lash," Sarah said and looking at her daughter wondered when she would learn to curb it with Liam Martin.

There was a hush in the room filled by the roar of the water in the locks. But they lived with that sound too long now to notice it. Instead they listened to the noises in the house and in the intermediate silences, and without being aware that they did so, to the thundering blur of gunfire from several streets away and coming through the open window on a wind of danger. Mollo shivered suddenly as if from the breath of ghosts. She looked at her brother shifting uneasily on his chair, his face turned towards the window.

"We should go," she said, knowing he wanted to.

"Where?" Sarah asked.

"Dalkey," Liam said.

"But will you get there?" Sarah was all surprise, and John saw that she sounded thorough-going again, as if the events that had led up to this moment were over. And, of course, they were. And that would be over, too, that thing that was happening out there in the sun. That too, would pass and tomorrow or the next day he would be back at his job, standing and bending alongside Liam. So far the Rising was successful, and the British who up to now had been unreceptive to reason and unconvinced by argument must realize that freedom is not something that anybody can be given; freedom is something people *take* and without which they perish.

Unable to maintain the caution necessary in front of his mother, John rose to his feet. He looked down at her and Sarah, unable to resist even had she wanted to, smiled back. The moments had begun to flow again.

"Will I wash the delf Ma?" he asked.

"Are you well?" Sarah stared surprise. "Sure you've never washed a cup in your life, why should you begin now?"

"In that case . . ." he moved towards Mollo and Liam standing at the door.

"You going with them?" Sarah asked.

"A bit of the way."

But Mollo knew he would part from them at the hall door. She heard Sarah's murmurings usher them out and ahead of them saw John jump the stairs and caught the grin he flashed back at her before he disappeared.

3

Christina Swords let go the brass handle on her door and turning to John Goss shook her head. No, she had not seen his Da. Maybe he was out in the yard. John nodded thanks and sprinted down the few stairs that led from the hall into the yard. Christina watched him, then went towards the hall door, perpetually ajar. On the steps and against the railings Alfie Doyle, looking as if he was having trouble with his groin, lounged with his white well-kept hands dug deep into trousers pockets. Christina came to a halt beside him, her clear gaze searching for some show of the pleasure she always imagined should be there when they met and never was, for his glance and greeting were as usual; non-committal and silent.

"I rushed," she said, and got for response the slow slumberous smile of a child coming from sleep. It was enough and in the glittering present she forgot how hard won it was.

Christina was thirty, and in the laundry where she worked, and in the house, and around the canal, people said, 'There's no flies on Christina Swords,' which meant she was more sensible than she, an unmarried woman her age, had any right to be. Of all the things Christina might have wanted, she wanted a wedding ring; and of all the men she had put through her hands, Alfie Doyle seemed the most likely to give her one. Though How and When,

27

only God and Alfie knew. Christina didn't. She had asked once, and because Alfie didn't consider the question merited an answer, he didn't make one; but his shrug was enough for Christina, and the interpretation which she put upon it she believed, her belief urging her to further more stringent denials, to go without. Oul' wans mouthing at doors commented at first pityingly on her poverty, on her lack of the odd pair of new shoes which she was forever in need of, or a Sunday coat to go to Mass in, and then left her to God in the aftermath of the shock they got when she suddenly and without warning spent money on a brass door-knob.

Christina's acquisition of the door-knob was the last grand gesture of sending two half-pennies astray that she was ever to make, and that had been two years ago, for now she kept out of her wages just enough to exist on and handed the rest to Alfie every Friday night to be put away in the Post Office, and if anybody had asked her, which nobody did, she would have thought that a brass door-knob was something you could feel and look at even if you had nothing to eat.

During those years of Friday nights, Christina had wondered often and long if there wasn't enough money behind herself and Alfie to get married on, but whenever she ventured to ask he always said no, and she herself had never kept track of the amount.

Alfie Doyle lived in the street around the corner from the canal with his widowed mother who, after the death of her husband, began the legend that Alfie wasn't strong and was unable for work of any kind even if he could've got it. He supported the fallacy by developing a stoop as if his body, too, was harboring the germ that had killed his father. He took an inordinate pride in his little boy looks and thin baby fair hair which both Christina and his mother loved. He wore jazzy blue and grey striped suits and pointed patent leather shoes. He read the Nick Carter Magazine and saw no reason why his mother shouldn't last forever. But if, by some remote chance she didn't, a man with his brains in the right place must know what road to turn to . . . and Alfie knew. He turned to Christina chaining her to him with the promise of marriage.

There was nothing in Christina's looks or character that either pleased or touched Alfie. He disliked the strong clean cut of her.

28

Her height and striding walk. She did not fit. She was a discord. As if she had strayed out of some other place. Her eyes, often surprised, glossed over things as if they would make do – but behind them you could see her mind rejecting. In the tea shops which they occasionally frequented she ate the cakes put before her and for which she paid – unlike the rest of her class and the other women he knew who not only thought it unladylike to appear as if they were ever gripped by the pangs of hunger, but also that the signs of an appetite in a woman did her irreparable harm in the eyes of a man. Repulsed by the un-seductive hardness of her body, he made no demands on her, but to give some semblance of reality to the relationship he would sometimes, around the roads of Herbert Park where they walked, hold her to him darkening his voice with murmured requests, safe in the knowledge that she would not grant them. He hated then her lack of deception for from her there were never any whimpers of ruin, just a straight 'No! I can't!' as if he didn't know that before him she had given it away like snuff at a wake to fellows who, on wet nights when their pockets were empty, gathered like monks at prayer to play cards in the hall and disappeared singly into Christina's room and came back with faces relaxed and muscles and body limp and with a matter of fact jerk of the head said, 'Next please.' But he knew she thought that as long as she held out on him it strengthened her chances of the marriage she so desperately wanted. What she didn't know was that he suffered no privation. After his erotic play with her, after he had forced himself at the hall door to feel her up, he beat it down to Wexford Street where Agnes Oats, who would never work for nor hand over a penny to any man living, waited, all white and big and ready to burst inside her blouse, in the shadows of another hall for him.

A breeze lifted a lock of Alfie's baby fine hair, then died a death under an explosion of gunfire from the next bridge along the canal.

"What was that?" Astonishment clouded Christina's eyes, and overhead a gull paused to turn and wonder before it soared in frenzied excitement from the rage and turmoil begun in the streets near the Liffey and now spreading with paralytic fits beyond them. "Something's up." Her bewilderment was lost in a new

29

roll of firing, topped with single, short but bigger and more savage explosions that sank into a minute silence before the guns again jumped into the air freshly wet with death.

"It's the Republicans!" Alfie said. "The extravagant bastards are blowing up the city."

"What for?"

"To get the English out."

"This way!"

"Prayers won't shift them."

"Then maybe the gun will."

There was a silence, and Christina withdrew her attention and gave her mind again to the immediacies from which it had flown. "Where will we go today?" she asked while her eyes examined his new blue suit, a suit she hadn't seen before. "That's new, isn't it?" She tried not to sound inquisitive.

"Me mother got it for Easter," Alfie said. "She had a club to get," he added as if his mother's plenty needed explaining. Which indeed it did.

Christina's thought was not new, and neither was the one that followed, because she had never understood how his mother, who earned to the penny what she did, managed the constant weekly instalments off something, which was what 'having a club' meant. Christina herself hadn't a penny left out of her wages after she had done what she had to do with them. And God alone knew when she had last put a screed on her back! And it wasn't for the want of them either. Her hands went to the frayed collar of her gray coat.

Through the dull despair of poverty and the indecency of want she had gone all her life. With never a soul to ask if she had a mouth on her since the day she was born, and even now, when all she wanted was to be brought to the altar, she was paying for that herself. But when? When out of the pittance she was able to save would she have enough even for that. Money! Where did people like her get money from? Christina didn't see John Goss until he had taken shape on the thin blown edge of her reverie and was giving an answer to a question Alfie had asked.

"Bray is as safe as a bank, Alfie," John said.

And Christina saw him quiver solemnly for a moment then

dissolve into sudden shapelessness. Her throat went tight with terror.

"Not Bray!" she said bringing it up and out.

"Why not? And where then?" Alfie asked as if he didn't know and mock her dread of the deathless sea.

"The mountains." Her lips moved stiff. John Goss had become solid again and now she was suddenly ashamed her fear might have been observed.

"But would this have spread out there?" Alfie asked and he meant the gunfire that was now a distant rumble, and Christina watching knew he didn't want to go within miles of the mountains and would get out of going if he could. But some things should not always be easy even for Alfie.

"No, it wouldn't." John had seen and now he winked at Christina; and she smiled back or parted her lips to ratify their sudden and unexpected alliance.

"But listen!" Alfie turned to John. Because if anybody knew the turn of events in this bloody uproar it would be John Goss. "Are you sure?" he asked.

John looked at Alfie as if he and his questions were some great and intolerable pressure from which he wanted to escape. His dark glance swept the canal, the sky and the cloud forms free of hindrances – and then he answered Alfie's question although Christina thought he couldn't have heard it.

"I'm not sure of a God damn thing Alfie, except that before this day is out Dublin will be free of the murdering bastards and the country, with the help of God, will be a Republic!"

Alfie tittered. "Jasus! and youse are the desprit lot!"

There was in Alfie's remark and titter the vicious mockery of the Dubliner. It was the belittling voice of the rabble John Goss heard and he knew it. It was the bitter begrudging voice of the slack-mouthed and slack-jawed who wanting to be the reason for everything were the cause of nothing – the self-advertising and self-styled 'literary' hacks of Dublin – the grown old without reward – failed solicitor novelists and glib civil servants – the merry Irish American widows and liberated bull dykes all nibbling like mice at other people's ideas on the back and center pages of the tabloids, and sniping at the Republicans and their betters as they arse-

31

licked and shadow-boxed for advancement in the wake of each other and the constipated ruins of the city's newspapers' editors.

From the night behind him, long and dark, with turmoil and blood, John Goss stared out over the heads sagged against him and beyond to the men panicking towards him and the men who were running away, a night crazed with motion and screamed sounds and himself in the middle of them astonished. He looked at Alfie. But only Christina saw that the eyelids on the eyes were contemptuous.

"See you!" he said. And moved and took the path before him in sure and certain strides. They watched him go in silence.

"Rebel!" Alfie said.

"John Goss?" Christina stared.

"The man of thought has become the man of action." Alfie sniggered.

"I don't believe you!"

"You didn't know?"

"How would I? I've heard him talk of course, but I never thought . . . He could be shot!"

"Yeah and wouldn't that be terrible? Some people can't appreciate. Only don't go mouthing. I don't want that pack down on me." Then, "Come on."

"John Goss a Rebel!" Christina said, or thought, and thought began to occupy – a vague determination to find out for herself if what Alfie said was true. But how? And did it matter? It was just . . . Some things come to life of their own accord. The hurt was an old one. She had imagined it gone. Lost. In that lost place where all we never had stands waiting. And here it was coming back over the same instinctive track, the same old falling leaves. She had forgotten. Or imagined. But only fools imagined that in time *everything* was possible, *everything* forgivable. Some things were *not* possible and everything was *not* forgivable. A pang of immeasurable bitterness that was physical caused her to stumble as if she had lost the use of her legs, recovering their power only after Alfie, in peevish complaint, asked if she couldn't walk proper an' what ailed her. To restore mental order she put her hand on Alfie's arm before her mind, struggling to keep pace with her body, took up again the thread of thought. Contrary to popular belief

32

suffering did not purify. It was all very well for the priests and their prayers to go on about forgiving those who trespassed against us. The priests like the rich were insured in heaven against the calamities. And John Goss of all people! Christ! Nothing is ever what you expect. The only certainty is death. All she had ever wanted was to get married – to some fella who expects a clean shirt on Sunday to go to Mass in, his dinner on the table every night and his regular fuck Saturday because you're married to him and he owns you anyway. It wasn't all. It was what she had prepared herself for after she had stopped reaching to the heavens to handle what wasn't there.

From looking ahead at nothing she saw the swan in motion on the green sullen water of the canal. She had never liked the canal. In fact she dreaded the canal. She had never liked swans. And this one was aiming straight at her. And couldn't be prevented. Like thought that won't be cut. The swan was sprouting jagged diagonal teeth and its head at the end of its long rubbery neck was gyrating vicious like that terrible destructive dangle between a man's legs. Christ the devastation that could cause. Endless. Secretive swans were. Like the Rebels. Secretive and treacherous and you never knew who was one and who wasn't. The dazzle of white slid noiselessly and serenely by. She shot a side glance at Alfie and wondered if he knew what sleep his words had raised her from. She pushed on.

At Harcourt Street Station, Christina followed Alfie into the train's crowded carriage, and while they fought for foot room her mind turned back, aloof and searching, to the house.

4

The house was quiet now. In the hall, in a lusty palpitating gold and red of fire, Mollo Goss and Liam Martin stood. They stood close, so close that their bodies had ceased to be either a comfort or a protection. They could feel each other's heart beating painfully erratically as their breath mingled or was ripped from them in bursts of sound that had begun to choke the throat. Above them a door opened and a woman's laugh skeined with mocking stridency the emotion surrounding them. The house shuddered. The walls stirred. The hall was all movement. Perversely Mollo hissed anger at the intrusion into the moment. She pushed him away to stare into eyes that in no way reflected her own honest and suddenly violent relief. "Come back," he said, and his words did not come right out of his mouth but lay just behind his lips, and his eyes stayed half closed. He reached and drew her to him. She could feel the thrust of his thighs and the beginning suction of her own. "Mollo," he began, swallowing hard because speech was difficult, "marry me!" She could just hear. "Yes," she said, knowing it was safe to do so, for the intrusion would avert the wide range of debates with which so many similar moments had ended. She felt his beginning kisses. He was devouring her with kisses that were abandoned for touch and words that were heavy and thick as blotting paper and dark with a passion of

34

senses that they both knew must be resisted. Against his lumbering voice she opened her mouth and into it he shot his tongue like a blunt eel struggling down into the deeper and darker ferny depths of the canal. It was how she had first seen him, she remembered. Holding in his hands blunt eels that he had pulled struggling out of the canal. "Get away from me," he said and thrust her from him with his thighs. The buttons on his flies strained to keep the upholstery down. His hand went to feel for what might have happened. They were intact. He glanced up and round the bend of the stairs, like the prow of a ship, Janey Reilly's mother, Harriet, came blundering in a rush away from the old maids behind her.

"Like the Little Flower I'm always where I'm needed!" she cried.

"Not this time, Harriet!" Unappeased sensuality blurred Liam's voice.

Harriet laughed and glanced back at the women behind her, who she knew full well had just come out of Esther Quinn's room. "God I never heard youse behind me," she said.

Which was, as Sophia Doran knew, a damn lie and only someone as lightminded as her sister Mathilda would believe otherwise. Sophia nodded a cool greeting but Mathilda, with the young face of an old bright child, smiled hers.

"We were up with some breakfast to Esther Quinn," she said, "but she's asleep."

"And, her statue's covered!" Sophia trumpeted.

"Aw Jasus! Not again!" Harriet cried, and thought that she had never yet come across Sophia Doran first thing in the morning without spending the rest of the day regretting the encounter.

"Are you sure?" Mollo asked and even in the dim light of the hall saw Sophia's cheeks turn a chocolate-purple.

"Positive!" Sophia Doran blazed. She resented being questioned by Mollo Goss and couldn't understand her blank amazement, for Harriet, after the first shock, was taking the news in her stride. But then the Romans were like that. Even the young and pretty ones like Mollo Goss with her trim figure, tapering neck and copper knot of hair, like a girl in a locket. A primitive, pagan and thriftless pack the Romans were when you got down to it – and that outburst from Mollo Goss, just another manifestation of their heathen worship of false idols to which they attributed all kinds of rigmaroles, invented by crafty Jesuits to keep in the depths of ignorance an island of backward peasants. Sophia munched and on her face hairs stirred as she thanked the Lord for her Presbyterian ancestors.

"You're standing there grinning like a cat with canary feathers to account for," Harriet said.

"It's my sense of humour," Sophia grinned or munched.

"Ah, well, with the help of God and His Holy Mother, no harm will come to us today." Harriet turned to Mollo. "I've a drop of water above from the Grotto in Mount Argus, I'll sprinkle it round the place when I come back this evening."

Mollo, afraid of what her face might be showing, made a pretence of tidying herself – while beside her Liam stood and waited for the moments to carry him out of reach.

"Esther's asleep now," Mathilda said, and watched Mollo fold herself into her plaid fringed shawl.

"So you said," Harriet replied and thought what gaums the old maids were.

"She's been poorly since Saturday," Mathilda said.

Harriet liked Mathilda Doran, and many was the good laugh they had together when they met at the pipe in the yard, and there wasn't an ounce of badness in the creature. And as long as she could arrange a life she was content. But she had a slate missing. How else could you account for the things she came out with – or the way she spent her days looking for, and finding, rooms her sister Sophia had no intention of taking. Turn you white, sometimes, the way she went on about the lovely rooms she saw . . . and around Ranelagh she was as well known as a begging ass in her search for them . . . but as for that other fuckin bitter black Protestant with her airs and graces and who spoke words as if they cost . . .

"Maybe Esther should have the Dispensary doctor?" Mathilda dared, knowing that while the others were with her Sophia wouldn't chastize.

Harriet laughed. "What Esther Quinn needs, the Dispensary doctor doesn't have. Why there isn't a thing wrong with that wan that a well-stacked man couldn't cure."

"Rubbish!" Sophia sliced the air between them. "Men are not the answer to everything."

"True! But they do fill a woman's life with little or – if she's lucky – big surprises – and, like Hail Marys, chain her fast to where it is she wants to stay," Harriet said. "Ah, but I'm forgetting, Sophia," she added blandly as if a cut at the other was the furthest thing from her mind, "you wouldn't know, never having had one."

Sophia munched. "From what I've seen *one* wouldn't be enough, for most of the women in Dublin seem to need two, three, even four."

All right, you vicious oul' bitch, you've got your own back: but Harriet was damned if she'd let her see it. She laughed easy, setting in motion the large solid gold loops of her earrings. They bashed each side of her face while her black eyes, caved under brows matching the doubtful black of her hair, glittered in angry expectation. She looked at Mollo. "I'm taking the kids over to Drumcondra to see me sister," she said. "A lovely place she has over there. A pair of rooms you could turn stallions in. I can't stand the north side, but I must say . . ." She couldn't stand her culchie craw-thumping brother-in-law either, but it was somewhere to go and saved her from having to look at Alex all day, and besides the kids needed the bit of air, and tonight when she came back and after she'd put the kids to bed, she had Darky to hurry out to. "Where are you going Mollo?" she asked.

"Dalkey," Mollo said, and didn't add that now Esther Quinn's altar was covered she no longer saw the use of putting one foot before the other. Because that would have meant explaining her fear for John. Harriet would have understood about the altar. And the old maids would have understood about John, for she was certain the people in the house suspected him of being a rebel. But suspicions were one thing, and Dublin as always was crawling with the informers the British traditionally relied on; those men, women and children who would sell their own mother for a lousy half-crown.

Into her sight Janey Reilly and her brother Willie jumped and stood staring with blank indifference down upon the people assembled in the hall.

"And where were you?" Harriet asked.

Janey glanced down at her fresh-whitened runners, still wet and gray, before she answered. "Waiting for me shoes to dry," she said. "Where do you think?"

"Another short answer like that and I'll tell you!" Harriet's voice had risen to a shout and Janey's muttered insolence into it went unheard. By Harriet, but not by Jeremiah Hudson who had come up from his room in the basement.

"I'm sure that child sprang from you fully grown Harriet," he said. "I'm also convinced that parents and children are only accidentally related," he added. On such a contemptible enemy Janey let fall a cynical eye. She saw him move in to take possession. Saw him greet the women and smile a happy smile, as he loosely linked himself to Mollo for a second, and all the time, she noticed, without ever once taking his eyes off Liam Martin. Out of her own fixed, arrows shot as she brought up the fear and panic that had made him who wasn't yet old, old, when she told him what it was she had seen in his room. Because his fear and rage was not what she had expected she had lost her nerve, and seeing, he had taken courage and slammed the door in her face. People were always slamming doors in her face. And she knew why. What they were looking for was a beef from the heel up thick. A plattered-face biddable fool. A knee-bending arse-licking dunce who didn't know any better and who would flatter their complacency like a glass. But she wouldn't. She saw through the night games. And the hypocrisy. She saw through the unholy antics. The forward gazing – the prayers lisped at Esther Quinn's plaster statue – the chiselling cheating and wormy lies – that wasn't confined only to this house or the people in it but was going on all over. But one of these days she would do something that the people in this house, especially, would not be able to forget or forgive – or slam doors on. One of these days she would get her own back on Christina Swords and on Jeremiah Hudson. And she had *seen* him. And what she saw flared up in her mind's eye. The haggard drained face smothered with paint under a black wig, with long pendant curls that touched the shoulders the red woman's dress left bare. Him, and that other man in the brown suit. *And she had heard him.* 'Lie back, my darling, lie still.'

Now he kept a coat hanging on the back of the door and she

38

couldn't see into his room – but she would find a way – and through her mind fidgeting for possibilities, she looked at her brother, and turned away impatiently from the smooth fair head, the baby-fat through which she could see no signs of emerging anything, let alone manhood – and from the metal framed glasses, cracked, and which were supposed to have straightened his eyes and didn't – though about that you couldn't be sure because through the cracks you didn't know whether he was looking at you or not. He was a fool. A coward. She would gladly be rid of him. He was afraid of his own shadow. She made an elbow and cupping her chin in her hand turned on him a bandit's eye, and then because she hated Drumcondra and her aunt whose dizened face under the gilt and cracks of color was mean and as plain as day, she began to curse silently under her breath while she waited for her mother to go.

"We can't expect our lives to remain unchanged," Jeremiah Hudson was saying in answer to Harriet, while looking down at his feet for the combed-out fur of the cat he was seldom without.

"A good rebellion might liven things up a bit," Harriet said and swept wide, then drew to the Connemara shawl that had come to her from her mother and which was kept for Sundays, Bank Holidays, Weddings and Funerals.

"You see yourself at the barricades, Harriet?" Jeremiah laughed.

"I might if old age wasn't nudging. And if I didn't have enough fighting to do to keep the bit in me belly and the roof over me head," Harriet said.

"Mr Nolan in the dairy said the Rebels were only boys, and some of them still at school," Mathilda Doran said.

"Yesterday Mrs Reilly said they were louts," Sophia said.

"Did I?" Harriet looked her straight in the face. "If so I take it back." Her glance flew to Mollo and her mind to John, who rumor said was a rebel, but she had shelved that piece of know-ledge because it wasn't safe to know with what foot your neighbor kicked. But she wished to Christ she hadn't opened her mouth, for here was that bitter black Protestant turning her words into something they weren't.

Sophia munched. "Come, Mrs Reilly, stick to your guns!"

Then on a stream of treacle, "You're not offending anyone here! Or are you?"

"I don't know in the name of Jasus what you're bladdering about," Harriet answered.

Sophia leant towards Liam. "You do, don't you, Mr Martin?"

"No! I don't, Miss Doran!"

"She's talking about the rebels." Harriet's voice spilled bitter over her old antagonist and under the thick folds of her shawl her arms tensed, as her son Willie came and pressed himself against her.

On the stairs Janey sat and waited for what she hoped would come, but there was no burst-up, for while resenting the reason that made caution necessary Mollo Goss moved to avert an anger that could end like many a little fire by burning the house down.

"We're off," she said, and to Harriet's relief her voice and manner was light and airy, sounding and looking the way she did when she stood in Camden Street and lured with her palaver – that was a lovely addition to the rest of her – the housewives to her stall and the money from their purses.

"Are you coming, Ma?" Janey got to her feet.

"I am." Harriet looked after Sophia turning into the back parlour: "Good-bye, Sophia, and enjoy yourself." Her slurred thick voice defied Sophia to do anything of the kind.

Mollo stepped from the hall into the sun on the steps. There was no sign of Jamesie Goss, and as her glance swept the distance before her, her mind sought John, probing the lanes and streets of the city where at this very second he was being killed or killing. She looked behind and up at the window on the top floor, and nodded the answer to the question Jeremiah Hudson didn't have to ask.

The canal was quiet, though from a few streets away they could hear the thunder of guns. On the canal a turf boat pulled by two black horses neared the end of its journey from Kildare. The horses' pace was leisurely, unconcerned. From where they stood on the steps they could see plain the face of the man steering. He wore a blue scarf, tied in a knot around his neck, and in his mouth a new white clay pipe with a cap on it.

"Poor oul' Ireland is going up bit by bit!" Jeremiah said and jerked a thumb at the sounds coming from the very heart of the city. "Christ, it's extraordinary how hard of hearing the English appear to be," he said thoughtfully. "But since they are, then I suppose the Republicans' policy of deliverance would seem to be a right and honorable necessity. It is about time the British government and people were made to understand that poverty, exploitation, ignorance and oppression are not after all conditions which nations can endure. Maybe now . . . maybe this time they will fold up their tents and go."

"Like hell they will!" Liam Martin thought it a wonder Jeremiah Hudson wasn't up and down on his knees at Esther's altar with the women of the house. The English had been Jackbooting it across the face of Ireland since eleven-hundred and seventy-two, and expecting them to get the hell out now was like standing over a dead man and telling him to get a cock stand. He looked from Jeremiah to Mollo and saw she had come to the end of prayer. He would have liked to add his petitions to hers; but since that wasn't possible he looked for John and found him against lids screwed up against the light. Saw John's face, about it a density, not of age but of youth. Saw the eyes approach till he felt John's forehead touch his, and for one split second felt the soft questioning of the lashes of his eyes. He blinked and stared up into sharp light. Fuck him anyway! But a man had a right to do what he wanted to do with his own life, and if he wanted to waste it fighting off an existence that the masses were content with and for the destruction of which they wouldn't thank, then let him. But, oh Christ! the humbug, the nauseating monstrous balls that would be spouted by every gombeen of a politician in the time to come, explaining away the dismal failure of a revolt that could only be an expression and in no way an achievement! That would take some swallowing, but he needn't worry, he wasn't going to be here to listen.

Into his sight four hackneys came, crammed with people from around the street and the lanes off it, sublimely unconcerned by the turmoil they were turning their back on and unaware of the chaos they would that night return to. He felt a tug at his arm.

"Will you look, at oul' Toby and Mary Ann Flood?" Harriet screamed her amazement at a couple beside the jarvey on the

41

first car. "Now what unnatural act brought them out into the light of day! Hey, Mary Ann!"

The old woman waved a handful of streamers.

"What happened?" Harriet screamed into a volley of calls and shouts, being flung by everyone on the cars, at them standing on the steps.

'As if they hadn't a care in the world,' Liam thought, and of course they hadn't, or if they had, hard experience had taught the working class of Dublin how to shelve them. For this one day at least.

"Someone has given Mary Ann Flood a whole new lease of life!" Harriet said.

They watched the hackneys take the bridge and disappear over it. And in the excitement left behind, Harriet with the rest of them moved on down the steps. At the door, Mathilda Doran stood nodding her head like a toy nodding to the touch of an infant's hand. She didn't want to go back into the house and to a room into which the sun never came, and where her sister Sophia was waiting. She wanted to go somewhere. Somewhere where the wind sang sad songs. And cones fell, and the wings of birds parted the heat.

Above her, from a window, Sarah Goss also watched them go, her dark brooding face crisscrossed with starched patterns of coarse white lace; Mollo and Liam were, as she expected them to be, alone; John was nowhere in sight.

TWO

TUESDAY

1

She must have slept, or something, for some-
time that morning someone had left a cup of tea on the chair
drawn up to the head of the bed. Beside the cup there was a plate
with two slices of bread and a rasher gone cold. Shaking off the
lusty drifts of sleep she hauled herself up onto the pivot of an
elbow and reached for the cup. She raised it to her lips, then
quickly put it slopping back onto the chair. "Shagging thing is
stone," she said. She rummaged round the piled flock pillows for a
cigarette, and finding one lit it. She dragged on it once or twice
then flicked it across into the empty grate. Through the rose-light,
caused by the decrepit red blind on the window, her slow glance
went scowling and reluctant. Not a large room, and except for a few
sticks of furniture and a shelf on which the shrouded statue of the
Virgin stood, was almost all bed. A large rambling thing of iron that
the drifting, musical, travelled Jewess she sometimes skivvied for
had given her. Mountainous with decaying red brocaded mattresses
that for some strange reason smelled of horseflesh and gunpowder,
and when Billy Boy Beausang was around, of whiskey and nico-
tine, and what he called 'Nectar'. In the bed, with its heavy and
clean linen sheets, Esther Quinn lay and waited for Billy Boy
Beausang. Esther was twenty-five and small. Her breath never
dimmed a mirror-face and her slanted greeny-yellow eyes never

43

asked unanswerable questions. Though not visible from the outside, she looked out onto the world from the depths of another woman. A woman whose hair was thick and black and kept wound around with the help of combs. The kind of hair which was forever coming down; too much of it, and too heavy. A dark eyed, thick creamy skinned woman, who spoke English as if she was coping with the demands of a foreign language and who laughing flashed spray like diamonds; who knew the rich and sinuous sensations of silk and sable; whose only disturbances and coquetries were muscular and localized; and who was endowed with that brilliance and deception that men who wore black pearl-studded shirt fronts expect. But, most of all, a woman whose body streamed like a landscape arum-white and gold and on which the sun fell from two enormous succulent globes of light and left in deep and blacker shadows the voluptuous ridges, valleys and gullies through which Billy Boy Beausang scampered.

With that other poor shuddering, sallow-skinned creature who seemed to be walking in the steps of someone about to die; whose hair was crimped and sparse and unlovely; who was all ankles, hands and intervening bones; who sometimes and without warning fell to the floor or into a chair in an epileptic frozen state of abandon and threw back her head and turned up white eyeballs; who thrashed and thumped and opened her mouth to moan, sob, to foam and drench her face with red or white or sickly green – and whose territory she was sometimes forced to re-enter – she refused to identify. With her she would have nothing to do. Without time or respect for the chapel's tinselled glory or supernatural tales of heaven and hell, Esther's belief in the benefit of prayer and the power of the Virgin was hearsay. Could've been the Virgin who sent Billy Boy Beausang along just when her need was greatest. Could've and if so God bless her and the mother who bore her. But she didn't believe it. Any more than she believed that the statue on the shelf over her bed could *see* or *hear* herself and Billy Boy Beausang. Oh yes, they fucked like animals but that was neither here nor there. What she did believe was that if you depend on something to any extent then you might as well learn to respect it. And the statue was hers.

Gave her an importance. And sometimes possession wasn't only a peaceful mystery, it was also a profitable one. What she didn't know, and would never have admitted, was that with time the statue had also become a dim and accepted apprehension lying quietly at the back of her mind.

Lying in her bed and with her attention narrowed down to listening, she continued brooding as she waited for Billy Boy Beausang, as the sky smouldered over the canal and in the far distance something she thought might be thunder sounded.

In the hall below the door was slammed open and banged to. The house rocked. Might be him. She stirred and plaited her arm into the iron flowers at her head as though to stabilize herself. For she had begun to shiver suddenly: all the old ironwork was rattling. In the rose-light dusk she held her breath when she heard a movement on the stairs outside her door. If that was Janey Reilly snooping she'd kill her. She waited, but the steps faded away and she thought she heard a grieving woman's cry coming from another room, but she couldn't be certain, for just then she heard Jeremiah Hudson call through the house for his cat. A terrible shagging pack. Her nostrils narrowed in judgement on the people of the house.

On the window the blind lifted in a breeze from the canal. Sunspots freckled and spread, shadows trellising the walls swelled to quivering shapes that were like the heads of fish and rose-red. Her head was eaten by the iron flowers. And so was her arm. She freed it. The rose-light flushed her face and arms as she let go and stretched. She stretched with her feet to touch the depths of the bed she did not fill. She lay and drifted into the rose-light that the blind on the window shed.

'Dear, dear! Aren't we women unfortunate? These terrible little accidents!' Onto the rose-red screen her lids provided, the abortionist came of her own accord. God! Nurse Madden hadn't crossed her mind in ages but if she thought about her now or began to, Billy Boy might walk in, for that happened. Just when the picture show began flickering, in he'd walk as large as life, and the grin . . . Oh, God! And Nurse Madden . . . Oh yes, and captured

Nurse Madden was assembled. What was it she said to her? No, before that. No, she'd go back. To the hall of brown wood, ugly and dark and the little room off it that reeked of Jeyes Fluid and camphor balls and against the dark mustard-colored walls the empty derelict brutal bed. She went to pieces at the sight of it. "What are you going to do?" she asked, as Nurse Madden turned the key in the lock behind her. "What do you want me to do?" "I'm pregnant," she said. "Who sent you?" Nurse Madden wanted to make sure she was no danger to her. And she told her, watching her pour liquor out of a bottle and knocking the bottle against the glass and spilling the liquor on to the dark and dirty carpet. It was just like a man to let her brave that room, and that woman, alone; she didn't know men could be such unfeeling animals then – but she did now.

"Your father?" Nurse Madden didn't even sound surprised. "Well go on!" She didn't have to, but she did. Misery alone would have made her. Anything to keep her from seeing the dresser, and in a blue chipped enamel bowl a pair of rusty forceps, red-handled scissors and beside them other instruments she'd never seen before, and on the floor beside the bed a swill-pail brimming with abominations. Wanting to fall forward and laugh with terror at the head coming up saying, "Well go on, go on, go on . . ." she told her, groping her way – rapping – fumbling – . Blood. It was just after her first. Frightened and nobody to tell, and her Ma not wanting to know. Watching her breasts grow bigger every day. Becoming snouts pointing up as if to blame. Frightened till the hair began to burst in glossy foliage and she discovering it. Sort of proud then. And waiting. And not for God to call her. But for something and not knowing what. A fella. Maybe. Then one night when her Ma was out her father had come in, off the boats where he worked, and after eating his dinner warming on the hob asked where her Ma was, and she didn't know and said and he just sat there instead of putting on his cap and going out like he always did and looking sideways at where she was standing at the table. He moved his body easy inside his shabby overalls, her Father did. He was dark and physical. There was no connection between them. She saw him shift his position easily on his chair and chew

46

on something with his strong teeth. He had that ease in his body, her father did. She thought he might get up and throw himself down on the bed the way he sometimes did, but he didn't. Certain positions of his body showed his manliness, she had noticed. Muscular. She saw from beneath eyelids. Saw him now laugh and get to his feet. "All ready to be picked, aren't you, Esther?" he said and half closed his eyes. She didn't answer because she didn't know what. He put his arms around her and she let him hanging dumb so as not to vex, thinking she might get the price of the dance hall out of him, and he was acting queer as if a hurry had come on him, but he was nice, full and blind and nice and smelled of boats and oil and she felt good. She didn't mind when he put his mouth down on top of hers. It was like they were drinking each other because his mouth was open and his lips were thick and full and hot. And then he asked if she'd ever had a fella and she thought he was tricking and that she was in for a hiding and she hadn't not ever . . .

Esther Quinn opened her eyes. A sense of anger had begun floating around her. Words came slickin, hiccupin from between her bare lips, while thought continued erupting in her eardrums. 'I could've drunk that bastard up! Oh yes, him! But shag him! And Billy Boy Beausang.' On the mantelpiece the Easter egg she had bought Billy Boy on Saturday caught her eye. In the rose-red light the red wrapping smouldered. Reminded. He would come now if she didn't think. Her anger broke around her suddenly and she began tearing to shreds the flimsy pink of the slip to free beneath. Naked now she slid further down and under her the matress sighed and sucked, before settling around her. She closed her eyes, searching, and searching and finding was dragged under again. Her father. The whites of his eyes in his dark face. The bristling skin and the lamplight at the back of his head. As he came slow but purposefully towards her, her mind began to root through, her parched mouth began to lap at every detail; she drank the saliva from his dark full mouth, dragged at the leather waist-coat; the striped shirt; the heavy metal buckled belt; the creases in the tight powerful thighs and between them the thing that bulged and bumped against her; to the big hands heavy and tearing until there was nothing on her and then him; the huge

47

shoulders and the long body dark and not only at the extremities but all over; right down to that never fully imagined thing which must have been there all this time and here she was only now discovering it; and afraid to, afraid to look at what he wanted her to see as he edged towards the bed; and stopping to show her and himself in the floor to ceiling glass her Ma had got for nothing somewhere and nailed to the wall; and then turning to face her his hands on his narrow hips, his legs apart and what he was wanting her to see rising and rising in tough and violent erection between them; and waiting, his eyes half-closed, until he saw her glance finally follow the fall of his; and then the hint of a grin, fleeting, a glint of strong white teeth as his hand went down and closed like a hand over a mouth. "Will I be able to get in?" he asked, but she couldn't answer. She stared, they both stared and watched the muscular contraction; saw the veins swell under the flesh and under the skin of his hand as it closed on the thing thrusting itself up and up in gigantic and triumphant proportions. It was like a savage furred animal coming up from a bush of undergrowth. She heard a cry coming in her; a throbbing; a bewildering hunger; he heard and took his hand away; she swayed towards him but he pushed her back with his left hand; his right hovered, he had only to touch his foreskin; spearheads of near seed burst through; her whole body was shaken as he bent her backwards onto the bed; he knelt astride her: in his right hand in the smokey lamp-lit room the hammer head of the man's phallus glowed. "If you start bawling I'll belt you," he said. But she didn't, even when he went in on her slow and then plunged and she knew she was killed. He was like a horse as big as a big black stallion. She lay, eyes wide open, and gathered his bursting flesh into her own enormous vacuum; her mouth screaming silent words that fluctuated between his brutal thrusts and the longed-for-death-blow. He kept on with it for a long time. And then he exploded into her, deep in, and she held him and sucked him out with strong sure movements and little cries.

And then it was done . . .

His tongue in her mouth was still. After a time her own moved against it. Stirring and then biting and begging and sobbing until he gave a great heave and taking possession reared up to mount her

48

again and again and again smothering her every time in a warm smell of oil and boats and wet and she didn't cry but held him to her . . . until they both lay killed . . .

2

Maisie had no sooner let Ba Fay go and settled
herself on the top step, when behind her the hall door was flung
open and Harriet Reilly stepped out, her black every-day shawl
thrown carelessly around her and held down on one side to hide
the bundle of just-washed sheets she was taking up to the pawn.
Maisie nodded her greeting and put aside the putrid state of her
soul and a conscience that allowed her to take a lover and reject
the teachings of chapel and priest and her lawful husband. With a
drawn-out sigh Harriet sat down beside her.

"Jasus, but there are days when I don't know which of me ends
to take my mind off," she said. She looked at Maisie. "Has Ba
gone?" she asked.

"Just."

"Will he be working?"

"Won't know till he gets there."

"And that wigger's altar still covered!" Harriet gestured to the
house behind her. "It's all I needed this lousy morning. Now I
know the humor this oul' bastard will be in," she cried. And
without being told Maisie knew to whom it was she referred.
"Shagging sheets are in flitters, and for spite that louser will
open them up like sails in a breeze just to shame me." She paused.
"Funny the way everything goes against us when Esther's
statue's blinded!"

50

"Shagging panic!" Maisie flicked the cigarette butt into the gutter. "And if there wasn't a sad lack of humor on me I'd die laughing."

"That other fucker wouldn't give me his suit this morning, not if I'd gone to him on me bended, though he knows bloody well what I get on these won't keep him fed for a week. Well, he can tell his shagging belly his throat's cut." Harriet nudged Maisie, who looked up to see her husband Hammy coming towards them.

"And where did the night fall on you?" Maisie asked, her glance hardening as she took in the stubbled grin and the boxes he carried in his arms. "And what are you colloguing there, Robin Hood, or need I ask?"

"No harm in asking," Hammy replied. "But first have a decco!" He set the shoe boxes down onto the steps and began to tear them open. Maisie stared at a dozen pair of men's boots, brand new, and a box of passion rousers.

"Not what you expected, is it?" Hammy asked. "And there's more where they came from." He began to rub the palms of his hands together as he watched Maisie's and Harriet's amazement.

"Jasus, wouldn't I be made up with a pair of them?"

Harriet fondled a pair lovingly. In her mind's eye she saw herself slapping them down in front of Christie up in the pawn, and demanding ten, or even fifteen shillings on them, and what's more – getting it.

"You wouldn't." Hammy looked at her. "There isn't a pawn office open in the whole city."

"You're joking!" Harriet raised startled eyes.

But Hammy was in no mood for joking, as Maisie well knew, watching his glance linger speculatively on the new boots.

Harriet looked desperate. "But why?"

"Because it's shoot to kill day, that's why," Hammy replied.

Maisie reached for the box of sweets, tore the lid off and offered them to Harriet.

"Ah, have a nuttyer. Have a Passion Rouser, Harriet," she said unconcernedly, as if the pawn shops being closed had no importance for her.

'And well it mightn't!' Harriet thought, for whatever about her

51

'If I am barren' and how ever much her large eyes and great tits protested – her predicament wasn't a frightening one. There remained all the material advantages that Ba Fay if not God provided. Harriet helped herself to the sweets. "Passion Rouser, how are ya!"

"The whole town's in an uproar," Hammy said, gathering up the boots and putting them back in their boxes. "The Rebels are everywhere. They've even taken over the Post Office, and dug trenches around it."

"But what, in the name of God, has that got to do with the pawn?" Harriet could not understand why a state of affairs that didn't concern her should discommode her. Every Monday, for as long as she could remember she had gone to the pawn. And besides, only yesterday, in Drumcondra, that foul-mouth, craw-thumping, brother-in-law of hers had said with certainty that the Insurrection wouldn't last the night.

"Your brother-in-law is talking through his arse," Hammy said. "It's worse today. The bastards aren't happy, yet they want to kill us all. The whole city's ripped open and the Lancers charging through it in their thousands, hang, drawn and quartering everyone they leave their filthy hands on." He paused and an odd memory sprang to life. "Jasus, talk about the sacking of Rome!"

Unmoved by his rhetoric, Maisie said, "And where did you get the boots?"

"Looting." Without thinking Hammy spoke the truth and for no reason she could account for, and for the first time ever, Maisie believed him.

Harriet sat forward. "Where?"

"Camden Street. There isn't a shop left with a pane of glass in it."

"You mean there's no windows?"

"That's what I said. No glass, no nothing. Every shop from here to Dame Street bandjaxed."

"And that's all you got?" Harriet's mind was on a scene of plenty existing elsewhere. Hammy grinned. "No, it isn't." He laughed and did a few steps of a reel before he said "It's in business I am. In business."

"Don't lose the run of yourself, Robin, and end up in Mountjoy

52

jail," Maisie said dragging thought from the enormous wonder of what Cassidy's, the biggest women's outfitters in George's Street, would look like without windows.

"You mean a person could just walk past Cassidy's and put her hand through the window?"

"A person could back shanks' mare through Cassidy's window," Hammy replied.

And behind him, Mollo Goss came, unnoticed until she said "You haven't been idle Hammy." She pushed her empty basket cart beyond him before she sat down on the steps between the railings and Harriet, who drew over to make room for her.

"Can't afford to be." Hammy's gaze took Mollo in but it was on her breasts, pushing at the restraint of her white starched bib that his eyes rested, and he wished . . . because them dairies fighting a losing battle under that pinny were a lovely handful. He wondered why Mollo wasn't like Esther Quinn, who if you happened to bump into her in the hall or at the pipe in the yard wasn't above letting you fondle her tits to your heart's content, though God help her! they weren't the marvels she thought they were, but still and all she let a man have his fill. But then these touch-me-not wans like Mollo Goss didn't know what they'd been given them for, though if the truth be known he bet that big-pricked randy bastard Liam Martin got more than his hands full!

Maisie leaned across Harriet. "You're back early, Mollo," she said.

"Nothing to keep me out." Mollo threw her shawl off her shoulders. "Market wasn't even open." She threw Hammy a brief glance as she bent forward to look up at the house.

"Your Ma's out," Maisie said. "Went out this morning just after you did."

Which meant that John, who hadn't come home at all last night, hadn't returned this morning either, and so her Ma had gone looking for him? But where? Mollo remembered the blaze of her mother's anger that morning. Waking to find Sarah standing over her and to her only half-understood urgent questioning she had gestured towards John's bed in the far corner of the room they shared. "He went out without waking you that's all," she had

53

answered. "And made his own bed before he went?" Sarah pointed to the bed that hadn't been touched. "Well you won't cover up for him any more. And something else! You haven't done him any favors hiding from me his connections with the Republicans, if you but knew it. He hasn't slept in that bed one whole night this week has he?" she asked and waited, and Mollo hadn't answered, but Sarah saw the answer in the eyes raised to her before she hurried from the room. Now Mollo remembered that the whole scene had been carried out in a whisper, Sarah hadn't once raised her voice; for not for God Himself would she have disturbed her husband's rest. And at breakfast, Jamesie was still asleep. Mollo wondered if he knew John hadn't come home last night, or if Sarah, believing him ignorant of his son's affiliations with the Republicans, was trying to spare him the knowledge. She should go up, she thought, but reluctance to disturb his hard earned rest kept her where she was. Besides, what use was she to him? She had never had John's gift for pleasing her Da.

She turned to hear Hammy Collins say, "The English have said they will starve us out."

Mollo remembered what the dealers who had like herself turned up at the market this morning had said and nodded. It was a pity now, she thought, drawn back to immediate needs, that unlike the rest of the dealers she wasn't a money-lender, for that at least would have kept her going till law and order was restored or until the market opened again. But she dismissed the thought even as it came. Money-lending demanded a ruthless dishonesty she didn't possess. She couldn't lend a woman a shilling and demand four in return and on top of that load her down with four or five shillings worth of stuff she didn't want but had to take if she was to get the lousy single shilling she was in need of.

"But for Christ's sake, we're not Republicans!" Harriet cried, and let go her grip on the bed-clothes under her shawl, for she thought now it might not be necessary to put up with Christie's abusive mockery when he held them up for inspection.

"And how would you suggest the enemy differentiate, Harriet?" Jeremiah Hudson inquired blandly as he removed his postman's cap and sat down on the bottom step at their feet.

"I never saw you coming," Harriet said suspiciously, though he

54

had wandered into her sight the moment he turned the corner of Rock Street.

"What happened?" Maisie asked, eying the ringed dent his cap left on his forehead. "You weren't sacked?"

Jeremiah eased his spine against the railings as his gaze went to Hammy and the boxes of boots at his feet. "His anguished lethargy fell from him, and he leaped up into the day," he said and turning from Hammy to Maisie, "At my age a man's not sacked. Just retired and turned out to grass or locked up in some bucolic eleemosynary . . . I'm here, Ma'am, because there's nowhere left for me to go, the Irish Postal Department having decided, by decree absolute, that no post will be delivered today to me, to you, or anybody else in the city of Dublin."

"No letters?" The exclamation came on a scream, and Harriet's eyes went wide in amazement forgetting altogether that she never got any anyway, and that the only thing that ever came through the post to her was a diddly club card once a year.

"Jasus! It'll kill Harriet if she has to go without all the letters she gets," Maisie laughed.

"It isn't that. But the Post Office is like the army, and the government and the chapel . . ." Her voice died. She gazed perplexed, furious at her inability to express herself then shrugged impotence away when Jeremiah almost against his will began to describe a scene that wouldn't be stilled. "I saw a horse with its throat cut." He spoke rapidly. "Against the as yet unruined splendours of the College of Surgeons it bled to death. It lay in a great pool of its own blood, and with clouds of British bullets darkening the air, not a British soldier could spare one to end its agony."

"The bastards are saving their bullets for us!" Hammy said.

"Here's your Ma," Maisie nudged Mollo staring wide-eyed with horror at the picture Jeremiah had drawn. "What a terrible thing!" she gasped, as Sarah Goss nodded to her neighbors and sat down, black-shawled, black-hatted, beside them.

"What is?" She asked, as she began to remove the pin from her hat and the hat from her head, placing it carefully in her lap.

Maisie told her as Mollo got up and went to sit beside her. "The market's shut tight," Mollo said explaining her presence on the steps at this hour of the day, and as if that was the answer to the questioning look Sarah was giving her. Their glances held, then broke.

"I went over to see Teasey," Sarah said. Her dark eyes dulled with disappointment, and the horrors she had just witnessed, swept the balmy tranquillity of the canal. Everyone there knew Teasey was Mrs Goss's only sister who lived on the north-east side of the city, but Mollo alone knew her mother only made that journey when all was right with her world, when she could laugh and make light of Teasey's constant complaints. She knew also that Sarah was lying to still any curiosity her neighbors might be harboring about her unusual early outing and that she was still trying to keep secret a thing no longer a secret, for yesterday Mollo had seen behind Sophia Doran's hedging, and had concluded that if Sophia knew John was a Republican, then the canal knew. But the look on the faces turned towards her mother now betrayed nothing, other than a mild inquiry as they waited for her to speak, but Sarah had nothing to say, and to all intents and purposes she might have been a woman taking a moment's ease from the normal events of an ordinary day.

"You'll have seen something of the massacre that's going on?" Jeremiah Hudson suggested quietly.

"Couldn't miss it," Sarah said and under the hand she drew across her mouth, a hidden nerve pulsed with unanswered questions, beyond which her mind refused to budge.

"And they say two shiploads of Lancers were landed from England during the night," Jeremiah said and added. "Eight thousand in all: and very pretty they looked, too, I believe."

"A helluva lot of use they'll be now, against the millions of Germans and Irish-Americans coming to help us!" Hammy said.

"When?" Jeremiah asked.

"Today! They're here now."

"Well, they're the shy pampered lot if that's true," Sarah said. "I didn't see sight or sound of anything or anybody but Lancers." Her glance fell to the boxes at Hammy's feet. "A woman told me the Volunteers shot forty looters last night."

Before her accusing gaze, Hammy shifted uneasily. "The Volunteers are taking too much onto themselves," he said. "They should save their energy, guns and bullets for the politicians and the British army and leave decent innocent people alone."

"Hear! Hear!" Harriet was all agreement. "It's a queer shagging war when the Volunteers are going round the streets killing the wrong people. And while I'm at it who started this war? And what will we get out of it?"

"Justice! We hope. And we started it, Harriet," Jeremiah said.

"Why?" Harriet asked.

"Because we are no longer content with the strictly limited and not satisfying freedom of stray cats to ravage dustbins and fight in alleys," Jeremiah replied.

"We want the English out," Maisie said.

"And in their stead a Workers' Republic."

"But for Christ's sake what harm are the English?" Harriet asked.

Jeremiah laughed. "None if you don't object to being governed by aliens! And as I used to say before the new passions in the air obliterated any affection for the English that might have lingered in my blood – if we were wise, we'd let them stay as our guests. But *paying* guests, of course. After all the British in Ireland can't go on claiming the right to live forever like the lilies of the field."

"We want to be free," Hammy broke in.

"Or just equal," Jeremiah murmured.

"Free from what? And what's more important, will we be any the better off for it?" Harriet asked.

"That's beside the point," Jeremiah replied. "The fact is, a handful of men decided, without permission – either yours or mine – that the English must go, and the only way to persuade them is by force. Right or wrong; this means bloodshed. But we're not supposed to mind. In their innocence, the Republicans think that we, the people, share their obsessions, and the ugly and appalling truth is we don't. So now the Republicans don't only have the British – and in the north – the moronic anchorites of Orangism to contend with – but their own as well."

"Will it change things?" Maisie asked.

Jeremiah shook his head. "I don't know. Perhaps society remains unchanged. Revolutions? – rebellions? Perhaps all that happens is that the dregs come floating to the top! Perhaps

57

all this is just an opening of the door for all those people who have never ventured into the daylight, but who then crawl out. Dungeon – basement people. Revolution! The other day I watched a kid kicking a stone embedded in the ground; under the stone there were insects; thousands of blind scrambling insects. Given power, insects would grow as tall as people."

"Where's it all going to end?" Sarah asked but nobody answered.

"Well, I must say it's a bit shagging much bringing murder and slaughter down about our heads for no reason," Harriet glanced at Sarah as she spoke, but if Sarah heard she gave no sign.

"I suppose that centuries of unparalleled political thuggery, evictions, famines, jailing, torture, poverty, and ignorance isn't enough?" Jeremiah suggested.

"Jailing, torture? Assorted jelly babies? When did all them things happen for God's sake?" Against Harriet's cheeks her earrings slapped.

"Didn't they teach you anything at school?" Hammy asked.

Harriet's glance took aim. "What school? The only schooling I ever had was in scrubbing the Goddam floors for the Jews on the South Circular."

"The possessor classes – buying themselves the luxury of servants for a few lousy pennies," Jeremiah said.

"Be Jasus! And you're the right stranger to life, Hammy Collins," Harriet cried.

"Hundreds and hundreds of people there was, round the Post Office in Sackville Street, as I came by; and half of them screaming filth and abuse at the Republicans, God help them!" Sarah Goss spoke suddenly out of her own musings.

"For doing the dirty work of the world," Jeremiah Hudson replied and continued thoughtfully. "Fifty or sixty years from now, the new feudalists – those implacable place-hunters and piety-painted toughs who rule over us – will be screaming the same filth, the same abuse, at the very sons and grandsons of these same Republicans."

"Well, you have to admit, nobody asked them, or their grandfathers, to fight," Hammy Collins said.

Sarah let her glance fall on him. "That's exactly what the *whores* said, gathered round the Lancers and their horses this morning."

"When the English are not gunning us down in our tracks they're laughing at us," Jeremiah said quietly. "And is it any wonder, for only this very morning the ladies of Baggot Street kept open house for the Lancers, and were out with their butlers, lining the pavement with food and hot drinks as they rode by on their way into the city from Kingstown."

"Ladies how are you!" Harriet cried. "If they were hanged for being ladies they'd die innocent."

Sarah was nodding her head silently. She had no difficulty in believing or visualizing the scene Jeremiah had described. She had seen for herself. Men and women all over Dublin playing deaf to the cries coming at them from the city's tangled ruins from heads smashed to pulp with the butts of rifles. She remembered the crowd of men tearing from a wall with vicious spite the Rebel posters asking for recruits to The Cause. She saw again the crowds surging through Sackville Street and around the Post Office, barricaded with sandbags and horseless drays, adding their sticks, stones and bottles to the bursting rifle and machine-gun fire coming from the Lancers in and outside the buildings opposite. Her search for her son had led her finally to The Green where she had heard the Rebels had taken over. But at The Green the gates were locked, and inside four youths lay close together, riddled with British bullets, and against the railings another – little more than a child – with his jaw shot away – made feeble silent gestures for help with stumps of arms from which the hands had been blown. "They can't be moved till nightfall," a man at her elbow spoke to her, smothering the scream of terror rising in her. For a moment she had believed that one of them was John. "If they last, their companions will get them as soon as it's dark," the man, tall, stooped and about the same age as herself, dragged her from the railings to which she had run, back across the street to the shelter of the houses. "They're keeping themselves to the middle of The Green," he said anticipating her question, for beyond the dead and dying Volunteers nothing moved, though from the windows over her head and behind her, British soldiers were pouring a constant

59

stream of fire into the foaming greenery of the trees. "A couple of attempts have already been made by their pals to get them," the man said, and he looked back and up at the buildings behind them before his glance rove the length of The Green. "But they didn't stand a chance, their pals didn't, and had to leave them there. All four sides of The Green is surrounded by the British," he said, speaking now not only to Sarah but to two young girls, one carrying a baby in her arms, who had appeared beside them.

"They haven't a chance," the girl with the baby said, as she eased her breast into the baby's mouth under cover of her shawl.

"And nobody in this city of saint-hunters cares!" The man, his face rouged with consumption, as long afterwards Sarah was to remember, shook in sudden rage.

"Have you someone out, mister?" The girl with the baby asked.

"My son," the man said. "He's seventeen." He tore a blue handkerchief out of his overcoat pocket and drew it clumsy across his eyes.

"Like myself, God help you!" Sarah's gaze rested long on the strange sight of a man crying.

"My brother is in The Green!" The girl, who could have been older than the one with the baby, spoke suddenly. "He's Sheila's husband."

"Oh, God, where's it all going to end?" Sheila's young eyes in an already old face implored.

"Up in fuckin Mountjoy! Or in the graveyard of Mount Jerome! Thass where!"

Sarah saw the big dizened woman grow slowly from the pavement, sway and bend towards her. She felt the soiled warm gust of the purple woman. She felt her kohl smeared eyes. Saw the wet lips that nights and scores had pulped. She would have touched to confirm that what was bloated and shattered had once been a light footed slip of a girl laughing, selling fruit, vegetables, and Friday's frozen fish, alongside Mollo.

"Ninety!" Sarah said.

She moved to touch but the woman drew back. "I hope every one of the bastards is shot!" She roared her curse and from the crowd, violently anti-Rebel, there was loud encouragement. She lurched towards Sarah who loosened her grip on her shawl and

60

stepping back unfolded her hands from the fists they had become.

"Go home, Ninety!" she cried. "Go home in the name of God," she said her voice slurred, her eyes sweeping threateningly over the crowd as she cautiously distributed her weight while her gaze darted to The Green across the road, and beyond the railings, to the dead and dying Volunteers.

"Ah, shut your face and let the poor hoor have her say!" A voice from the crowd cried the crowd's belligerence.

"God blast you! Who cares what she has to say?" The girl with the baby handed over the sleeping child into the arms of her sister-in-law.

"We care," someone laughed.

Ninety, as though dodging blows, began to drag at her purple satin coat, screaming obscenities as she did so while she struggled to get at what was beneath. And the crowd, thinking it a row begun between Ninety and Sarah, and not yet ended, began with the Dubliners' vicious love of a rucky-up to shout encouragement, the shouts fading to mocking titters, the titters to silence as Ninety ripped and showed her broad mutilated chest. From both breasts the nipples had been hacked off.

"Look!" she screamed to show wounds from which blood still flowed.

"Oh, Jasus!" The crowd murmured.

And Sarah said, "Dear Christ and His Holy Mother!"

"Who did it to you?"

A man stepped from the crowd. "The Rebels!"

Sarah would have blocked her ears. Now her veins ebbed, which had flowed before.

"The Rebels!" Ninety stared. "Maybe! The lousy bastards!" She wasn't sure. She didn't know. Men. They had wakened her in the dawn from her sleep in the doorway in some lane. "Love," they had called her, "Love." She began to cry. "Love!" the little carrot-headed bastard had called her and all the time the foxy fuckers were butchering her. She began to scream her pain into the rifle fire over her head.

"Someone should do something!" A man shouted.

"The Rebels should be tarred and feathered!"

"If it was the Rebels!" A mild looking woman spoke mildly.

61

"And who else could it be?"

"The Countess is above in the College of Surgeons."

"Having her picture took!"

"Or keening over graves of hope and pleasures gone – while all the time trying to see from here to London with tears in her eyes."

"The Countess is a patriot!" The girl with the baby cried.

"The Countess and Maude Gonne are shagging English Protestants with idle hands and full bellies," a woman shouted. "And what's more the daughters of English soldiers! Don't you stand there and talk to me about patriots! The pair of them are smug untalented English Protestants out to make a future for themselves. They couldn't do it in England so they come stravaging over here to put us all in our place and incite the scum of this city to rape, murder and plunder. Patriots! Be Jasus! If they're ever hanged for being patriots they'll die innocent."

"Ah, but if they were hungry or dry! Or if patriotism was costing them anything?"

And Ninety, coming to a halt before the girl with the baby in her arms began to spit a burst of fresh abuse into her face.

"I hope everyone of the buggers is hanged, drawn and quartered!" she screamed and reached – but the latter made alert by the antagonism of the crowd, who were now moving in, anticipated Ninety's move and parried it with her open hand. With a twist of her body she sent Ninety sprawling and the crowd released from tension, began to take sides. In a moment, Sarah had lost her balance and was reeling against the shop-front behind her. She lay where she had fallen until hands reached out and helped her to her feet.

"Quick ma'am." The old man was handing Sarah her hat and looking around for his own.

She let him lead her out of the crowd which had shifted beyond them. And in King Street, when he stopped to look back to catch another glimpse of the dead and dying men behind the railings of The Green, she walked on. When she remembered him again she was climbing the steps of the parish priest's house and ahead of her, polishing the placid and obedient hall door, a servant was pausing long enough to tell her that Father Robinson wasn't at home. She saw the dismay in Sarah's eyes. Heard the labored breathing, and hoped next time she came calling on the priest she'd know enough to go to the side door of the kitchen and not be killing herself climbing steps – intended for the use of her betters. But then, some of these oul' wans from the lanes and tenements of Dublin had the cheek of the devil, you'd think the priest had nothing better to do but be here at their beck and call at all hours of the day and night and dip his hand into his pocket every time they ran short of an article to pawn.

"I wanted to talk to him," Sarah said, as though she had surmised the other's thoughts.

"Well, he isn't here and won't be back till dinner-time."

Sarah knew she was being dismissed, and yet she stood there, baffled and lost. No, she corrected her statement silently to herself, not to talk; and her glance came to a blind halt on the grey square stone of the solid wall of the chapel against which the house was built. She wanted Father Robinson to say something that would ease her dark and bewildering misery. Beg him to do with her son what she had failed to do. She wanted the weight of the Church's authority to prevent him, not only from destroying himself, but from destroying Jamesie as well.

"Have you somebody sick?"

Sarah looked back from the chapel wall to the woman's face. She shook her head.

"In that case, your want can't be desperate." The eyes between thick lids probed. "And if I was you," she said, "I'd go into the chapel and say a little prayer of thanks."

Sarah regarded her in silence, tempted, and she turned away suddenly lest she give utterance to the words that crowded thick behind her lips . . . 'Thanks.' Thanks for what? Thank an uncaring God! Thanks for rearing a son who could lie and cheat and play at soldiers, throwing his life around like snuff at a wake, a life not his to give if he would pause long enough to remember who it was he owed it to, what he owed to that man upstairs, a loving man, a kindly man, a man who had poured his own life into him, and for what? What thanks was Jamesie getting and what thanks would he get, for the lifetime of love he had in wild extravagance given this son of his? Dear dear Christ! Sarah paused, brought to a halt by the desperation of the thoughts coming at her. Able to see again, she saw that Jeremiah was watching her, though it was seconds before the knowledge penetrated.

"You've been a long time gone," he said and he alone saw, rather than heard, the escaping sigh.

"I was thinking."

"You were, God help you!" Harriet said lightly. "Lost to the world you were. Where were you at all?"

"All over." Sarah rose to her feet, and towards her came her son John, his strides quickening at the sight of her. "Your brother's come home," she said to Mollo, and turned her back and opened the door and closed it behind her with a clatter on the flash of his grin, white against his dirt and sweat-stained face.

3

But it was with quiet caution that Sarah moved
around the room busying herself with the preparations of a meal,
while Mollo, after a quick glance at her face, went to stir the fire,
low in the grate, into new life under the perpetually steaming
black fat-bellied kettle on the hob. Only John was still watchful,
fear of his mother's expected wrath keeping him where he was
near the door, his dark glance sliding from her to his Da huddled
in sleep in the big white bed in the corner.

"I'm waiting." There was no pause, no sound that could waken
the man on the bed, as Sarah moved between the table and the
dresser, nor did she look at her son as she spoke.

"What for?" he asked, and, taking courage from the misleading
even tone she used, moved from the door towards her, coming to
an abrupt halt when she drew back from the kiss he would have
placed on her cheek.

"Christmas!" she said. "And this time I want the truth! Where
were you all night? No, it's no use your looking to her," she said,
intercepting the glance he threw Mollo. "You'll not get her to carry
out your game of lies and deceits with me any longer."

"Out." John said, and behind him Mollo lifted herself from the
fire.

"With the Republicans?" He nodded and saw a nerve pulse

across her mouth, while into her eyes momentary confusion sprang which she impatiently tried to wipe away with the back of her hand, the gesture childish and utterly useless. Against the table she leaned all her weight. "You said you were finished with them," she whispered and tried to rein in the blind anger flooding her. "Only the other day . . ." She bent across the table towards him. "You gave me your word. You said you'd quit. You swore..."

"Anyone listening would think you were dealing with children," Mollo said. "Ma, they're men!"

Sarah ignored the interruption. "You told . . ."

"So he lied to you, Ma," Mollo said with irritation. "He had to."

"Shut your mouth."

Mollo stared from one to the other, marvelling at the self-repression her brother had cultivated in the face of Sarah's behaviour, for he stood meek, allowing her to berate and bully him as if he were a child again, and made no attempt to defend himself. She felt a twist of pain that was love, and then, strangely, pity for the turbulent never-fulfilled longings within him which she thought he shared with his Da and which she had only ever been able to guess at. She smiled suddenly up into his desperate gaze. "You look terrible," she said wanting to bring the scene to an end.

Roughly Sarah pushed her aside. "Why did you go against me in this? Why did you say you'd quit when you hadn't?"

"Because you don't understand!"

The bitter laugh was flung at the broad expanse of the back he had turned on her, and slapping away the restraining arm that Mollo reached towards her, Sarah flung herself in front of him. "But you understand! We've seen to that, your father and me; we made sure you'd understand. We kept you in school long after others your age were out earning their livings. We schooled and educated you so you'd understand: the warnings of death, the threats, the reprisals. Is that all we did? Was that what your father meant when he said you had to be learned?" Her hands closed on his open jacket. "The only thing I don't understand is you! I never have! I've never known why you had to be different. I've never understood the fever and obsession with this miserable country that rides you like a nightmare. I've never known why you couldn't be like the rest of the chaps round the place. Or what the demon is that's devouring your guts and pushing you into an early grave. And for what? In the name of Jesus, and His Holy Mother, what for?"

"Ma, if you don't know I can't explain. You, and my Da, are set in your ways. You and others like you have accepted . . ."

"I know," Sarah interrupted. "An English King and an Italian Pope!"

"I can't explain. Can't make you understand."

"What?"

For a moment he did not answer. "This dream. Maybe that's all it is. A dream. Or some lunatic humor of the moon."

Sarah drew herself from him, and speaking in a voice that she tried to make steady said, "Dreams! To paper the walls with pound notes? To put some Judas politician with his shoot-to-kill politics on top of the Pillar and call him Nero? Some red-neck farmer's son or civil servant corner boy who can't even keep his nose dry or his arse clean and who, tomorrow or the next day, when you and the likes of you are in your graves, will claw and crawl his way back into the big pay and arms of the British Imperialists! Is that the dream? To give Hammy Collins and the rest of the rabble a day's looting, and idle English women the opportunity to scutter street corner eloquence, and fill the cemeteries? Is that the dream? And what about your father's dreams? What about him? He wanted to get out of this place; leave this dark strife-torn and poverty stricken kip behind him. He wanted to run from the ruins, the hovels, the ignorance, hunger and filth of this city. To go where he could make something of himself, but he was stopped: first by his father and mother, who couldn't go without the few shillings he was bringing in; and then by you. Yes, you! *And* me. Jamesie Goss's son John – you came, and because of you, he committed himself to this and the pittance he was sure of. What about his dreams? To see you make something of yourself? To learn you, to teach you? And what is to become of that man if you end up in the gutter with a bullet in your back?" She paused, her face distorted with a rage that masked the torture of her mind that had no outward showing.

"Oh Christ! What is to become of that man if anything happens to you? He has given you his life. All the sweet long years you took from me, souring and ravaging the heart and soul in my body." The accusing voice rose in a hysteria made more frightening and terror-ridden because of the restraint that was being put upon it; and on the bed Jamesie Goss moaned soft as if her despair had reached him and he turned his face to the wall. The movement and the cry, unheard by Sarah, was sensed by her. She stopped speaking and, quieter now, rushed on, her words thick and muffled like a voice heard in the dark, John thought as he lowered his eyes for a sight of her, stunned with the unrealized, and unthought of, and unknown things she was saying.

"Christ sent you to scourge me, but your father . . . you owe that man something, for it was for you, the curse of God on you! that he committed himself to this." Her gesture swept the room, but it encompassed more, it took in the whole span of Jamesie's life from the day he brought her up the aisle of the chapel and put the ring on her finger – it closed round and included unfairly his lifetime of failures and it foretold his ending as a night watchman in a factory, the only job he had ever been able to hold – it took in and embraced the love she had just accused her son of robbing her of, the one and only sin she would not forgive him.

But her Ma was wrong, Mollo thought, for you couldn't lose what you never had and Jamesie had given all he had to give to his son to the exclusion of Sarah and herself. She looked at her mother, listening, every word serving as a thorny reminder of the little and sometimes big cruelties that his father's love had subjected John to all his life, and which had until now never been really understood by her, though she had sometimes guessed, and as it now turned out, rightly.

"What about him? What thought have you given to that man?"

"Mother, leave off!" John's teeth clattered with sudden cold. "What do you want of me?"

He whispered, as his father stirred in his sleep. And over the wild thumping of his own heart he could hear the wilder uproar of hers.

"Nothing," she said. "For myself, for the peace and love that belonged to me are indeed gone, but him . . ." She paused, stupid with the struggle of her own unresisting grief and fear that he had heard the terrible things she said, "he must not be nailed down into his coffin by you. You owe him that. You owe him his life, or what's left of it."

"What do you want me to do?"

"Quit."

He closed his eyes to shut out her voice, her face, twisted with a misery he couldn't bear to see – strength was gone from him – he stood in darkness – his face dirt-streaked, quivering, shattered, her accusations swirling in on him – and all were nightmarish – they seethed and swirled – he wanted to protest – or slide down. He was trembling now and his mouth was dry. Her voice pursued him.

"I can't," he said.

"Not even for him? Ireland, and Ireland's cause means more to you than he does?"

"No!" His voice came up from the depths.

"You must."

"It's too late."

The loud fury in Sarah made no physical sound. She saw his eyes search her and then the room as if, she thought, he was some-how dead, devoid of thought and feeling, scanning an existence in which he did not belong, a world to which not even his love for Jamesie could return him. He would do what he felt he had to do, and without understanding the strength of his conviction or what inner need drove him, she knew that nothing she could do or say now would stop him. He was a stranger. Or she was. She looked away, around the room the way he had, and her eyes came to rest on Jamesie, and though she was silent, she shouted the pain she was feeling for him at the full pitch of her voice. It seemed im-possible he should not hear her frenzy speech, but he didn't and on a gasp the storm rose up inside her and spilled itself in tears onto her face; and into the strident tension of the room, Liam Martin came after his unheard knock on the door.

Sarah turned away over to the dresser, and after a shocked pause at so normal an intrusion into the abyss into which they had been plunged, Mollo alone emerged to meet him. But something of it showed in Mollo's face and in the stoop of John's shoulders and Liam, tuned to Sarah's moods, guessed the cause.

69

"Are you not working?" Mollo hurried to deny, and at the dresser, Sarah made an effort to ready herself.

"No," Liam said. "Nothing at the market?"

Mollo shook her head and looked at John as if he might supply the answer. He didn't.

"Have you a drop of hot water, Ma?" He took off his jacket and began to roll up his sleeves. "I want to shave."

Sarah went over to the fire and took the kettle from the hob. After pouring some water into the white enamel basin, she put the kettle back.

"Hammy Collins tried to sell me a pair of boots as I came in," Liam Martin said and laughed.

"What's funny?" Mollo was vexed by an ease out of place on the air of the room still throbbing like a festering sore from the furies of contention.

"Nothing!" Liam replied. "It was the number of sweet shops the kids are looting I was thinking about. And why the hell not!" he asked. "Making the most of *their* opportunity, having the feed of their lives; tasting things they never had before and probably never will again. One thing, though: until *they* go to their graves, the Easter Rising, will, for them at least, have a sweet flavor."

"Is that why he's cleaning the filth and dirt of the streets off him, so that the kids of Dublin can have a feed of sweets – and he can go to his death smelling of soap and water!"

In the glass over the mantelpiece Sarah's glance clashed with John's.

"Is that what this is all about?" she asked.

"No it isn't!" he said and turned from the glass. "What we want won't be given to us as a gift – or as a peaceful present like a candle given by a shopkeeper with the oil at Christmas. If freedom is ever to come to Ireland then this Rebellion is the only thing that could have happened."

"But other countries . . ." Sarah began.

"You can't compare what's happening here with what has – and will – happen all over the world in the next hundred years . . ."

"So we're different? There's no cause like Ireland's cause?"

"Ours is an older one. Eight hundred years old. It's feudalism we're fighting; eight hundred years of oppression, exploitation, hunger and tyranny; the abuse of all human rights, and the total denial of any. I remember you yourself saying the English had turned us into a nation of serfs. You said we had their bread and their circuses but no rights. Political or otherwise."

"You've too good a memory, that's the trouble. The Irish have a great memory for wrongs, the unpleasant and the ugly, but none at all for favors."

"The English and the affluent would agree with you. They are now saying we are committing another new depravity."

"Well, the English should know. It's their barbarities and atrocities that sowed the seeds for our depravities. But that's another matter. What's important now is that you . . ."

"Mother! I can't come and go as you please. What's happening out there isn't a rucky-up – and it won't be pushed aside just because *you* don't like it – or because it happens to be discommoding the brocaded and plush-covered – or the landlords and shop-keepers and all the others who've grown rich by corruption and extortion. This isn't just the despairing cry of the overstrained tolerance of a long suffering people. If that's all it was then men castrated of their will wouldn't be risking death in yards and back lanes; and in the dark of night men, women and children wouldn't crawl from their holes in the ground to show us the way . . ."

"Like the whores," Sarah interrupted quickly, "and the well-fed, well-dressed, craw-thumpers gathered round the Lancers this morning? And the others out in Baggot Street to welcome them as they came in off the boats."

"No! Women breast-feeding babies, old people, children, point and guide us on our way; no longer willing or content to crawl and die in poverty and disease; men and women rediscovering that they are human after all. Mindful of what they were made for, and of what is happening, and of their part in it. Convinced as I am that we are right: and just as certain. They'll fight! And not just from Party devices, nor self-aggrandisement of hack politicians, but from life – *for* life! For like us, they also have found again the courage to exist."

"Do you really believe the things you're saying?" Sarah addressed her son's image in the looking glass.

71

"I believe in the dignity of man. In justice and in freedom and if I have to I'll fight for them."

"And die." Sarah drew the back of her hand across her eyes and turned to Mollo. "Better waken your father. He may want to take another look at the son he brought into the world, for it might be his last."

A sudden commotion on the canal claimed attention. Sarah tore her smouldering glance from John's face, but all she could hear was a shout that died in the blur of shots from many rifles. She clutched John's arm as he sprang past her, but Liam was before him; and pitting his strength against him pushed him from the window.

"It's all right." He shook off Liam's restraint while his eyes went in a frantic search of the room. Mollo grabbed his jacket from the back of the chair and gave it to him.

It was heavy, she thought irrelevantly before the reason shot her mouth open in a protest she never made.

"Dear God!" Sarah grabbed and held her son to her, while over her head, his eyes met Liam's.

"Liam!" Mollo's cry stopped Liam in his tracks, and as he turned back to reassure the door was flung open and a youth deathly pale met him head on. Younger than Liam he stood in the doorway bare-headed and rain-coated. He looked rigidly at John – then bared two rows of irregular teeth and said "New day, brother!" He stepped in and closed the door behind him – sized up the room and everything in it, then gestured towards the bed. All eyes followed his: and skipping past the thought that under other circumstances should have caused wonder at anyone being able to sleep, John said, "My father."

"Better not wake him." The intruder's voice dropped. He looked at John. "We should be on our way."

"He's not going," Sarah let go the back of the chair she had been clutching. "He's not going out of here to get himself killed – I won't let him!"

"You won't be asked, Ma'am."

"He's my son."

"He's a soldier."

"And what's left of him after, the dogs can have?"

72

"Take it easy, Ma'am," the youth spoke in an undertone.

"I'll take you easy!" The room rocked with Sarah's contempt. "I'll gut you if you don't get out and down them stairs. Playing soldiers and running round giving orders before you've finished scuttering yellow! Who in the name of Jasus do you think you are?"

The youth snapped to rigid attention. "I'm a soldier! And I've had enough oul' guff from the mothers of Dublin this morning . . . and if you don't shut your mouth I'll shut it for you," his voice shook in husky uncertainty, and in one quick and nervous gesture he had pulled a revolver out of his rain-coat pocket and was pointing it into the room.

"My God!" Mollo stared, hypnotised at the revolver cupped in hands softer and whiter than any girl's, and which she would afterwards remember as the loveliest pair of hands she ever saw.

"Put that away!" After the first pang of fear John spoke before anyone else could.

"Make me?" The revolver shook slightly in his hand.

Sarah's sudden laugh lashed scorn and anger. "Aren't you the daring little bastard!" She pushed herself in front of John. "If you think I'm frightened of your gun you've another think coming!" She flung herself forward but with a fist to her chest she was sent staggering back and at that very moment John struck – his arm cleaving the space between them like a knife and the revolver dropped to the floor.

"I'll get you for this you sly fucker!"

The threat followed the shattered silence and was made just as the sight rushed from his eyes as against his windpipe John's knuckles dug. His eyes turned upward, his legs jerked as his feet left the floor and then John flung him from him. Released he lay buckled, his face naked and sickly-green. On the very verge of collapse he stayed where he was until Sarah lifted him to his feet and pulled him towards the table where he slumped in a chair turning his face this way and that as he fought off the sickening mist clouding his vision. Reason reasserted itself as he sipped the water from the cup Sarah held to his lips, and when John putting the revolver down on the table beside him said "Put that away," he heard and obeyed.

From his dissolved shapelessness the youth dragged himself to

73

his feet. Rejecting the hand John held out to him his mouth quivered with a bitterness John had not bargained for.

"We better get moving." He stared hard at John.

"You don't have to go," Mollo spoke to John.

"But he does!" Sarah's voice stabbed. There was no escaping, she knew. No turning back. No running away, for where were you to run to? One way or the other you were killed. End up with a British bullet in your belly or an Irish one in your back, you could have your pick, Missus, but you get no change from either, an' what more d'ya want for ninepence, a bargain's a bargain, Ma'am, and death the only certainty.

"Aw, God! What did I ever see the sight of your face for?" The cry was wrenched from her as she watched her son go towards the window.

"It's orders, Ma'am." With some apprehension the youth spoke quietly.

"Whose?" Sarah turned from him to John. "They are sending you to your death and you don't even know who *they* are. Who are *they*, who issue the threats, the warnings, the orders? Is it the cross-bred with his hankerings after power and celibacy? Are they the red-necked culchie politicians – rattling out their humbuggery like scutter out of a babby's arse? Or are they the bankers and the big landlords with their diseased louse and rat infested tenements! Who are they God! Who are they?" Her hair had come loose from its neat bun and streeled onto her shoulders, and from its thick mass, hairpins fell.

"Why did you come back here today? What misguided notion brought you back?"

"I don't know," John said but nobody heard.

He stood taut as leather and thin as grey light. Through the white lace curtains the sun filtered and fell on his face. On an expression of sleep and solitary mirrors. There was no heat in the sun, only light, wafer thin and cold. The cold passed through his bones. He should not have come back. And wouldn't have if the raid last night against the British arms depot had gone as it should have gone. But the quick arrival – the quick attack – the quicker get-away – had not worked and he alone of the men with him had been caught leaving the building by two British soldiers.

He had gone quietly with them for about a dozen steps, and then suddenly he shot his elbows out as if to force two mountains apart and breaking the hold they had on him made his bolt for freedom.

With the British soldiers at his heels he had gone like a hunted beast from one side of the city to the other – screamed at, shouted at, laughed at, through streets shadowed and soundless and scattered with dung straw and paper – through others where people turned faces to roar abuse or mouth words and directions he couldn't hear – and all the time and at the very last minute – pausing to draw breath – or double back and away from streets where British soldiers flanked by the police were carrying out raids on the verminous wrecks of tenements, and with vicious spite smashing bits of furniture, pulverizing delf, beating up the inhabitants – wreaking a ruthless and savage revenge on men, women and children for sins they had not committed.

At last finding himself in a familiar area of factories and warehouses – and just when his only concern was to keep upright, not fall under the boots of the men behind him, he had found the opening he had been looking for and into which he knew he could escape. It was an unused concrete built warehouse into which he ducked and where he stood stupefied for what seemed hours before he could even raise his head. He was roused by a sound. Had he heard something? Wasn't that the scuff of hobnails on cobbles?

He listened.

Silence.

He tilted his head to one side and listened. They had gone and he hadn't heard them go. He had led the British soldiers into the maelstrom of a foreign city. He felt great. Suddenly. He could have applauded himself on out-running, out-maneuvering the enemy; he had been quick witted for sure, cunning as he ran for his life as he had never run before. But then after all he had been covering sure and certain ground so perhaps getting away wasn't anything to brag about. No great achievement. And he hadn't done what he set out to do. Nonetheless he had out-run, out-smarted the nailed boots; and the terrible scorch of breath trumpeting a monstrous urgency behind him and which even now in his head was still clearly audible. He had got away with his life. He had escaped! And not only a manhandling with fist foot and rifle butt – but jail or the wall of lace from the bullets of the firing squads up in the Portobello Barracks. And only Christ knew what else. For how many times had an Irish day come up to find a man sexless hanging from a tree? He suddenly felt on the verge of collapse. His veins were still throbbing thunderously from the chase – and under his feet the ground began to heave. He had a feeling of nausea, like seasickness or the stirring pangs of beginning lust. From standing he threw himself down on what felt like the rags of sacks that had probably been accumulated during the occupation of the warehouse by knackers or Republicans. For a long time he lay motionless on his back. He could see the streets through which he had run. Endless streets shuddering under the tramp of British army boots down the long long corridors of time. Hundreds and thousands of muffled, bent backed, hurrying soldiers, in puttees, with bayonets and guns while out of their way the Irish crept, crawled or were beaten. He remembered reading that the English Queen Elizabeth's declared policy during her reign had been to root out the Irish and exterminate them. Shē had tried to make Ireland one enormous graveyard. In 1582 one of her henchmen reckoned that apart from deaths in battle or by hanging thirty thousand people had died from starvation in six months. Year after year, unripe corn was cut down and ripe corn burnt by her soldiers, and the cattle the soldiers didn't need were killed or maimed, and long long after all resistance had ceased, men, women and children were hunted to death. Spencer the poet, himself a squatter, took over an enormous confiscated estate, described the condition of the very few who survived.

Out of every corner of the woods and glens they came creeping forth upon their hands, for their legs could not bear them; they looked like the anatomies of death; they spake like ghosts crying out of their graves; they did eat dead carrions, happy where they could find them; and if they found a plot of watercresses or shamrocks, there they flocked as to a feast for the time, yet not able long to continue there withal; that in a short space of time there was none left.

76

And ever since then the English had been trying to complete the butchery of Ireland and the Irish that Elizabeth began . . . He turned over on his side and rummaging around the sacks found the stump of a candle and a box of matches. He wanted to strike a match and light the candle. He wanted to see the candle flare and flame in the dense darkness. He wanted to chase the ghosts away. But with so many hands raised against the Republicans who knew what threat might be lurking in the sinister darkness. His teeth clattered. When they stopped the warehouse was dead silent. In the daylight this place would be large and long but now in the dark its limits were undefined. He listened. He heard slabs of silence pile one upon the other. Like certain kinds of music. He waited for the heap to be made, till from outside a wind came sawing and rasping, a thin gritty wind blowing off concrete and damp cobbles. Now that it was no longer a matter of life and death he must try to be calm. To plan his next campaign, his next sortie, but at that very moment and without warning the Enemy got him.

From inside.

At that very moment he became detached. He experienced total solitude. It felt as if something inside him had been knocked to pieces. He suddenly realized that he was alone in a warehouse in a lane in a city in which he had been born and reared. He knew a hundred people in this city and was on hail and farewell terms with a hundred more. A stone's throw away from where he was now in two rooms at the top of a house he had a family; a father, a mother, a sister, and in other rooms in other houses all around them were men and women he had known all his life. And yet in all of Dublin at this very minute there wasn't a single person he could run to. Was there anyone anywhere? His family? His friends? He could hang and cover the invisible walls of this place with their portraits and did. His father, his mother, and Mollo! But were they his? Was he theirs? And his Republican comrades; he ate, slept and fought with them; but did he know any of them, did they know him? He had a home, but was it his home? He had a mother, but was she his? Was he hers? 'You are not my son,' she said, 'otherwise you would be different.' He had a father, but was he his? And did not his mother stand between him and his father?

He remembered his very first swim in the canal, standing in the soft warm mud; the water lapping around his chest; and Mollo and the other kids shaking him loose to follow some distraction in the street; leaving him standing rooted in the mud in that long and wide expanse of water and emptiness on his own; needing help, suddenly, desperately, but not knowing where to look for it – or who to ask – or how . . .

But there was no water lapping at his chest now; no soft squelch of mud beneath his feet; it felt as if the world he was now inhabiting was made of harsher stuff; of cobbles and concrete and empty space; he was standing on a murky strand of subterranean gravel surrounded by space. Waiting. For something to happen – some gigantic event to swallow him down. He wanted to scream but his breath choked and knotted in his throat. But scream what? And who would hear? Who would understand? Outside of his skin there was nothing . . . Then a bell sounded in his head. He had heard it before. Heard it when they clamped the ether mask to his face to take his tonsils out. A slender note that seemed to come from thin glass just before he went under . . .

He opened his eyes.

And with a trollop's indifference the darkness shook, exploded and recovered . . . Consciousness came back and jumped and fretted and pulled like a boat at its moorings to be away. He was returning from that solitary land in which no human voice or fellow footfall is ever heard. He had been there before. And so has everybody, he thought. Some for a whole lifetime, others for a second; but everybody at some moment of their lives must have known that chilling world of streaming silence of ash and sleep and desolation; since it's free to *all*; it's humanity's lot; a condition of existence; people are completely detached, completely alone, completely left to themselves . . . Contrary to popular opinion – *Every man is an island* . . .

On a rage of intolerable loneliness he shut his eyes and when he opened them again – outside the warehouse the horizon had tightened its grip on the smouldering earth and standing over him a man said, "You made it then!"

"I made it." John got to his feet.

78

"Load of murdering bastards!" Sunny Cullen's powerful face crinkled into a laugh.

"Heard you hadn't pulled it off and came looking."

"And you knew where?" John threw his Commandant a hurried glance but there was no criticism in Cullen's voice, no pause in the speed of stares. A middle-aged man wearing a dark brown over-coat broad-chested and purposeful. A pillar of the Republican movement and a voice that like a cannon could bring bodies up from deep waters.

"I always know," he said, and asked, "how long have you been out?"

"Sunday after Mass," John said and didn't add that for the three weeks before Easter he had been on every raid carried out by the Republicans against every British arms depot in the city. But Cullen knew and half-believing in the rumors that had been leaked to him now passed them on to John. Irish-Americans in their thousands, he said, were crossing the Atlantic by barge and boat, all answering the call; and along the coast of Kerry the Germans were landing in their millions, and bringing with them every conceivable modern weapon. That this was pie in the sky nobody wanted to know. Not even Cullen. After all, it's very difficult to maintain a suspicion. Nevertheless in the grey dusk of the warehouse the look he shot John was filled with irony.

"So what now?" John glanced round the warehouse. It showed nothing. There was not the slightest trace of the night past. Nothing except the small heap of sacks.

"You better grab some kip or you'll be no use to us or yourself," Cullen said. And now there was a hint of criticism in the heavy voice. "Can't afford a repeat of last night's fiasco! Just remember to report down to Kevin Street around five." He hadn't looked at John as he spoke but at the door the glance he turned on him was calm, clear and fatherly.

Cautiously John stepped into the lane down which smoke from near and distant fires drifted. He looked in both directions but the lane itself was empty. "See you," he said, and with his shoulders hunched against the morning's cold, went one way while Cullen went the other.

At first he had thought about going to the Salvation Army

Hostel for a bed – but a sudden overwhelming need to see his father made him retrace his steps – and because it was early, too early to risk his Ma alone – he headed for Whitefriars Street Chapel, where he sat dozing through the first two Masses and halfway through the third he got up and made for home.

But he should not have come back. And why the urgency? Why had Cullen sent for him?

"If you cross that door today don't come back."

His mother's voice hacked. If that's how it has to be, he thought. Around his mouth and nostrils there was a dew of sweat. A strange lifelessness had come over him. He felt as if someone other than himself was crying inside him. He turned to the bed in which his Da lay. The light from the window slashed his Da's face to the bone. And today his body under the bedclothes seemed to have grown smaller. He had to remind himself that his Da wasn't a young man any more. Even so it had just happened. He moved and for the first time in his life was unaware of Sarah as he bent and kissed his Da. He was kissing, he felt, not his father but an old man. From the bed he moved to the door the youth held open, and without looking at Sarah went through it.

The youth took a last look round the room and the people in it. They stood like statues. But there would be ructions, he could tell. The oul' wan looked set for strife. And what about the oul' fella in the bed? Hadn't stirred. The oul' bollix! More than likely drunk! Stoicous! Dubliners! A bitter fuckin pack!

He closed the door.

"Ah, Jasus! Will you watch yourself, Mister? Have you no manners or what?"

Janey Reilly clutched the bundle of bedclothes her mother wouldn't be needing for the pawn after all – as the youth tore down past her. And on the steps outside, Christina Swords laughed her answer to the question he threw her in passing; but it was John Goss her eyes followed. "Ireland's with you, John!" she called as he turned the corner into Rock Street; and to herself she said, 'It is in its la-la, you bit of a child.'

THREE

WEDNESDAY

1

With the sanction of the Lord and the dis-approval of the people, a British gunboat came up the Liffey and poured shells into Liberty Hall. And at noon, while the city's chapels were ringing the angelus bells, martial law was proclaimed. In the streets people stood and scrapped old rumors and began new ones of how the Rising was going or talked about the ambush of the British officer and three soldiers in the Park. Through the streets children bolted, exploring the skeletons of burnt and blas-ted buildings, and bolted out again with British bullets quickening their feet. For children don't believe that grown-up people will actually kill them. But they did, and the screams of their dying was drowned under the louder screams of gunfire.

But it was spring. And a crude brash sun shone white to take the harm and pointless agony out of death as it rode with the wind, free and unfettered by *Gesummarias*, scapulars and St Christopher medals, through the new green of trees that were a torture in themselves – before it swooped, luxuriously scarlet-robed in a gloriously impartial streel, onto the narrow and broad streets, pausing here and there like a heart-beat to observe its own passing, its own strange and spectacular beauty. The city, aware, was too much involved in, and animated by, its own indiscriminate bombardment to keen over the destruction death

81

left in its wake . . . in the daylight; but when night fell and the sky was crimson with funeral pyres, Maisie Collins gave a hooley.

In a crimson dress, a deep crimson, inseparable from the lines of her flanks, her thighs, her breasts, and wearing every scrap of jewellery she owned and some she didn't, Maisie stood at one end of the room and surveyed the fruits of her own and Harriet Reilly's labor. Splendidly lit by three oil lamps, no crevice of the room was exposed to the dangers of mystery. The big double bed had been taken down and stored out in the hall. Along the wall opposite the fireplace, two snowy covered tables, one of which she had borrowed, stood and proclaimed that the material world was, after all, the one and only. Among the sparkle of glass and the glitter of silver, two cold hams, taken from Smyths on The Green, stood up beside rounds of roast and corned beef, swiped from Doolins in Wexford Street; loaves of brown and white bread, slabs of rich cake, jellies and serious blancmanges, apples, figs, nuts; whiskey, brandy and black-bottled bottled stout; and in the very center a huge, ornate, solid silver bowl of punch – made especially by Ba. In a friction of excitement, of people arriving and people leaving, Maisie eyed the silver bowl of punch uneasy in her mind, for Ba Fay could say what he liked about it being a ladies' drink, but she had distinctly seen two bottles of brandy go into the making of it. To prove its innocence, he had given her a couple of glasses, and no mistake it was very nice and was helping her cope with the hazards of a gathering for which she was responsible, but she'd hate to have to swear to the priest on the altar that she was cold, cold sober.

Through the orchestration of lights, glass, food, and a mutually appreciative exchange of opinions going on between those passing and repassing, Maisie looked at her guests who had arrived early and had risked or were now risking, and they were all looking suspiciously unlike themselves. All except her old friend Judy Madden, who was still her own burnt-to-an-orange-brown-sober little self as she entered the arena picking nervously at the feathers trimming the neck of her dress and peering over them and around for the first sign of treachery. She saw Judy pause to frown

82

black over the loaded tables before moving on to settle beside Harriet Reilly sitting on her own on the only sofa in the whole house.

"I see that certain poor souls around here have decided not to go hungry either," Judy said to Harriet just as Ba, urged forward by Maisie to attend to the wants of her guests, bent and let his hand rest on her knee.

In his white shirt and blue suit he was looking rakish.

"And Judy the only capitalist among us and not drinking." He aimed at her his most stunning grin.

"A Vimto, Ba, a Vimto," she said when she could, and just managed to keep herself erect as his hand shifted and closed tight about her knee.

"Isn't that the right oul' ram," she said, after him moistening her lips at the prospect, just as 'The Sphinx', who had arrived with some others, drew up a chair and sat down beside her. The glance Harriet and Judy threw the lethargic somberly black-hatted and black-coated woman was one of criticism and, as with all Dubliners, was and for no reason, hostile. Prepared to carry on as though she wasn't there Judy and Harriet did no more than nod and from the deep folds of her fat, 'The Sphinx' stared stonily back.

"You're like a rose," Harriet shouted to Maisie going past with Jeremiah Hudson.

"She'd plunder attention from any rose," Jeremiah replied.

"She's upsetting that man's sober decencies," Judy said.

"It's just as well you can't see what she's doing to mine," Ba said, as he returned with Judy's drink, bringing an extra one for 'The Sphinx' without being asked. "That will put lead in your pencils."

With rapacious hands, 'The Sphinx' and Judy reached.

"Oh, Ba, you shouldn't!" Judy looked imploringly up from the sparkling amber punch in her glass. She could have been asking him to take on a responsibility, or accept a sacrifice.

"Well, here's to another lovely war," Harriet said, into the clash of voices growing vigorous as people adjusted themselves and found their tongues, and as 'The Sphinx' slowly raised her glass of stout, the only drink she ever drank, to her lips.

Judy downed her punch and turning on the disbelieving smile, with which she sometimes rewarded those she found herself amongst, cast an eye on Maisie standing now with Ba and laughing at some whispered remark. The woman was no class, she thought, seeing Maisie rest herself against Ba for a second as one of his hands curved round her breasts, but you had to give it to her, she was a beauty, and too good for Ba Fay. Although it was nothing short of a miracle, the change finding him had brought about in her. For even Judy admitted that the truth known had to be recognized, and who better than herself knew what the truth was? But Rose was right! And them tits of hers were having a terrible struggle with that dress. She turned to Harriet.

"Its new isn't it?"

"What is?"

"Maisie's dress."

"It is."

"And yours?"

"Thanks to the Famine Queen and the Republicans."

"You're getting your queens ballsed-up!"

"I know it, but I'm right about the Republicans. Up the Republicans!" Under the liquid action of the purest, subtlest silk Harriet stood up in a moss green flounce and froth to salute, then sat down again.

"That's the advantage of having nothing. You can't lose it." Judy offered her smile to the room and the blare of the gramophone. "And if you don't mind my saying so Harriet – you, and the rest of the working class, have *nothing*. But flag-waving, my dear, never filled anybody's belly! And what about commerce? And the little man? Like me for instance? I'll lose the shift off my back if this Rebellion goes on, for its already causing havoc to my ladies' trade so it is."

"What about me, Judy Madden?" A big pink woman was shouting big. "The best hustler in Dublin, and not able to hustle. And now the British have brought in martial law, Jasus only knows when Dawson Street and the four sides of The Green will see me again."

"Ah, be spartan, Martha, for Christ's sake. Pretend it's Lent and give your poor oul' chassis a rest. After all, men seven nights a

84

week for the past ten years must be having some effect."

"It is, Ma'am. It is." Martha Liller laughed raucous and drew back from the young fella she was dancing with, to bounce her breasts with both hands. "It's oiling the wheels and keeping the engine purring. But look and long, Judy, look and long."

Judy watched Martha dance away and beside her 'The Sphinx', whom she knew slightly and disliked, said to no one in particular, "Mary Pickford for President!" Judy turned back to Harriet.

"It's the exodus that's fretting me," she said. "Because all my ladies, like the rest of the gentry and moneyed classes, are packing up and going back to England . . ."

"And taking with them everything they can leave their thieving hands on!" Harriet said, and turned a bland smile up at a black stranger. She heard a woman say, "If I'd known what the world was going to be like, I never would've bothered me arse about growing up." And beside her, in an anxiety she could no longer disguise even had she wanted to, Judy asked, "What class are they at all, at all?"

"Who? Your ladies? Or the brave bastards that sent the British gunboat up the Liffey this morning to bomb the town and leave us all corpses?"

"Neither!" Judy clamped disapproving lips over small pointed teeth. "The wans doing the looting."

"Oh, now there I leave you," Harriet said. "But I'll tell you something for nothing, Judy Madden; the groans you hear coming from them tables is the direct result of two days' hard work. And so is me own and Maisie's finery."

"Youse took all youse could and forgot to thank God. I thought so! The figs from Tunis and the oranges from Spain."

"Whiskey from Scotland, and brandy from France."

"Jasus, youse will die roaring!"

"And Luther's at peace with God and himself!" Jeremiah Hudson had come to join them, bringing with him handfuls of fresh drinks.

"And as for that dizened, double-dyed hoor of Babylon!" Judy said up to Martha Liller dancing by.

"She's like some old Divinity disguised, aren't you, Martha?" Jeremiah raised his glass.

85

"What's coming between me and me rest is what'll happen to this kip of a country if the English do clear out," Judy said. "For fifteen years now, and in the midst of breeze and blast, I've been going round the best Protestant houses in this city, buying and selling the grandest of second-hand clothes. Now what I want the Republicans to tell me is this: who, and what, am I to replace them with? For with all due respects, our own crowd of penny pinching craw-thumping muck-grubbers – God help us – will never be up to them."

There was a raucous bray of male laughter and the more impudent thin reeds of girlish giggles at one end of the room, and on the chair beside Judy 'The Sphinx' stuck her nose into the glass of stout in her hands and downed it in one loud gulp. She sat back, "All right then," she said, "Charlie Chaplin for President, and fuck the lot of youse!"

As a business woman who was on speaking terms with the great and near great, Judy could not allow herself to approve of any kind of eccentricity. She glanced at Harriet whose laugh at 'The Sphinx' had burst from her and said, "The Republicans are turning this country into a randy-voo for rowdyism."

"Ah, drink up for Jasus sake, Judy," Harriet said finishing off hers and looking after Jeremiah going to get her another.

"I don't see Chrissy Swords, or the Gosses?" Judy said, and asked, "Did Maisie not give them an invite?"

"She did," Harriet wiped the laugh from her face. "But Chrissy's out and about her business in the dark, and surely you heard about the Gosses!"

"Heard what?"

"The Republicans took John out yesterday and eyes haven't been clapped on him since."

"I didn't know John Goss was a Republican."

"You would if you'd been listening. But then your hearing isn't what it was."

"Is anything?" Judy asked wryly.

"You heard about the shooting of the British officers in the Park this morning?"

"Who hasn't? And it was only *one* officer!" Judy corrected Harriet. "*One* officer and three soldiers." For the details of the

86

ambush had taken precedence over the news of the proclamation posted on the walls all over the city announcing martial law, and even over the fairy tales published in one newspaper that the country was at peace again, and even over the sight and sound of the British gunboat bombarding from the Liffey the very heart of the city.

"The Republicans didn't give those poor bastards a chance," Ba Fay came with Martha Liller to a halt beside them.

"The bastards manning the British gunboat didn't give us much of a chance either," Harriet's smile was feline but friendly.

"Ambushed an officer and three soldiers, and after blowing the head off the officer, they bundled the three soldiers still alive into the car and set fire to it."

"Oh, Christ!"

Ba watched the shock on Martha's face.

"You must be the only one in the city who didn't know," he said, forgetting – if he ever knew – that Martha seldom, if ever, saw the light of day.

"Jesus, aren't they the right heathens?" she said. "Have they been caught?"

Ba tossed back his drink. "No, but they will be. And Jasus help them when they are. The English have been going through every house and yard with a fine comb since morning."

"I hope they catch them!" Martha spoke with quiet vehemence.

"You would, you vicious hoor!" one woman remarked.

Some of those gathered in the room audibly agreed with Martha, while others hushed mouths in full or half-emptied glasses.

"The room is humming with accusations," Jeremiah said.

"Well, it's only natural a thing like this would cast a gloom over the proceedings," Judy replied.

"Perhaps! But I was just thinking: how people who, up to now, haven't cared one way or the other, and who've maintained a singular reticence about their own particular sympathies, have suddenly sprung into voice and violent protest at the death of these four men in the Park, and loudly demanding – like you, Martha – retribution upon the guilty."

"And how do we know it was the Republicans?" Harriet asked.

"We know because they left one of their own men behind them," Ba Fay said. "A young fella killed in the skirmish."

Harriet caught Jeremiah Hudson's eye. "I hope . . ." Her voice trailed, as above and around her voices began mounting.

2

Christina Swords turned the key in the lock of her door. She was on her way to Rock Street and Alfie Doyle, who had not showed up when he said he would. Behind her Janey Reilly came creeping up from the basement, from the frustrating hindrance of Jeremiah Hudson's locked door. Hearing the darkness move behind her, Christina's hand froze over the gap of her open handbag and thinking it to be somebody from the hooley, and probably drunk, asked: "Who's there? Who's that?"

"Me."

Christina spun round and out of the darkness Janey came in white. A new white pinny, and a large white butterfly bow in her hair.

"Oh! It's you! The smiler with the knife!" Christina dropped the key into her bag. "Just try to keep your light fingers off my property."

"Who's touching it?"

"You were! Yesterday *and* the day before." Christina went quickly towards the hall door.

"Watch it, mister!"

Janey heard the scream and flew to look at the two men who had with brutal force slammed Christina back against the jamb of the door the second she opened it.

"And where do you think you're going?" The question was precise, the voice English.

"Around the corner." Chrstina forced an answer from a long way back in her gummed-up throat.

"What for?"

"To see my fella!"

"What's his name?"

"It's none of your business." Christina made an attempt to push past, but again the arm shot out and knocked her back against the door. She could smell the whiskey breath.

"Easy."

"You're drunk!" She tried to draw back from both men; but one of them continued to follow, to press himself against her. "Stop that!" She cried when she felt what it was he was doing.

"Let me pass!"

"When I'm ready!" he snapped in anger.

A thud of fear shook her. "If it's Maisie Collins's hooley you want, it's the first door on your left."

"Is John Goss in there?" The eyes, hidden in shadow, took in the blinded window through which the sound of confident voices came.

"He isn't," Janey spoke for the first time. Christina looked down, only now aware of her though both men had held her in their sight from the beginning.

"Are you sure, little girl?"

"Of course I'm sure!" Janey sounded annoyed. She certainly wasn't frightened. She half thought the taller of the two men fingered money in the pocket of his overcoat.

"They took him out of here yesterday," she said.

"Who did?"

"Well, it wasn't the Chapel Man." She hoisted herself to the tedious level of communication. "Ah, some snotty-nosed redneck with a gun in his hand. I know. I saw it when he passed me on the stairs." She paused to touch the crisp sleeves on her white pinny – her long stalk of a neck. The face continued to remain mysteriously opaque.

"John Goss is a Republican," she said.

"And dangerous, wouldn't you say?"

90

Inside Christina a breath came out as a laugh. "If she would she needs more than her head examined. You must be out of your minds, or you're looking for the wrong man. John Goss dangerous? He's as gentle as a girl. John Goss wouldn't hurt a fly."

"You'd know?"

"Who better?"

"The man we're looking for is a Lieutenant in the Volunteers. Tall, dark. Mid-twenties?"

Christina nodded. "What do you want him for?"

"We want to ask him some questions. And that's all you need to know." The taller of the two men eased himself closer. "And for your pains we'll cross your palm with fifty nicker.".

The breath was offensively close, almost against her mouth as if he was about to seduce or command, but Christina did not even try to draw herself away until she heard Janey's urgent demand: "What's he saying? What's he saying, Chrissy?"

She drew back then from the mouth, the blast of breath and tried for a sight of the faces hidden by the brims of hats. Now that the first significance of his words reached her, she felt she could laugh or just vomit. The fools whoever they were. Wanting John Goss because they thought he was dangerous. To whom? To what? John Goss worth fifty whole pounds! John Goss, who imagined God had given it to him to stir his tea with . . . Him a Lieutenant in the Volunteers? The dreamer under the solace of the drifting clouds . . .

"Ah, no, it's not the same chap, it can't be," she said, at the slowly developing vision of that afternoon three years before when she had tried to drag the sixteen-year-old into her bed – and might have succeeded if the furnace of her own body hadn't prevented it – hadn't made her sick-witted . . . hadn't . . . a furnace of an afternoon inside and out and full of murmuring contact, and a scorching wind prick-teasing with languorous fidgety spite, the bare branches and the naked white trunk of the dead tree in the landscape of the yard. A heavy-limbed dragging afternoon and her anchoring the swell of clothes on the line, and under the tree, him, untamed by the heat and stripped to the waist, kicking, with soft thick thuds, a football. And him, then lusty slim and olive skinned, holding his dark head under the gushing tap – the cool water

91

washing, foaming out over the head, the broad contracting shoulders and the long spined back down to the worn-thin, blue, faded pants that showed his all. And herself and without warning wanting. Wanting to touch, to hold, to reach through the thick hush, the risen mood, the tenuous flow of light and wind and tree-shadow trembling on his wet shining body. Herself devoured with an excitement that came in slow thumps, or blows of terror, and wondering if she dared. Then tightening all over, she had laughed with him – laughed a prostitute's invitation offering offering . . . a towel she said because she couldn't think, and told him to come and get it, as she hurried to blind the window to tell the world to keep out – to peel – to touch hidden surfaces – to wait in a voluptuous torpor. She could see even now the wet head and standing horns of hair, and the laugh on the wet mouth before his eyes latched in sudden shock, and then veiled in smouldering beginning lust for her strong white nakedness. Stiff with innocence he had allowed her to struggle with the buttons on his flies to get at the hard swell, which was thick and brutal and as long as the day, and which in her manipulating hands became a monstrous velvety snake un-winding with involved grace; its arrow shaped head sliding up and up uninjured, as though from some long sleep, before it sprang into rigid and violent life. Teased beyond reason by that, and by his crude but sensual hand suddenly cupping her warm furry center where a pulse throbbed like a fiddle, she allowed herself to grow incautious – and by foul naming the acts she wanted him to perform she had succeeded only in offending the fastidiousness of the male who failed to overwhelm the man. He had pulled away from her then in a stern withdrawal and puzzled rage, trembling in sudden revulsion from the nightmarish mess of the thing she had murdered, and stood over her nauseated by the sight of the feast she was offering and upon which he had almost gorged. She tried pleading then – begging as she might in a famine have begged bread – crying out for him to appease the want that strip-ped bare and exposed nerve-ends in her chastely white body, panting her moans beyond the horror growing in his eyes at the spectacle she presented: at the hair streaming and sodden with sweat; at the glazed eyes; and the convulsed jerks of the thighs. Women's thighs, flesh folded and garter marked, rounded,

92

mountainous, and in the valley between a pit, a quivering dense mouthing jungle from which his senses reeled until, grown savage from her own despairing hunger, she tore wildly at him, smashing the sight, with a red-crazed blow, from his eyes. She could still hear her 'Jesus', her breathed 'Jesus'. And his shouted bewildered pain while she continued to plead, to beg, to scream. Even after he had gone and she was alone again, she had gone on crying, crying, giving wild vent to her own torment for the thing she had lost until . . . She roused herself and raised her hands. They smelled of. In a blaze of anger she flung herself down on the bed. And settled. And spread. *You wash up as far as possible – and down as far as possible.* It was an old music-hall joke. *But you musn't touch possible.* She did though; she crushed it between her hands as though to cauterize a wound until an unfamiliar scent of some unrecognizable herb invaded, and finally emanated from her body. Onto the ceiling witnessing her self-exposure she projected that young bastard's image. He had rejected her smoothest offerings. The fucker! Would he now? Would he? Through the distorting dusk he came to mount. To separate the mounds of glossy foliage with the weapon he held in both his hands. She spread to receive. To arch her hips until from the depths of the mounds she had been rubbing together bursts of scent, of near seed, shot and scattered in a reckless waste on the bed under her. 'An ugly substitute.' It was, but only when her anger broke and only after the glaucous haze cleared.

Afterwards she blamed him for the shame that made her keep her eyes down and her gaze averted when they met in the hall or in the street, the shame turning to bitter mockery as the weeks and months went by, and as she learned. In the laundry girls mouthing. The world they said was cluttered with men useless to women. Men incapable of having a woman. 'Empty Forks' they said and tittered at what they imagined was a physical absence. But there was no comfort in that. She knew better. John Goss lacked nothing. Except the will, she thought until a girl in the street brought a bastard into the world, and the street said he was as likely to have fathered it as the next. She herself had seen them together. She herself believed. And mockery gave way to nagging spite and hatred and she had furthered the rumor. But John Goss had stayed single and the girl in the street had married somebody else. The longed for revenge had not materialized. Until Alfie told her he was a Rebel, but after long thought she had decided against using that piece of information. Besides she didn't know how, and even if she did she wouldn't have dared. The Rebels were shooting informers, and the soft knock on the door in the middle of the night led to the walk from which you didn't return. But wouldn't it be the height of John Goss if his banditry brought him to a cell in a prison or if he was found one morning hanging sexless from some gibbet. That would be a sight for sore eyes. She'd like to see him after the British were through with him.

But she shivered when one of the two men touched her.

"Shag off," she snarled, while he whispered where it was she should come if she had any little bit of news that just might interest them.

And he would have lingered with her if his companion, who had already gone beyond them into the hall, hadn't called for him, and if Christina herself hadn't gone running in terror from a risen vision of her own inferno.

3

The groupings of Maisie's assembled guests
had changed only slightly. At the music end of the room, in her
professional body, Martha Liller summoning up all the reflections
that had ever faced her in the glass and shining with her own gor-
geous pink vision was singing 'My Lagan Love' – and at the other
end and cutting in unpleasantly and unavoidably a young animal of
a girl, with that staggeringly insolent aspect of Irish women, and
whose eyes had something of the explosive violence of splintering
ice, was trying to destroy a man with thundering blows. Forced at
last by inquiring faces to take notice Maisie and Ba when they
did move did so like sheet lightning and for some seconds it was a
matter of spitting and gnashing of teeth; of flesh on flesh; of
claws, fists and a dangerous creaking of borrowed match-stick
chairs and swinging cups on dresser hooks. From the dust up
Maisie surprisingly emerged almost unscathed but Ba came battered
with vicious scratches of fingernails running down one side of
his face and with his brilliantined hair standing up; if it had not
been rooted to his scalp, it might have taken off.
"Honest to Jasus, I never get a drink on me or begin to be happy
but something terrible happens." Maisie said, her words thicken-
ing inside a beginning lower swelling lip. Revolving in desperation
and looking for a hiding place she flung herself down on the

upholstered sofa beside Judy Madden and Jeremiah Hudson and gulped in one go the drink he pushed into her hand.

"Underprivileged and oppressed by the British we may be, but no one can say we don't appreciate the higher things," he said, and he could have been laughing his voice was so high and clear.

"It's Esther Quinn's altar!"

A cause had to be found for the beginning ructions and a cause was found, voiced in a whisper that flew from mouth to mouth and ear to ear, from one drunken island of unconcern to the next, and reached Judy just at that moment when the hooley and what was taking place at it was about to go beyond her.

"I said when I heard oul' grunting cunt was that way again that we could expect neither luck nor fortune to attend us or ours as long as she kept the light of day from poor sorrowing Mary; for the Cross of God falls on us every time Esther Quinn needs a man. An' Jasus! but she seems to have the want of them more often than's natural!"

"Don't we all?" Maisie rushed to defend the face on the pillow in the blinded room at the top of the house.

"Ba Fay was good for you," Judy said. "But what is it that makes a woman like Esther Quinn demolish herself and everyone round her for the first little louser that claps an eye on her?"

'I could enlighten you,' Maisie thought. 'If I had a mind to.' But she felt too remote to reply. Besides the room was still shaken. Not indeed that she would compare herself and Ba Fay to whatever it was that held Esther to Billy Boy Beausang. Ba was good for her, Billy Boy wasn't good for Esther. But *she* knew what it was like to be tied to a man who was neither a man nor a husband to you, and what could happen to a woman. *She* knew what it was like to need someone. Anyone. She remembered explaining to Ba that very first night in the pub: 'I had to. Had to get away from my father and mother. What I didn't know was that I was swapping one lot of drunkards for another.' But Hammy was a lazy drunkard. And he didn't beat her. Though she was beaten, all right, by something else; Ba had seen that, too. When she met him. She was standing on the canal stirring the fallen leaves with her foot and looking up through the branchy pitch of fall at a Druid moon.

96

Instead of the straight-bodied woman nature had intended her to be, she was fleshless, bent and straddled. Her face gray, her mouth an old draw-necked leather bag shut tight against the laughter for which it had been shaped. She was shoving her hair back with a string and already, although she was only twenty-eight, it was showing inroads of white. And nature hadn't intended that either! Ba said the only thing about her that wasn't bent were her eyes, strange untouched brown eyes that flashed blasting anger when he first approached and kept their urchin's caution even after two whiskies and a hot rum in Quinlan's had aged the acquaintance. Ba said she looked as though she needed the rum. Right from the start Ba was good for her. Fixing her up like a Christmas pudding she had laughed guzzling the rum in burning gulps. Enjoying the strangeness of laughter and him, and thoughts, childish, and drifting like cotton-woolly baa-lamb clouds, until into their laughter, Hammy had sidled, fey, slack-jawed and waiting – waiting for the drink Ba bought him, fawning and intimidated, until she couldn't stand it any longer and got up and went out, not caring who followed, not even caring then that it was Ba.

"Of course some need men more than others!"

Judy Madden's voice intruded like a grievance.

"Like me!"

"Ah, no Maisie you were different."

"Balls!" Maisie said. She knew exactly what had been said about her in the streets' favored crannies by the fierce, the mean and the scapular strung. About what happened to a woman who turned her back on the angels and her face to the beast – and about the number of bastards she'd bring into the world for Ba Fay. Only she hadn't. And he had wanted her to have his child. It was one of the first things he told her, even before she went with him that night. It may even have been the thing that made her go. But it hadn't been that simple. Not when you thought about it.

And she did.

Remembering how close they'd come to walking their separate ways, for one minute they'd been spitting venom at each other in a stand-up row and the next he was asking her up to his place for a drink.

"What's the matter? Got to put it somewhere?" she had asked, reshaping her mouth.

He laughed or she thought he did slightly.

She laughed back bitter. "Am I right?"

"What are you looking for? A man with gumdrops where his balls should be?"

"You think you're the only pebble on the beach?"

And little did he know it, but he was.

Or perhaps he did. His face softened suddenly and his eyes under the fall of hair on his forehead darkened. Unaccountably he had stepped back then and gone stalking around her – subjecting her to an examination more brutal than she deserved. It was a long time since she had been looked at, a long time since she had given any more than a passing glance to her image in a shop window and she hadn't liked what she saw. Dominated by his serious eyes she had stood there hovering the way the mind will between two uncertainties – seeing herself as she used to be before she slipped into the gloom of night to hide the way a child will, gifts abandoned – and not knowing whether to hit him or curse him. But she had done neither.

She was nothing to write home about, he said, and asked, "Ever had a child?"

And that wasn't the class of question men around the place asked, and caught up in surprise she said, "No, why?" – and smiling, did so only with the mouth and a little bitter the face of the incurable still to be stricken with its malady.

And he told her: she needed to ease up; good body if she didn't fold it over in the middle as if she was nursing pain; eyes in profile rounded – well slightly – the temples big, square – white throat, softly rounded chin – giving off a sensation of beauty but without its details. And all the things wrong with her he could set right! Shagging cheek! A *schkutzim* the Jews she skivvied for would have called him. A gurrier whose own disqualifications were massive and who in insolent arrogance refused to hunt down a single one of them. Unskilled and uneducated and with that about him that told you he would reject servitude in heaven for sovereignty in hell. A man with two women already and more children than you could count by both of them, and here he was carrying on like the gold-toothed – the smooth-textured – the prosperous and the broad – hustling another. Be Jasus a fella as randy as he was should open a brothel or be married. Why wasn't he?

"Because one woman wouldn't be enough for me," he said out of his thick soft bemused lips. And simply, as if he was saying: I believe in the Father, the Son, and the Holy Ghost. It was a miracle the priest hadn't been sent on him, she said; but he had.

Ba shrugged massive. "I told him to get fucked and gave him a tanner for the plate."

And she knew he had. He would do just that.

She gave him a smile and asked for a cigarette and he gave her one and lit it.

"Maybe we better knock it off," he said.

She dragged on the cigarette, then into the leaf of darkness spread across the arches of his eyes she said "I'm about to become your third or is it your fourth prostitute?"

And without another word and holding hands like any pair of lovers they began to walk up into the darkness of the lane. She hadn't expected it, but it had happened, and what followed – in Ba's room – was unexpected, too.

"Poor Esther!" Maisie said, and realized she had done so only when Judy said "Poor all of us!"

"Speak for yourself!" someone laughed just as the door was burst open and those near it were sent staggering back and shouting murderous oaths as the two strange men entered. From between them Janey Reilly edged her way and sidled through the uproar and the crazed ill-omened distorting flare of lamps to stand beside her mother. There was considerable commotion. Some of the guests rose stiffly to their feet, while others, older, drunker, continued conversations too grave to be interrupted. For what seemed a long time Judy and Maisie stared then Judy remembered to scream and Maisie flinging off golden visions clawed her way to her feet just as Ba abandoning Martha Liller moved to intercept the grim intruders, who were doing no more than scanning with flinty unease the shocked room.

"They are looking for John Goss," Janey said, in a voice of calm hard insolence. Angry because her unasked-for presence

99

during the search the men had made of the house and the yard had yielded nothing, to them or herself.

A barely perceptible ripple stirred across the room.

"That's all," she said. "They want John Goss."

She threw a glance up at her mother then at the blank faces turned towards the men at the door, the room so quiet now that she could hear the usually unheard roar of the water tumbling into the canal locks at the bridge.

Someone jerked out a small laugh.

"Well they won't find him here," Ba said.

"Have you any idea where he is?" The man speaking gave no sign of life; his eyes could only be glimpsed through his heavy lids.

"You've looked above?" Ba asked.

"He isn't there."

"Then I wouldn't know where he is."

"You Peasants never know anything!"

Ba's face hardened. "It's group thinking," he said.

"Are you Irish?"

"Yes. I am. And I'm also a British ex-serviceman."

The eyes Ba couldn't see slid past to the big ripe smile of Martha Liller.

"Ask the man to have a drink," she bathed her cheek in Ba's, her mouth melting within a few inches of his own.

"Are you as ignorant as he is?"

"Worse," Martha's eyes were full of sly laughter, and on Ba's arm her hand acted like a brake. "But come in," she said, at ease under the close hard scrutiny, "And take a load off your feet." She chuckled at the stranger softly. "You could talk me senseless if you were sitting."

The room stared. There was no way of estimating the degree of its approval.

"And that's not all he could do!" Judy recovering the power of speech, spoke up; and beside her one of the men came to a halt and flicked with his fingers the feathers at the neck of her dress. "That'll do you Oliver Cromwell! None of your freemaking! I'm having no truck with the enemy!" She stepped back onto Janey Reilly's foot.

"Ah, will you look out, you blind bitch! Can't you stand on your

100

own two feet?" She pushed a fist into the thin bony hip and ducked the swipe Judy aimed at her.

"Well, come on, Ba, what are you waiting for?" Martha slipped her arm around Ba. "Give the men a drink and a bit to eat. Love does no reels on empty bellies."

Ba looked for permission to Maisie who nodded just before she stuck her nose into a glass of gin.

"And now," Martha said, her eyes full of benevolent life and her mouth curved back sensually over milky teeth, "Take it easy: for none of us here are Republicans."

She appealed to the room. "Am I right?"

"You are Ma'am!" The room or part of it acquiesced readily, eager and willing to fly past the pause that for a few minutes had torn into their detachment from the world's urgencies, and now with a great spurt of energy hurried to mend the fabric of ease woven by the full and plenty of food and drink.

"I'm going," Jeremiah Hudson, slightly drunk and suppressing anger, got to his feet.

"Where?"

"Back to my room."

"What for?"

Jeremiah could have been an actor rehearsing the role of an old man with a beautiful character. He looked at his examiner. "I'll not be guilty of having betrayed, *or* belittled, my country-men!" The smile he smiled was excessively bland. "Besides," he added as if to take the harm out of what he had already said, "I'm engaged in the study of old Irish."

The man with Martha, certain that what he most looked for wasn't to be found, was prepared to take what was, and his glance dismissing Jeremiah followed Martha, moving on hips gloriously balanced towards the sofa now miraculously cleared.

"Time after time down the miserable generations, we have not only forgiven our own, but worse, much worse, we have forgiven our enemies," Jeremiah addressed the room before he pulled the door to.

"Play a record!" someone shouted.

And on her chair beside the sofa 'The Sphinx' rising up and out of her stupor roared:

101

"Hands off me till I quench the bastards!"

Laughter went up a tone and became strident.

And on the sofa the man beside Martha removed his hat and settled back.

"You should have come in long ago," Martha said, and smiled and snuggled. "Ah, but sure we have the night before us. The whole long night . . ."

Cloudily, indolently, he felt desire spread through him. "No!" Martha cried halt as the hooley rattled on. "After," she said, as the room closed round them.

4

The night sky was clear of clouds; those which had mitered the city all evening had shoved on, maybe towards less sinful places, condemned by the bearded legend to lesser penalties. Over the bridge a British Army lorry thundered and in the overhanging branches of the tree under which Mollo Goss stood, birds were twisting and turning to settle; to flex muscles; to shake dew off feathers; to shut out memory with the drop of a lid. Along the almost deserted canal a moist wind harping its own sorrows was blowing through open windows of dusty lace; through houses asleep or pretending and all dark now, Mollo saw, except for a light from an oil lamp lowered to a glimmer in her own room.

"My Ma's home," she said.

And from the water's edge; the squeal of a water rat; tin cans; dead cats and used frenchies; Liam Martin came back over the trampled grass.

"She should not have been out," he said. "Doesn't she know about the curfew?"

Mollo explained. "She was out looking for John."

"I could have saved her the trouble." In the trees' dusk Liam Martin's eyes were black sockets.

"I tried myself this morning but all I found was that red-neck

103

Cooney who I know is John's Captain but he wasn't wearing me. Said he had no idea where John was or anything about him."

"Why did you want him?" Against the tree's bark Mollo's face was very white.

"I just did," Liam said, and paused as if he had memories or thoughts to reorganize. It was after the news of the ambush in the Park that he had gone tearing through the city to look for John, driven by directionless fears for his safety; despite the weight of his own conviction that John and all he stood for was against such tactics as the burning alive of men, even one's own enemies. But just the same he had to be sure. Absolutely certain that John had no part in the crime in the Park, for that was what the atrocity had become, a crime – outside politics and the tactics of war. And he could only be certain of John's innocence when he asked and John answered.

"But that Cooney is an implacable bollix," he said, looking at Mollo from a thoughtful distance and speaking irritably into the frenzied scream of a late gull skimming the ruffled water of the canal. "I know the Republicans have to be tight-lipped but surely to Christ my seeing John for five or ten minutes wouldn't destroy the party or harm the Cause!"

He had found himself facing the wary and watchful Captain Cooney in a room very much like the one into which the Captain had been born. Surrounded by the inevitable rhetoric of excited young men with shy or staring eyes, ready and prepared for martyrdom and from whose ranks no doubts would ever raise the notes of an anthem; and others – the Adjutants and Commandants with silent sullenness stiffening their dialogue as they eyed him and talked among themselves – some looking like out-and-out fanatics or professional agitators. He remembered with sharp clarity the threatening dead eyed circular stare of Captain Cooney sitting at a table littered with papers and the remains of a meal, and on the wall behind him the dark framed picture of Saint Agatha the mutilated claiming her own sliced-off breasts. After hearing what Liam had come for the Captain had risen to his feet and with shaggy eyebrows and parliamentary attitudes had accused him of coming to rob the Cause of a good soldier at the behest of a 'mott' or a gut-greedy bitch of a mother whose only concern was her belly and dread of facing the rent man empty handed at the end of the week.

"My Ma hasn't stopped crying and praying since that fella took him out of here yesterday," Mollo said. And saw her mother in black down on her knees at Esther Quinn's shrouded statue this morning – and in her vast unmade bed Esther Quinn in her pink camisole and with her hands down between her thighs angrily edging back from unwilling consciousness; her moist mouth brilliantly enamelled; the whites of her eyes seeming to be flushed with blood and struggling against something she didn't understand and was afraid of. Eventually Sarah palsied and ponderous with sudden age had come to the end of her confused and blasphemous prayers and taking hold of herself had allowed Mollo to haul her from the sag she had become and lead her from the woman on the bed and the rosy glow of Esther Quinn's own gulped protests.

"My Ma will lose her mind if anything happens to John." Mollo drew the jacket on her shoulders close. "As for my Da . . . About him I don't even want to think . . ."

"And will they win aself?" she asked after a pause, and she meant the Republicans, and Liam was so long in answering she imagined he couldn't have heard.

"No," he said, "they won't," and he made his answer a statement and flat like a contradiction.

"What'll happen then?" Mollo asked and tonight her hair neither pinned nor ribboned lashed about her.

"Nothing," he said. His glance went to the bridge, the sweep of cobbles and then the canal that sometimes, like tonight, smelled the way the whole of Dublin did of age and dirt and sour creeping damp. "When the shooting stops we will all go back to sleep," he said. "Back to being manipulated by our own and the British in British interests. To pandering to the priests and the chapels every whim. To our craw-thumping and saint-hunting and satisfied waiting for nothing. To our rain and drink-sodden hankering for oblivion and carefully contrived ignorance – to our praying for the Pope's intentions and an early diddly – to believing we are the Pope's, the Saints' and God's favored – to believing the civilized norm is here; the oddities elsewhere; to our sanctified poverty, dirt, disease and fizz-bagged illusion of achieved perfec-

105

tion – and since living is something that happens in spite of ourselves – to our unquestionable right to hairy bacon and cabbage dinners on Sundays – and at the end of it all to holy and grand funerals . . ."

"And the men doing all the fighting?" Mollo's question slashed the dusk like a knife.

"Oh, they will become the quare, the round, the crooked and cornered. They'll be slagged and hunted and hated for on this irredeemable dunghill it has never mattered a damn about doing something well or badly; the sin the Irish don't forgive is simply that of 'doing' at all."

"So like Maisie Collins's Novenas and my Ma's prayers at Esther's altar this morning all the killing and shooting will have been for nothing?"

"No, because the Republicans have now begun something that others in the future will be compelled to finish. And also because among us there will always be the honest and only half asleep like John who will continue to see Ireland as a Utopia once the enemy have gone."

"And will it be – that?"

"No! For when the British go from here; those who take their place will be the Cooneys and the sons of the Cooneys; the jackals, hyenas, red-necks. The collaborators with their arses and feet covered for the first time in their lives. The petty and vicious and unimportantly wicked – the avid and disorderly, the hurried and grasping, and whose only dealings with life are second-hand – the gurriers – time-servers in an alien interest who will grow pot bellies and opulent crotches and become purple men stout with a fury of accumulated dishonesty – and then, and because it takes a skilful and courageous thief to get first-hand plunder, they in their turn will use the gun, the knife and the jails to keep everything 'exactly as it was when . . .' "

A silence fell between them. Cats in yards were limbering up for the night and slashing and gnashing toms. Along the canal whores with patent-leather mouths and acquisitive eyes risked the curfew to seek substance from shadow. Acclimatized by now to the greening dark Mollo caught glimpses of them trying out the port that poured purple as they settled or streeled from tree to tree dredging up voices between glugs to shout invitations to the night and then savagely and obscenely cursing absence.

"I should go in," she said, and her hands going up to remove his jacket from her shoulders came to rest instead against his white shirt chest as his arms went round her.

"We should get married," Liam said.

"We can't till this is over. Besides what about America?"

"America won't take off."

"Maybe not. But you've set your mind on it."

"You've set yours on things you've never had."

"It's different for a woman. A man wants more than just a home and children."

"Such as?"

"You wanting to emigrate. My Ma says a man can turn in on himself with disappointment."

"Your Ma's the powerful philosopher."

Mollo's too desirable mouth made a straight line.

"I want to get married now," he said, cupping her face between his hands and speaking rapidly, thinking to down her doubts as they rose. "We can afford to. We can find a place tomorrow and furnish it. And . . ." His arms fell and went around her again and against her body his pushed forward in a randy pelvic stance. She felt excitement begin to stir in him.

"You'll have to," he said.

And she would. Or let him go. He wouldn't hang around for ever. Marry him now and stay at home! Why not? Give him what he wanted now? What she wanted. Herself and the children she'd bear him could replace his cravings for distant scenes and faraway places. In his need of her she'd be enough for him? As he was for her. She loved him. Her Ma loved her Da but even now and after all this time his eyes could still blaze in a blind fury of desperation. And America? But he had just said America would wait. Till when? The blood in her hands began to run a little faster as the threat of exile receded.

"There's no reason for waiting," he said feeling his way past questions his hands on her body were answering. From the black sockets his eyes were he saw that ghost of a smile people give when the mind begins to forget. It touched her red mouth and spread to

107

show a beauty that neither blazed nor startled but which had, in the fine bones of her face and the sane unflurried eyes, a refinement of coloring and structure that made him easy.

"No!" she said. "No reason." And was irritated suddenly at finding recurring in her insistently a phrase used by her Ma.

'A woman has no right to litter with hindrances the path a man has set himself or deprive him of his peace of mind.'

The voice came at her with the mingling of their breaths and, with wilful obstinacy, a scene shaped itself up. It was Sarah speaking and it was summer, and they were sitting on the steps herself and her Ma when Harriet Reilly's husband Alex came out of the house behind them and her Ma looked up to bid him the time of day. But there was something about him that stopped her, and he spoke before she could. "I landed myself a trollop," he said. "A whore," and though there was no outward showing, her Ma said afterwards he was crying inside. "I went walking and whisking my eyes about for trouble – and found it," he said. "She told me. I knew but I didn't want her to tell me. Didn't want to know about the young bucks she was shoving her legs apart for. That way I could pretend . . . that way . . . She laughed at me and named them! Named the young fellas she's having it off with! She named them!" He cried as if he couldn't believe what he had heard or even what it was he was saying, and before her Ma could get to her feet he had gone running past them to the locks and threw himself in. It was when they dragged him out with the grappling fork, battered but alive, her Ma said that. "And God help me! I should know." Sarah had added. "But he *knew* about Harriet," Mollo protested – she was only twelve then and *she* had known, or heard about Harriet and her free and easy lusting for young men. "I know, but in his heart and soul he was ready not to until Harriet herself said so." "But he made Harriet what she is," Mollo said, "doesn't he see?" "No, he doesn't. People don't," Sarah said. "We never pause to accuse ourselves. Most people live their whole lives waiting for someone to tell them they're innocent."

And afterwards. Days afterwards. Sarah said: "You can rob and deny a man his dreams, but what Harriet Reilly has done is kill Alex's; I'd like to believe there was a difference, but, God help me, I don't think there is."

"Mollo?"

"Yes?" He noticed her eyes were no longer stars.

"About America . . ."

"Yes. But after, after . . ." The ship was taking its usual course.

"I'd better go in," she said. She felt cold. But cold can be overcome. She handed him his jacket as they went back across the cobbles to the house.

"I wonder if your Ma saw John or heard anything?"

"I'll tell you tomorrow." She raised her hand and touched his face and as she did so conscience tore to shreds the near smile she threw him as the hall door swung to behind her. The hooley had come to its end and now the house was still. On her way through the hall she met Christina Swords coming from the yard. They bid each other good night and she heard the door of Christina's room close as she reached the door of her own.

Sleep crawled in after them by the dark hallway . . . sleep . . . that unpeopled annihilation where voices blend and battle without pitch . . . sleep to make easy the easy who received its communion open-mouth like penitents at the altar-rails – sleep to feed the doubts of the unquiet and the miseries of the unreprieved who stand in the dark at doors through which it refuses to come. In all the rooms cups and saucers stood still upon dressers and tables on floors that sagged under beds shrouded in coughs, huddled in corners against flowered wallpapered walls riddled with holes stuffed with fillings of insect powder through which the bugs came red in the blood-red glow of the altar lamps, while round the ghosts of fires clothes still soaking from the lines in the yard hissed steam on lines of twine or the backs of chairs.

From roof to basement dreams crept.

FOUR

THURSDAY

1

The dawn, on a scourge of wind, comes through the hall door Christina Swords left open behind her last night, and onto the cumulative stench of sleep coughs like bricks are flung through the doors of rooms to stir with granite strength the lusty drifts through which Christina Swords struggles towards consciousness.

Chaste but ready for possession Christina, dreaming in her red-raddled-walled room, glides brass-slippered through a dream brass-glazed with buckles off shoes and dance frocks from every second-hand shop in Kevin Street. If it glitters it's good, she tells the antelopes bridesmaiding her down aisles of trees chapleted with orange blossom bridal veils and hoofs as she goes to marry Alfie Doyle before the High Altar in St Kevin's. At the great gothic doors of the chapel waiting to make sure of her is Father Robinson himself, his cheeks gilded like trumpets and dressed in the flaming red of a Cardinal. For Christina Swords doesn't get married every day. This is an occasion, Christina! His eyes soaked white with moonlight are turned on Christina and the thousands unbidden that have come to her bed. An occasion. For hope. For make-believe. For the conventions. For crubeens and cabbage and champagne in silver buckets. For the glitter of brass and the blaze of diamonds. For handshakes as watery as promises. For Grandfathers and Grandmothers and icon-faced Sarah Goss. For her son John and furs and flowers of red. Great sounding rivers of red. Peculiar shades of red so loved by our sister Esther and the Jews on the South Circular. And rattling in the barbarity of her tarnished and spangled grandeur and imposing in her stiff dress of brass and red watered silk Christina authoritarian, imperial, goes like a tight-rope walker through the scarlet clamor of the thousands flanking her and in the Chapel, from out the crowd and coming level with her that blood-sucker Janey Reilly pocketing money and withered dreams – pushes her way and raising her face on her thin little neck bares teeth that are sharp and spaced like a cat's.

Chrissy!

Like an animal wanting to escape when it's already caught Christina rigid with tortured amazement shouts help to Alfie standing under delicate sweeps of crimson lace held up by gilded cherubs. He is wearing a blue British Army jacket and under it a cataract of green trousers. Will someone claim this decent Christian woman Father Robinson says. And Alfie does with a wink, a solemn double wink and she knows he is ready to put the ring on her finger. You are acceptable to Alfie and most acceptable to the Church and to Our Lord Himself, Christina Swords. Father Robinson is talking down to her from the pulpit and above him in the vaulted ceiling Christina can see an upright in badgered flounces hanging from a gibbet. It's a terrible thing for a woman to go manless for the whole of her natural, Christina Swords. I know, I know, Father, she answers and milling round her the crowd with ill-humor creeping over them and sudden violent rage frantic in their teeth bear witness. Who better? Who better? Christina Swords has chased and lost many a man. And made wanting a husband a sinful perversion! Christina! Christina! From the crowd stretched and crouched like figures in relief a cat's claw strikes to wound, to lacerate and in the howling mob of sullen flesh a lone voice begins to shout Christina's life around her. Crying for the ruined loveliness of her pomp that was the pomp of cathedrals and chapels and circuses, Christina begins to search for the coppers that should be littering the wavy floor under her dreamed footsteps. She had some in her hands for the kids for the

112

grush. But the floor is bare and her hands are empty. Coppers were unlucky. Coppers found their way into dreams for no good. Christina Swords remembers in her dream. With her hands outstretched to ward off flesh and brass teeth bristling to consume she goes on felt feet towards Alfie. But Alfie's not there. Unlike the Little Flower, Alfie's never where he's needed. Alfie and the chapel have unravelled into long passages and ropes of silence. On the white quilt Christina Swords's hands unclench. The marks of her nails are impressed on her palms. And still asleep her eyes below her lids flow in tears that never reach the surface.

In her bed in her room under the roof Harriet Reilly waking from her nocturnal activities in a deep sweat spies the dark face of her husband Alex veined in cobwebs and falling asleep again sees him diminished and only half himself breaking the grievous and rusty six long years of silence between them. She sees the black bristle of beard and the sliver of tongue and hears an almost unrecognized voice lick out thick throated words that taunt, accuse and reveal secrets she'd scarcely made known to herself: shut up, Alex, she cries and shouts trying to silence it and when she can't begins to sing. Singing for lost moments in her life, and streeling a waltz that is an invitation glides through a roughed out luminous landscape in which a younger more exquisite version of herself stands in the foreground while beside her Alex Reilly intones: And wasn't you the dainty dish to set before the King! The scapular and medal-strung little Miss Shannon. To Mass in the mornings and devotions in the evening and between the paternosters and ave marias trailing your pussy like thread through a tapestry across every cock stand you could lay it on. What an autopsy you will make Miss Shannon. The giggly eye-rolling and hip-swinging Miss Shannon. With the mind and body of a lumberjack hiding behind the fey voice of the little Irish whore lost. Some nice little pieces there, Alex Reilly, your oul' Ma whispered. Them is as fresh as the morning. In her dream Alex's hands on Harriet's breasts are callous uncaring. Grass that's never been trod on, your Ma said.

And they were mine, all mine, your Ma said. Making no mention of the merrymakers that had been coming and getting for years before me. Forgetting to tell me that fuckin' you would be like beating a goose to get a pâté, Alex Reilly the chicken butcher gives a laugh through which the bed springs groan. Buck up Alex you're not dead yet! Harriet cries and her words worn by much use have in spite of herself a certain shabby tenderness. No thanks to you Alex tells her. And no laurels either for the hot life I poured into you. And I was good at my work. Like the heart you were a wonder. Kept at you all shagging night every night! Couldn't get you off me Harriet agrees. And when you weren't screaming for more you were wanting my hands to reduce its size. None of us ever know when we have found what it is we've been looking for, Harriet says. Insatiable! Little Miss Shannon. You should have buried your dead, Miss Shannon. It was unwise of you to hide only the body and leave the feet sticking you. And now whisper me this, daughter. What young buck's bastard first fattened you up? Was it Tom's or Dick's or Father Robinson's? Can you hear me, Harriet? For if Alex Reilly isn't laughing loud now he's not crying either, Alex says, and in her dream Harriet sees him lift his head, black now with forgotten black thatch. Because I wasn't anything you ever priced you broke me up, Harriet. Only because you expected too much of life, Harriet replies. Suddenly emptying his bewildered mouth in screams Alex turns on her eyes that have been defeated and mournful for years. She would have touched him then. If she could she would have sucked up his screams of enormous bitterness. She would have touched his mouth, his eyes, his receding back, but already Alex was a footfall.

At Harriet's feet in her bed, her son Willie awake in the slumbering dusk listens for sounds on the edge of silence. Settling sighs of stone and board and packed rooms inhaling and exhaling constant wind. He wonders what it would be like to be a stone boy. A separated stone boy hacked off a headstone. What was it like never to shut your eyes, to be forever reflecting the same ceiling, faces,

furniture, dark? Be like he is now without identity and unconnec-
ted. In the dusk Willie's face is gray and puzzled. It is the face of
a victim. A victim of some terrible exploitation. All night long
someone was playing mean scurvy tricks on Willie. They were also
making thunder. Bolt after bolt of thunder. A cataclysm of earth and
sea. Did it stop? He raises himself up on his pillow to listen and
hears a nearer sound. He stares through the dusk for a sight. On
the scrubbed topped table almost touching his end of the bed a
rat is sitting on its haunches beside a sugar bowl. Neither he nor
the rat stirs. In the space between the eyes of the boy and the rat
meet and hold like two distant and unrelated lives mingling for a
moment in sleep. Then the rat turns; thumps the floor as he lands
on it, not in fear, and slowly moves away, dragging his long tail
into outer darkness. Willie watches his going and lies back down
again. And with the suddenness of pain he is aware, then, of
loneliness and isolation, of an overwhelming sense of loss and
gray nothingness.

Alone in her chair bed under the window Janey indifferent to the
dreamed stares of the sternly respectable and already anticipating
the hundred injustices she will encounter that day, opens her
eyes and mutters aloud her necessity. Stunned with sleep she
reaches through the jumble of bedclothes for her pinny.

On the stairs going down to the basement a bucket filled with
water, deliberately put there the night before by Janey Reilly, is
sent crashing onto the flag floor below and sounds the supper
gong through the African night of Jeremiah Hudson's dream.
Watching himself, he scrambles to his feet and begins to shift from
foot to foot with excitement on the blenched Inch-a-Day shaded
floor of the stoep. Behind him, from the dark depths of the square

115

red-bricked house, the clatter of plates on bare wood goes unheard and the tired voice calling stays unanswered.

Beyond the low brick wall before the house and over the red sandy earth between it and the 'sheep-kraals' a man as long as the night past and Calvinistic black in the warm sweating cicada-clouded evening pounds loose limbed towards him, faceless under his double-brimmed terai that forms an awning over his broad shoulders. With a shout the youth of ten that's Jeremiah goes to meet him. Going in ecstatic and painful restraint past the drooping brazen faced sunflowers that have outstared the sun all day – past the clumped-thorned and glinting leaves of the prickly pear every step taking him closer and closer to a collision with the man who then stands his head a little to one side, his forehead knit asking questions. Jeremiah half-suffocated with the weight of heat and breath and sudden desire flings his boy's body against the great long limbs and reaches above them, shivering in a sensual and just this minute discovered unknown and inexplicable longing: his hands grope blind, through the thick cloth of britches to get at the man's heavy bulge on a level with his pink mouth and with a cry of ancient hoarded pain he sinks his face in – unaware of the terrible silence that has come, now that the man's laugh has stopped. The darkness, lasting a moment only, is smashed, and in a violent flash turns red. Against his smooth flesh is the sandy red earth, and along his lips the grit of sand mingles with something that's sticky sweet and indescribably strange. In deference to obedience he staggers to his feet and stands reeling on legs no longer his, moving through hardening pain towards the man backing from him as though from a leper. His name, thundered from the man's big chest reverberates and multiplies in places where hoary monsters wallowed in mud and into his sight the Biblical dark-bearded bony structured face of his father looms – the caved eyes which could and had flashed back at him only passionate flashes more thirsty and infinitely more desiring than the love glances of any woman – and which had added their own fuel to the great burning – are now black and dulled with accusing anger. Stunned by this age-long horror which only long long afterwards will he be able to account for or understand, Jeremiah, his tongue a stiff curving terror in his mouth, leans forward to vomit his

116

fear; but around him arms, and over his father's voice, his mother's low and sweet at first, rises strong and abusing while against her throat he whinges quiet his own occult misery. Shaking on the shudder of a past that's still vibrating Jeremiah turns over on his side and pulls the bedclothes up closer to his face, drawn, haggard and childlike, on the flock pillow on the bed in the convent-neat and blinded room.

2

The clattering bucket that failed to wake Jere-
miah Hudson woke his gray cat hugging the last of the fire's heat
from the white ashes on the hearth and brought it with yelling
impatience to the locked door. The animal's persistence succeeded
where the clattering bucket had failed and on the bed Jeremiah let
go sleep and from his gummed up throat flung a muttered curse
onto the room's stunned pause. The cat, thinned out with rage,
glared red-eyed and spat retaliation at the man who because every
morning is the first was having to drive and drag and haul himself
to do her bidding.

Unresigned to what he knew was prepared Jeremiah shoved
the bedclothes off and slid his feet to the floor cringing back the
way he always did from the icy flags while against his cracking
ankles and uncertain shanks the boneless furred body lashed and
clawed. Wanting to get back to that warm place from which he
had been flung Jeremiah swore and tried to kick the cat off but it
stayed an unmoveable weight against him – and then in the open
door – and as if to demonstrate an emotional life of its own –
stood with its nose raised to sniff and test the outer darkness of the
passage with the quivering antennae of senses beyond which it
refused to budge. Blind to the cat's natural caution and still
reeling in the dregs of sleep Jeremiah thinking the door to the yard

118

shut moved to open it, shivering against the chill of damp that seeped through bones and walls and stone over which he shambled dazedly.

"Blasted cats!" Jeremiah said. "One of these days I will free myself of . . ." A snarl of hate behind him went unheard as ahead of him a breath stirred and lurching sickenly, he pulled up, panicked into full wakefulness. But the movement had been so swift, so silent, it could only have been imagined. Might even have gone unnoticed if his mind's ear had not heard his own clotted cry still tearing itself from his severed head. Through the violence of blood throbbing and prickling in his now functioning veins, he staggered nervously and stared frantic through his own death rattle and shock of fright and then dismissing the moment as a trick of the mind or the hour was about to push on when a clear unmistakable slur of sound reached him.

There was something or somebody in the dark. But who? Or what? And at this hour? A tramp, maybe wandered in from the canal. Or some other poor clawing survived monster who like himself had had enough of living and was wanting rest. In the passage the walls and the ceiling were moist, and now and then a drop, slowly collecting, fell from the ceiling to the flagged floor. He stood and listened and submitted himself to expanding terror and from somewhere in the lowest depths of his mind was aware that ahead of him something vast was painfully vaguely forming. A curtain of cold sweat gathered on his eyelids, waited to fall.

"Who is it?" His voice feeble and dust-colored uttered unknown to himself.

"John Goss."

Jeremiah could have screamed or blubbered shamefully.

" I didn't mean to frighten you." A hand found him and rested briefly. It would have reassured if it could. Like rain against window panes in the dead of night or the touch of hands in childhood. It brushed along his bare arm before it was withdrawn and he was alone again.

"What is it?" He asked when he could. "What's up? What's going on? Your father and mother have been out scouring the streets for you."

"I know. I heard," John Goss said. From the dark reaches of the

119

passage the gusting sexuality of his breath trumpeted and shattered. It was frontal and aggressive and had in it sounds wind has that sweeps down from hills before the sun has sucked it up. John Goss had become a body again. The darkness reeked.

"You should go home," Jeremiah said. Under the cover of the dark he drew his slack self back from something that could have stopped his breathing keeping pace with his heart.

"I can't."

John Goss muttered confusedly.

"Then why have you come back?" In Jeremiah's voice was something that never showed in his clouded eyes. Calm now, he wished he had his cat's propensity for seeing in the dark.

"I had nowhere else to go," John Goss said.

And that would have been his answer, too, Jeremiah thought. He would have liked to rub his hands over surfaces.

"I don't know what happened, and I won't ask," he said, "but what do you want?"

"Somewhere to sleep." The voice lifted, crowded the extensions of space.

"I haven't a bed but there are two paillasses on mine. You can have one of them." Absorbing with the intensity of his ear the sounds of the house, Jeremiah spoke and acted quickly for up through its crib and bones somebody was a busybody. "Come on," he said shuffling back to his room and with his head skewered on a pike John Goss followed him. In the room Jeremiah, like an ant woken by the sun, no longer poisonous but livelier than ever, hurried to raise the wick in the lamp from its glimmer; pull a pair of saggy-kneed trousers up over his limp jack and frozen balls and push his cold feet into old carpet slippers – marvelling as he did so at his own and humanity's wretched trembling acts of faith, while behind him with his back to the door John Goss stood dwarfing the room and staring round it: at the table drawn up to the fireplace and neatly set for breakfast; at the bookshelf with its well worn books; at the deal scrubbed dresser of sparkling blue delf; at the bed in the corner with its rumpled bedclothes; and then at the door beside the bed that led to a room that had never been used. Aiming a sideways glance Jeremiah saw him hesitate, then limp across the room to open it.

120

Right now John Goss would doubt everything seen, done or spoken, he thought.

He said, "It's amazing into what little space the human soul can be crushed. But it is clean," he added blandly, and it was. Scrupulously clean and bare and except for the door there was no other way out of it. The window that had been there and on a level with the yard had long ago been blocked up to keep kids, busybodies and rats out, Jeremiah said.

And asked, "John were you in the Park yesterday?"

The reply was slow in coming. "Yes, I was." In the smoky glow of the lamp the fevered eyes of the one met the clouded gaze of the other and held.

"And now to save you the embarrassment of asking me to go . . ."

Jeremiah planted himself between him and the door.

"I didn't ask and I'm not going to ask what kind of soldier you are, or were; all I'm doing is sniffing after reasons."

"If I stay nobody must know. Not even my father or mother."

"If that's how it has to be . . ." Jeremiah said and whatever his thoughts may have been he was keeping them to himself. "You look tired," he said.

"I am."

"I'll get the bed ready. And then make you something to eat."

As if his body had forgotten its soldierly bearing John Goss moving awkward and stooped-shouldered turned in his own space in the small room. His hollow cheeks were covered by a dark growth of beard – his mouth set rigid against pain and the sudden debate of thought. In the grip of an inward cold he stood studying the room and Jeremiah with fixed and seething eyes from beneath heavy and swollen lids. He should not have come back to this house tonight – but he had. Like an addict going towards nar-cotics mindless of the depredation and misery his being found here could cause. But, no. That wasn't true. He had thought and then he had stopped thinking and like a man on gur with a murmuring mind he had run, crawled, through the smells, the horsepiss, the despair and sleep of others devoured by lice and plucked at by men and women whose every aspect like his showed weariness, poverty and age – limping his way from one yard to

121

another, from one doorway to another, stalked by fear and pain and scourging gusts of near grief – only this time nobody had come out to point the way or lift a hand to help. Until . . . Jeremiah was old. Older than his fifty odd years would account for. And now that he could see him he saw that his face was as pale as cheese in the lamplight and that his eyes had a pink and ragged look. He tried to remember what he knew about Jeremiah and what the canal said of him – the all-knowing, omnipotent canal, whom no bolts could bar, or blinds blind – the canal said, poor old Jeremiah. Born unprovided for except in the provision of himself. He belonged to nobody and the canal belonged to him only by accident. Old and uselessly wise. Deluging their minds the canal said with the useless, the doings of the bramble, the oak and the elm; or switching from them, in his orderly manner, to Irish history during the reigns of the four Georges (about which he knew a lot), to the price of bread, the cost of coal, or the jagged organ tune of man's existence (about which he knew even more). The Bible and book reader, the canal said. The African with the white skin. The man lover from the other side of the world. Womanless with his womanly ways. A true woman – born for the very functions that some women have to shoulder whether they like it or not. Contented with his darning an' his mendin' an' his washing an' with his rough an' rowdy cronies from Guinness's making love to him in his parlour.

Offering help now that could land him in trouble. Offering without encouragement. And if accepted what then? Would this one offer have a sequence of others? It might! So it might! – but right now he was in no position to chase after mights; he had to have certainties. And what the hell! If all things are in all men would it matter if it did? It had once before, only then ignorance had allowed him to accept the proffered gifts wrapped in rotarian phrases and afterwards . . . The stranger's tenuous smile in the unset features was guileless and he had taken the cigarette and then because the inclinations of others can't always be guessed at – the drink in the pub and the offer of the bed for the night. Gullibility was then and still was something to be wondered at, he thought now as he watched Jeremiah tear his own bed apart to get at the mattress he was giving him. And as he roused and shifted himself to help Jeremiah he remembered that the stranger's cadaveric lips showed white teeth in his lean face and then the narrowing eyes bearing down on him in the white bed and the lowering hurried mouth with which his body fused. All night long and in almost frantic succession the stranger's mouth went down on him and in the morning that was spattered and puddled under a sky ashen gray with rain clouds – excitement had continued to mingle with unexplainable panic as he trudged with his collar up through the bitter biting streets. Afraid not of what had happened but afraid that what he felt might show, he had gone that day and for days afterwards directionless in his mind and reluctant to face riveting sight.

He didn't then but he knew now that there was another side to all mens' lives and thoughts. But of that the canal and the world knew nothing and said nothing, as the way of the canal and the wise world is. All life is a dream; his Da sometimes said – and so if cats and Bibles and rough lovers from Guinness's keep it from becoming a nightmare then so much the better.

Leaving Jeremiah behind him in the little room he limped back into the lamplight – and with a suppressed groan lowered himself into a chair beside the table – and then lugging his mind back from where it had taken him he said, "I understood, Jeremiah, that it was the duty of every citizen to refuse assistance or support to the Republicans."

"I know!" Jeremiah spoke quietly behind him. "I've read and heard the slogans: 'Beat them into the ground and bury them!' But in spite of them we continue to fight our little battles alone, son; you your way, I mine."

"It could square things for you if I was found in your room."

"You won't be. None know me for a patriot! Besides at my age I'm damned if I'm going to allow myself to be intimidated by England's henchmen and arse-lickers about who or whom I invite into my own little parlor. And, furthermore," he said and now he seemed, as old people do, to be speaking to himself, "it isn't me you should be giving your mind and attention to – but to whatever it was that drove you back here tonight." He paused and looked at John Goss in straight inquiry and also in a way that till now he had avoided; at the jacket and shirt spattered with

123

stains and in flitters; at the black hair branding the forehead; at the sickle of doubt on the heavy black eyes aglitter in the underbrush of lashes stabbing with their every rustle the pallor of the battered flesh beneath; and what Jeremiah saw hurt him – and attracted him and it hurt him. It was something between pity and sympathy for this man and the dark rough beauty that had settled upon him. A beauty that bordered on the dark and the tragic; that seemed to threaten innocence and hint at some odyssey from which there was no return; and over all a long aching silence that filled your mouth with longing and disquiet and reached right down to where your balls are. This man with the sometimes, as now, eyes of a child whom a long day's play had saddened – worn out with protest and who had run for cover to this hideout – this place embattled from the maiming and fugitive play of angels. Had come to this stone flagged and one windowed grave – this Golgotha – seeking shelter, not from a drunken husband like some of the women who from time to time hid out here, not like others out of reach of a destructive meddling priest or a chiselling Jew come to collect his pound of flesh; but from something more terrible, something that could not be fought with promises or dreams, maybe from something that could not be fought at all.

He remembered the two strangers at Maisie Collins's hooley and then for no clear reason hymns – menacing dark German hymns sung on a doorstep in wet summer dark and in winter on chairs stuck in among ferns, grandfather clocks and gilt mirrors that reflected endlessly the dark and ponderous furniture of an unfashionable century. And as if the unrelenting past was a weight that had settled on him he shuddered suddenly – and fighting off a slight drag in his voice he asked, "And who would even think of looking for a real live Republican in Jeremiah the cat's?" His attempt at a smile was hindered – but his shoulders melted under the collarless blue shirt and hung and streamed in sudden folds on his thin frame.

"Is it me, sir?" He pantomimed his question and narrowing his blanched eyes to slits held his head sideways. "Me, shelter a Rebel?"

The flicker of humor his antics kindled on the dark lips of the

124

man on the chair went unseen by Jeremiah, but not by Janey Reilly, who hearing the crash of the bucket on her way through the house to the yard had come creeping down to the depths of the basement to investigate. Unaware of the cold vigilance of the eye at the keyhole Jeremiah paused in his pantomime.

"If it's safe you need to be then this is the place," he said. "Here, where all is that never was. Where daylight never comes and where God has gone from. This accomplice that like a well-trained dog hides even the evidence of my occupancy." He paused. "That is except in nightmares." In nightmares – in looking-glasses crowding nightmares Jeremiah saw himself beaten up, mauled and weeping. A sleeper in an unknown land – adrift among the hymns, the ferns and the furniture – rummaging his way through the wigs, creams and rouges – through the lace ribands, stockings and women's dresses – his head framed in the semi-circle of a black or golden wig with long flowing curls – his face raddled rouged and painted – and under the paint and the powder and in spite of it – the hide of time – porous and sleep worn, mazed with boundaries, frontiers and transactions – the whole of his life showing through in ugly deteriorations.

"A man has to be mad to see into the past or the future," he said. "But I think my queer habits will have made you secure here," he added with a laughing irony.

"I don't think either of us are sound of mind, Jeremiah," John Goss said and got up from the table to stretch tendons Jeremiah thought. He watched him pace the floor in silence then sit on the edge of the bed. He sat forward with his legs apart, his body crouched, his hands taut between his knees.

"In my case thoughts may not be strides any more," Jeremiah said. "But I at least gave up believing that this dunghill was worth preserving a long time ago."

"I am not trying to save the world!" John replied, his eyes on a stretch of awareness going round the room.

"Perhaps not," Jeremiah said. "But *you* are still kicking at walls you can't bring down."

"Haven't you at one time or another?"

"Oh, all that's buried is not dead," Jeremiah said. "But we never get up the true enthusiasms a second time. Also belief leads

125

to commitment and eventually loss of self. Though in my case that would be no loss. Also age catches up with a man, and then Reason asks, who or what men fight wars for? Not for the likes of me." He shrugged. "Nor you."

Going down on his knees at the hearth Jeremiah put the match he had been searching the mantelpiece for to the sticks and the paper in the fireplace and then from the bottom of a sack took bits of coal which he placed mechanically among the flames jumping to consume.

Against the barred and only window below street level the wind and gray of early morning was flinging itself in throaty spasms. In the fire the flames burned steady like candles in chapels for the troubles people had entrusted to them; Jeremiah's thoughts ran in their own line: Behind me sitting on my bed is a man like a young beast cutting first horns and with a look on his face I could follow the way I would a witch-fire. Follow that rigid mouth and those heavy black eyes anywhere. He is an addict to death. But then so are we all addicts to death. Life is but a journey to the place of execution and death. Though why this particular man should have chosen this place to break *his* journey is something I don't know. Standing he is taller than me. All of six foot. Could eat off my head. It's how I will see him. And his unrecorded look. As if he was being tested by continual blows from someone unseen. Trying to sort out the world the way the spatulate fingers of a surgeon will try to trace the diffusions of a tumor.

Coming here to disturb the long dead. That paleness will rot my sleep. I will see that also in nightmares. Framed in flowers in nightmares. And I'll lie on the floor the way I sometimes do now. From some terrible aching of my body that would in its misery be flat with the floor. Or lower. Lost in burial. Blotted out like him. Erased. Wanting no trace of ourselves left to ache upon the stone. I can feel the tracks my hands and feet have hewn out on these flags. Hacked out every second of my own torment. The hands and feet of years devouring stone. I sometimes just kneel on this floor. Or like a medieval abuse I lie on it face down.

If I were to turn my head now I could feast my eyes on that

126

outraged mouth. On the heavy eyes that before I've seen shadowed if not with an understanding of my needs, at least with a mysterious puzzlement of my desires. And I'd be safe looking; for a man like you would hardly want to smash your fist between my eyes, for never having shared the particular want that has driven me all my life you have nothing to fear, nothing to strike out at. I could have loved you John Goss or – and now thought comes slow, reluctant – a man like you, and I hesitate upon that admission as though I could reject the idea of second best, but it has been second and third and even fourth best all my life, hasn't it? I have asked the question and answered it. Isn't it for everyone? Don't most people make do? Or are left sideways with misery and looking as if they were waiting for something they had been promised when they were children. There is no justice. The gnaw of want and endless eye-searching gaze is not the prerogative of the sentient being writhing in impotent anguish in the ranks of the secret brotherhood haunting the *pissoirs* and cottages of the world. Everyone is on the prowl for someone or something else. You have only to scratch the surface anywhere – look to see the never ending search which furrows the air as eye is turned to eye in desperate hope and lingers for a second's duration, then unrecognized and unrecognizing, pulses forward to pursue its furtive or open quest . . . for the somebody that that bearded queen in heaven was supposed to have made for everybody.

Mother! Behold thy daughter!

Wanting to stand up and reach out and touch, Jeremiah stayed where he was staring fixedly into the fire and holding his head at sudden attention while against his knees his hands waited to perform yet another act.

"I will get you that promised something to eat," he said, and getting to his feet went about doing so.

"You sometimes sound like my mother," John Goss said.

"We are not alike," Jeremiah replied. He stood for a second between John and the fire. "But free of the world's bounty and with no string attaching us to any cause, we don't have to blind ourselves into making allowances for the one or maybe two sins we ourselves are not committing."

127

"I've never understood this question of sin," John Goss with a dissection by knives of light going on in his head had to force his voice.

We see what we see but nothing more, Jeremiah thought. He said, "That's not surprising since you don't see the sin of the crime being committed against you this very minute." You are a dreamer John Goss. An idealist, he thought; and a fact like a dog would have to bite you before you recognized it.

At the keyhold Janey Reilly saw Jeremiah Hudson go to the press of the dresser and then go to its shelves and from them begin to take cups, saucers and plates. She saw John Goss. The light in the room showed him to her, where he sat and then stretched out on Jeremiah Hudson's bed with his arm suddenly thrown across his eyes. When she saw his movements become spasmodic and uncontrolled; when she heard him shout pain as he tried to lift his right leg and lay it straight beside the other; when she saw him act up like a wino liberated from all sobriety invoking charms; and when she saw Jeremiah Hudson stop what he was doing and hurry to his side, hiding him and the room from the keyhole: Janey Reilly knew that John Goss would be staying whether he liked it or not.

The dream had become a nightmare.

Softly in her runners, whitened specially for the hooley the night before, Janey crept away. Back up the stairs she went – smiling. Her head on her white gophered pinny – a strange white flower on a long stem – and gleaming like a white canal lily that folds its lips secretively on a fly.

128

3

"Did *you* know that as late as nineteen-hundred-and-eleven half the people who died in Dublin gave up the ghost in prisons, asylums, hospitals and workhouses? And that half the death rate was twice that of London, or that quarter of the population was housed in one-room tenements which even then were verminous wrecks of a once classical city?" Maisie Collins said as she closed the door of Esther Quinn's room behind her. "Well it's all true according to Jeremiah Hudson," she said, breathless from her stiff climb, her mind rampant with hustling thoughts, her vision blurred by impatience at herself and at the knowledge Jeremiah was forever imparting.

"I met him below in the hall just now and between him and them stairs, or Ba Fay's big thug of a stretch, one or the other of them is taking their toll of me." Feeling fat and over-pollened in her cotton overall, inside which her easy going body was given full play, she moved around the room then walked across it to the window. About to yank the blind down off the window she remembered the ritual and leaving it as it was came back towards Esther and seated herself on a chair at the table. "Go wan, get that down before it goes cold."

Esther hanging on to the ironwork of the bed hauled herself up and throwing off the fantasies in which she had been lost for several days began to sip the tea and eat the fried bread Maisie had brought and left on the chair beside her.

"It's Thursday!" Maisie said brightly and wanting to recover cheerfulness.

Mentally edging away Esther swallowed a mouthful of tea and looked.

"I need hardly ask!" Maisie said. And didn't.

She was looking and smelling round the room, like a bitch where a dog has lifted its leg.

"You should've got up and come down to the hooley last night," she said.

"I should've. But . . ."

"Yes, and then he didn't turn up, did he?" Maisie could not resist.

Esther's face immediately tightened.

"Maybe a job came up!"

"Maybe." Maisie thought it unlikely.

"Or something happened," Esther said. The scream of a loitering gull on the sill outside seemed to confirm that something had. "But he'll be here today. If it's Thursday." Her look was questioning, even (Maisie saw) doubtful.

"Don't tell us you've lost track of the days!"

Esther had.

Maisie eased her hand across her belly.

"Where was I?" she asked, fighting off a sonorous melancholy she couldn't account for and trying to think of other than the thing going on inside her and that kept her changing her position on the chair.

"Are you sick?"

Although Esther had painted her lips into a big cupid's bow they were thin and straight under the grease.

"Something I ate," Maisie said.

"I could hear shooting all night." Esther's voice was suddenly convalescent. "The buzzing and the rattling never stopped."

"Didn't hear a thing." Maisie eased her position again. "Ba Pay didn't let me." She looked sideways up at the blinded statue

130

on Esther's altar. "Mesmerized, he keeps me," she said lowering her gaze as if in guilt and looking into the wide expanse of Ba Fay's throat – her mind floating in quick and pure contentment as she rushed to cradle his body. "Goes in on me like bees over fields of daisies that man does. And I thank God for him every day of my life."

And she did. Before Ba, sex to Maisie was cries in the night that bordered on despair. It was pictures, childlike pictures and the growl of a man mounting a woman and not the side her face was on. It was the drunken bubbling moments of lust that Hammy and his countrymen called love and which left her head rented with such misery that even her teeth weighed. A misery to be added to all the others of a hand to mouth existence and neither to be seen nor remembered; and it happened, thanks be to God and His Blessed Mother, in the dark to which it was mercifully confined.

To Maisie, then, Ba approached sex with all the luxury of a ritual, and his was the first man's body she saw undistorted by the ugliness of shirt-tails or trousers or the ill-formed glimpses of flesh seen in the ruins of a dying fire or in the degrading whimper of a guttering candle.

She had seen Ba in the full light of a fat round globed oil lamp, and he stood before her with the unconscious nobility of an animal naked, and brimming from every pore with life and juice as thick and as heavy as glycerine. Laughing loud for uncelebrated and departed innocence – she remembered now her fear at the last minute that first night with Ba and calling on God who, if he came, came not to protect but to assist at her own sinful destruction. She remembered begging Ba to let her go and not make her see, only stopping her blubbered whinging when he went quiet and when she thought he was decent again, and opening here eyes she had stared shocked and mute onto the charcoaled expanse of his body before her eyes dropped of their own accord and against her will down to where his smoking torch was.

"Christ, and wasn't she the prim one!" he had said, his voice sieved through paper wrapped round a comb – his eyes glittering like blackberries in a hedgerow – and then flinging aside all that

131

she had been born, bred and raised to believe about the sins of the flesh she had looked from his face to the unconscious beauty and changing architecture of his body.

Ba's body though slender was not thin. His skin firm and white darkened to almost night at the hair across his chest and narrowed to a pencil stroke down and over a cast iron flat belly. Long legs and narrow hips balanced a long back that broadened up to shoulders spread like twin mountains some distance from each other and, from the valley between, his neck rose long and thick like a pillar and supported a head that had none of that narrow-back mean look – a left over from the Famine which charred Ireland seventy years ago and now scarred many an Irishman. Ba carried proudly a beauty unblemished either by nature or politics as yet, and until Maisie's eyes climbed to meet his, he stood still under her scrutiny like a horse arrogantly poised and ready to mount.

Her, he said and she knew and felt his fingers undo the strings of her sack apron, the buttons on her blouse, stripping resistance from her layer by unnecessary layer and herself, her eyes robbed of focus standing throwing off shiver after shiver. She knew when his hands cupped her breasts and lingered before they slid down over the flitch of her ribs that she was now as raw as an onion, like himself, and in a sudden gust of panic explored the darkness pressing against her lids for the shame that she, a married woman, was prepared to feel at that very minute and – didn't. Convinced that its absence condemned her for ever from the sight of God and the corporal and spiritual world, she opened her eyes and heaving and protesting had tried to shake him off. But wasn't she the right thick, then, for she had even at that moment torn like a cat to get away. Her flight halted by his shouted lurch towards her. Against his opened mouth her own got lost, but they were without her knowing no longer protests, and when he led her to his bed she went – remote under her heavy hanging coils of hair – and quiet as a whisper . . .

Esther growing steamy with imagination was staring at her.

"Oh, God!" Maisie was trying to sooth her belly. "You shouldn't have let me go on like that about Ba and myself." She shook her head. "What was I talking about before that? Did I

132

tell you about Martha Liller and the fellas at the hooley?" She paused and thinking Esther's stare concurred, went on . . .

Esther looked puzzled.

"Goes in on me like bees over a field of daisies." The way her Ma's claws went in on her when she discovered herself and her father. "Where were you?" Her Ma had asked when she came back from Nurse Madden's. "I had a job." "You didn't keep it long." And at the fire her father scratching an armpit and pulling on a Woodbine. Esther wasn't looking at her Ma. She was looking at him, waiting for him to say something nice but all he did was stare while the thing in her that wanted to go back and be a child ached. "Where was the job?" Her Ma asked and hearing but not answering Esther wondered what her Ma would say and do if she told her. Told her what Nurse Madden had said and done . . . no tearing the place asunder with the strength of your trottle if I do you here and I will if my terms suit. "How much?" Ten quid cash down – and as she moved to go – what you must remember is that I'm a woman with all the prerequisites – chemist shop and hospital trained and up to my oxer with the results of that short dangle men carry between one leg and the other – though I've been told to my face there isn't a whore walking the streets of Dublin, nothing but saints and saint-hunters, and now that we've got down to business what were you thinking of parting with – and keep it low and speak it soft for I'm a demon when I'm insulted. THREE POUNDS! She could hardly get the words out and the other's blank stare had gone right through her. Three pounds ten, then; though she had hoped to be able to hold onto the ten bob.

"Done!" Nurse Madden said and while she took the money and hid it in an article in a cupboard, she began to glance furtive round the mustard-colored room avoiding seeing only the brutal derelict bed.

She had expected the room to show some trace of the things that had happened there. Some trace of the others like herself who had emerged from it maimed, degraded and enraged for life. Where for instance had that girl died whose body was found dumped on the steps of the house next door on Christmas morning? Was it on that bed? Or on the folded chair bed Nurse Madden was setting up even as she watched. The coppers in spite of proof positive had done shag all about it. Said they couldn't prove that Nurse Madden had caused the girl's death, although they as well as everyone else knew she had. It wasn't hearsay that if Nurse Madden went up to 'The Joy' she'd have company, for she would take the police with her, that they had been sharing in her criminal profit for years, for the blind eye they turned in her direction was nobody's secret.

Wanting to run from the nurse and the room she hadn't run. For where was she to run to? The world had prepared no place for girls like her, and if the church and the state had their way no place would ever exist. Supposing she died? Just suppose . . . Like the rest of us you would not much be missed and not much remembered – besides it's hard to kill a bad thing – here get into that bed and drink this . . . And she did and lay then without voice, without movement except for the now and then quiver of an eyelid until from the nurse's wandering hands pain came. But even so no protests. No screams. Until light came and went and Nurse Madden was telling her to cut out the roaring if she didn't want to halt the heart and hinder the progress of decent Christians like herself in their tracks.

It was when the nurse shoved a rag in her mouth and then tied another over it that she saw for the first time what she had not seen at first glance – the face bent over her – the haphazard and sagging structures of stroke and line – daubs and streaked guilt – smeared kohl and blotched rouge – and beneath the visible surfaces as if the whole fabric had begun to decompose the gullies and chasms and nudging folds of perished and splintered flesh – melting and spreading like wax into that space between face and shoulders. Wanting to escape the betrayals of maturation and rot and her own pain she had risen up to scream because she wanted to scream and felt and smelled the breath blowing at her. Fungi – heavy dishevelled – it was the breath of decline threatening consciousness – coming at her in blasts through a gaping painted mouth that reeked bitter of porter and Swansdown cream . . . "Cough it up, you whore!" But she couldn't. She was whimpering

134

on a thorn among the stench of excrement blood and the rustle of mauve paper flowers.

"A beauty," Nurse Madden said and it was wrapped in a rag. And she knew. In the ominous lamplight. Nurse Madden threw them into the fire or into the canal at Ringsend or out into the Phoenix Park or into the ditches along the roads beyond it, and sometimes they were found and it was put into the newspapers, but nobody, not even the papers, said they knew, and they did, who threw them there.

She might have whinged then for something she didn't know. When she saw again she had her arms and they were welted, and her tongue was swelled and her lips were skinned and raw, and at the table the flaking façade of Nurse Madden waiting for her return was complaining through the gobbets of meat she was chewing . . . I earned my money with you, next time you'll not grease my hand with a lousy three quid . . . next time . . . But what about the ten bob? She remembered. The ten bob? Maybe she hadn't had to give her the ten bob, but she did. When her Ma asked her to shell out some of the week's wages she hadn't a penny, until her father slipped her five bob to hand up . . .

"What are you laughing at?" Maisie Collins asked. "It wasn't any laughing matter." And she went on about Martha Liller and the two strangers at the hooley.

Esther nodded. Laughing matter, how are you! she thought, remembering her father's face that evening when she asked him for a half-crown . . . I gave you five bob today . . . He spoke in a hurry because her Ma was standing at the door talking with the chapel man . . . and you'll give me another . . . Narrowing his eyes for something that might be in store for him he asked "For what?" She didn't answer. She didn't have to. He knew. And when he told her to follow him out, she followed him. Stifling her isolated child's cry dying away under the chapel man's high laugh and the grinding of the iron trams.

135

It was easy after that. After she knew. He didn't feel nothing, her lusting incestuous father, and she hated him. Out of bed. In bed he smothered her with his weight and thick lips, but he stopped knocking her about because he knew better, not that she would've told her Ma, for she knew as long as she didn't he had to toe the line. There was also the money he gave her whenever she asked, and she wasn't shy about asking. They made love when her Ma was out, but she liked it best when her Ma was home and asleep and from her Ma's bed he came to her's staff in hand that even in repose spelled out the alphabet and up and doing stood like a mortadella at attention. She was glad when she felt him go in on her in the thickness of sleep driving at her in a way not always calculated for her pleasure and when her Ma began to grow tear soused because she wasn't getting it she could have laughed in her face for she said he must be spending himself with some fancy woman . . .

"But that wasn't all," Maisie's voice cut in. "They were searching the place for John Goss! Did you know John Goss was . . ."

Esther wished Maisie would go.

"I'll give no more hooleys." Maisie stood and stretched and stooped to retrieve the teapot and plate from the chair. Her eyes went above Esther to the shrouded statue of the Virgin. "I feel a need of Herself today." She turned from the bed. "Ba Fay will have to leave off me," she said, "I'm not what I was any more. Will you be all right?" she asked, with her hand on the door.

Esther forced herself to turn her head.

With a loud "Yah." Maisie drew the door to behind her.

On the landing Janey Reilly stepped away just in time.

"Did you hear anything?" Maisie asked.

"I wasn't trying to," Janey's gaze was quiet, contemplative, hostile. "I was on a message if you must know."

"So?"

"It was to Esther Quinn," Janey said slowly, deliberately.

"What about?"

"My mother wants to know if the altar's still blind; she wants to say a prayer."

Poor Harriet and her prayers! As if prayers would help for what it was that ailed her!

"Where is she?"

"In bed. She has one of her headaches."

"Tell her the altar's still blind." And as Janey turned away, "Tell her to get herself a Seidlitz powder!" "Esther's altar," Maisie muttered as she began the stairs. Poor oul' Mary caught between all our tortures. A past she was in no way responsible for and a present she couldn't share.

At the hall door, Sophia Doran drew aside to let her pass, while her eyes remarked the glimpse of breasts under the cotton overall that was all Maisie had on down to her naked feet. Christina Swords, sitting with her chin in her hand on the bottom step, didn't look up as Maisie settled herself on the step above her.

"No work for you either, Chrissy?" Maisie asked lifting her face to the breeze, her eyes to the heavens scattered with sheep-shearings.

"No, the laundry's shut down; and so is everything else in the city this morning," Christina said.

Maisie heaved. "And no word of the Republicans who shot that officer in the Park? I was above just now with Esther. Still no sign of Billy Boy Beausang, either." She glanced at Sophia. "A lovely day," she said.

"And meant to be lived in. The night for sleeping!"

Sophia's reproving voice was met by a laugh.

"The hooley kept you awake?"

Sophia drew herself tidily together. Maisie Collins was a loose sensual woman. Feeling emotionally squeezed out from her rage of the night past she turned herself at an angle that would exclude Maisie and saw Jeremiah Hudson coming towards them, his arms against his chest carrying a mess of lights wrapped in a newspaper.

"Are the shops open?" Maisie asked as he came to a halt beside Sophia.

"Only Claffey's and the bowels of the earth, Ma'am. The intestinal track, pouring with Irish blood and British bullets."

Climbing the steps Jeremiah came to a halt beside Sophia.

"Anyway you can't be wanting, Maisie," he said.

"I am." Maisie replied. "Ate me out of house and home, though

137

I must say there was enough food and drink on that table last night to keep the house fed for a month."

Jeremiah glanced at Sophia.

"I wasn't there," she said averting her head from the smell of the lights.

"You missed it." Jeremiah said.

Sophia was revolted by the smell of the lights; she unclenched her jaws with an effort to mutter, "I missed nothing!" There was the rise and fall of barricaded breasts under the smooth blue of faded cotton.

"When I wasn't being dragged from my sleep by two English thugs tearing the house apart in their search for John Goss – I was being kept from my rest by people who should know better! And I mean you, Mr Hudson," Sophia finished on a long painful expulsion of breath.

Jeremiah might have enjoyed a clash between himself and Sophia this morning if he hadn't been frightened by what he sensed was the cause of her attack. A nerve twitched at the corner of his mouth and the vague meandering stare that he had learnt to turn on and off at will crept into the clouded eyes.

"And what sin have I committed this time, Sophia?" he wrenched it out, but quietly.

Sophia munched, swallowed and might have been preparing to burp; but folded her arms instead. "It was bad enough being kept from our sleep by hooligans, and the hooley . . ."

"Ah, that's what's vexing you?" Maisie laughed, but mirthlessly.

Sophia ignored Maisie.

"Perhaps you would like us to turn the kip into a home for elderly ladies?"

"But when that stopped," Sophia continued, talking through the other, "to be kept from our rest for what was left of the night by *your* allegations! That man you had in your room . . ." She paused and gulping uglily to get it out – "Was either a lunatic or a wino!" Her swift glance sought confirmation or approval from the others that they couldn't very well withhold – but did.

"I didn't hear anything." Christina spoke up out of her sunken thoughts.

"You would have had you wanted to!" Sophia's face mottled as she drew in her mouth and stared from Christina to Jeremiah and waited for a denial or an explanation but none came.

"Ah, I give up!" Maisie cried and jumped to her feet before Jeremiah could move on his. "What with the English wanting to starve us out, Esther's statue still blind, and now you spouting balls about the hooley and men out of their minds in the basement, the country's going to the shagging dogs." On a level now with Sophia and Jeremiah she narrowed her eyes to fire her parting shot. "You're as cold as a witch's tit, Sophia and what's worse you're an interfering old bitch!" Briskly she pushed Jeremiah into the hall ahead of her. "Go wan outa that for Jasus sake!" she said and slammed the door to behind her.

Maisie Collins was a savage sensual whore! Sophia was perspiring with injustice. She glared down at Christina. "*You* must have heard the screams and shouts coming from Jeremiah Hudson's room last night," she cried. And stood prepared now to doubt whatever Christina said.

"I was out," Christina spoke without turning her head.

All night, was Sophia's swift thought. She waited, but Christina had nothing more to say. When Sophia, trembly and addled, finally went in, Christina's eyes continued their search for something they would probably never find.

4

Christina had not seen Alfie last night but she had seen his mother, and then only after repeated hammering on the door had Mrs Doyle grudgingly admitted her.

"I was in bed."

As though a martyr to the unreasoning demands of others, she looked at Christina, her eyes and mouth full of accusations, then clutching the man's jacket she wore over her shift lumbered back to it.

"I suppose you're chasing Alfie?" she said once settled under the covers again. "If so you've come to the wrong shop. I haven't clapped eyes on him since yesterday."

"Didn't he come in last night?" Christina glanced from the empty bed in the corner to the one where Mrs Doyle sat, beside the fireplace.

"No he didn't." Mrs Doyle's face was hidden under the wide flat brim of the black straw hat she had never been seen without. She wore it in and out of bed, and it hid her absolute baldness.

"I was supposed to see him last night," Christina said quietly.

Surly by temperament and clearly sulking now, Mrs Doyle grunted and leant sideways out of the bed to look at the fire and the bottle of camphorated oil warming on the hob and which, Christina knew, she rubbed on her chest. She nodded and Christina anticipating her want, brought the bottle from the hob.

'You'll get a piece of brown paper in the press,'' she said. "Heat it."

Christina did as she was bid and held the paper to the fire and when it was warm brought it back to the woman in the bed. "Will I do it for you?" she asked.

Mrs Doyle didn't answer but proceeded to smear the paper with the oil. "And he didn't see fit to tell you where he was going or what it was he was up to?" she asked, running the flat of her hand over the paper.

"No, he didn't."

"That's Alfie. 'Oul Go Be The Wall An' Tiddle The Bricks." With sombre and malicious glee Mrs Doyle seemed prepared to accept whatever behaviour might demonstrate a man's rights. "That chap's left hand has never known what the right one was up to," she said, pulling open the jacket and the neck of her shift and easing the oil-sodden paper down across her chest. She sighed at the contact then doing up her clothes again leaned back on the flock of pillows behind her.

"But where would he be? He didn't turn up tonight either. You'd think he'd have told me, wouldn't you."

"Well, if he didn't tell me, and I'm his mother," Mrs Doyle could have sighed for her unappreciated self.

"And I am going to marry him!" Christina said.

A dread that Christina might settled on Mrs Doyle's oil-sodden surface. "Youth calls to youth," she said, her stare falling directly on her visitor. "And Alfie is only a lad. And between you, me and the lamppost, Chrissy Swords, you're no chicken. I'd think long and hard before I set me sights or saddled myself for life with a man half my age." And now that Christina Swords was warned and reminded . . . "Besides, what would you get married on? I'm hard set as it is trying to keep the bit in me mouth without him landing in a wife on my floor. And I've no intention of letting him retire me to a bed in the Union."

There was no avoiding it; and it might sooth the oul' bitch.

"We've saved. And I'll keep on my job in the laundry," Christina said.

"Well, all I can say is there's a bigger hurry on you to get yourself a husband than there is on Alfie Doyle to take a wife. And I'd like to be sure you know."

From under the brim of her wide straw Mrs Doyle's eye sockets looked hollow.

" 'I'm in no hurry, Ma,' he's said many a time when I told him I'd go easier to my grave if I saw him settled first." She paused and when she spoke again her voice had taken on a direct note, softened with confiding candor as though she were neither thinking of nor talking to Christina. "Yes. Some decent little girl from a decent family and with a little something of her own at her back to set up house on. A little girl who'll age with him. But as he says, he's in no hurry. And can you blame him when you look at the poor shuddering scrubbers cluttering up the high and byways of this city. I'm concerned, Chrissy Swords. And my concern isn't unnecessary. He's not the strongest and would never be able to rough it or survive without his little comforts: a clean shirt a day every day; a bottle of milk; and in the evening his slippers and bottle of stout. He likes a good breakfast. And a meat dinner. Now them sort of luxuries are not picked up off the street. That kind of high living costs money."

"What kind doesn't?" Christina could not make her voice cold enough.

"You said a mouthful!"

"Will you tell him I was here?" Christina had to force it.

"If you want me to." Thoughtfully Alfie's mother aimed her deadliest insult. "Though I don't mind telling you, you're cheapening yourself running after any man. For speaking from my own experience of life a fella who has to be dragged to the altar isn't worth dragging."

Christina flamed. "Alfie's done quite a bit of the running you know," she said. Her hands closed tight on her practical handbag.

"I doubt it!" Mrs Doyle muttered and raised her face but the lamplight struck only her mouth. "You off Chrissy?" She said sinking back and arranging herself for death, it looked, rather than sleep: her eyelids so definitely shut.

Christina knew she had been dismissed. Her face recovered its characteristically direct expression, though her lips looked twisted; her shoulders humped: she could have been suffering physically. "Yes. I'm off," she said, suddenly drawing herself back up to her normally impressive height.

"Can I get you anything before I go?" she asked.

At least the streets had taught her not to show, or only in deepest privacy.

"Not a thing, Chrissy. Not a thing." Mrs Doyle had lost interest.

Christina moved to the door. "Good night so," she said, her going waited for in silence.

In the dark gap of the hall door Christina had stood and waited for Alfie. Her eyes had scanned the street, sinister in its emptiness, for only those who had to braved a passage, missing the calm clear beauty of the night as they darted through its unreal vacancy, keeping tight to the shadows. Once she had seen Liam Martin come with foxy caution out of the house he lived in opposite. And later, much later, Sarah Goss had come, a small black figure huddled in the folds of her black shawl, her stumbling walk as tell-tale as possessions: unconcerned with curfews, and neither knowing nor caring where the night fell on her, unhurried by the frenzy of machine-gun fire and the explosion of grenades that in the near distance never stopped.

From the hall door, Christina caught between her imperfections and her agonies had watched the red glare that crept to the sky and stole over it, and stayed suspended, riddled by gusts of crimson that streamed to greater and greater heights . . . unseeing, because Sarah Goss had reminded her of John and the fifty pounds the men in the overcoats had offered for information concerning him. Fifty pounds . . . you could buy a lot of luxuries with fifty pounds . . . a lot of meat dinners . . . you could get married on fifty pounds . . . Unseeing through the long hours she had waited, through the corrugations of dark and light, through the pounding of guns and, but for the guns and her thoughts, silence.

Christina, returning from the distance into which she had retreated, brought her mind from something rattling round inside her like the loose seeds in a maraca. The cobbled rise of the bridge appeared, its surface black and smooth as metal in the sun and – cresting it – the rare and almost forgotten sight of the brilliant orange of a farmer's cart, piled and pyramid-shaped with the hard hearts of Savoy cabbages and drawn by a black horse bravely astray in the city's tumult. Behind it, in rowdy exhilaration, kids and grown-ups tore or streeled sly with one eye on the driver, laughing and jeering his sworn attempts to fight them off, and she knew without consciously thinking about it that the farmer would lose, for the kids and grown-ups would follow the cart till it stopped or was forced to stop and then swoop with relentless fury onto its cargo.

Sitting up and back she let her joined-together hands fall slackly down between her wide apart knees and gradually became aware of the sudden hilarity going on inside her, unaccountable for the space of time it took her to be aware of the passing of the cart, and when it was gone she found herself listening to the roar of the water tumbling through the gates of the locks into the depths below. The locks and the sound of the water was some great pressure from which it was not possible to escape and Christina's fear of them had never been exorcized. As a child she had invented her own way of dealing with the locks. While other kids crossed the wooden footbridge on their way to school, she went by way of the bridge, her eyes shut, her lips squeezed together, her hands clenched to fists and with all her might forced herself to think: The locks aren't there. They aren't real. Just two gates. With water for boats running through them. Just remember you don't have to see them. You don't have to hear the water. Or see the locks. In that way she managed to fight her way slowly out of the horrors, and when finally she dared to open her eyes again she would have reached the decay of Ranelagh and be heading for Richmond Hill. But the canal *was* there. And the locks were *real*. And she turned her head now as from a blow, the movement pushing her dread and the desperate hum of the water to a thicker but distant rumble that had nothing of urgency in it and was, if you could offer the mind a distraction, almost blotted out. And Christina could; because Mathilda Doran, back from her reconnaissance of the rooms her sister Sophia would never move to, had come to a halt and hitching up her coat and skirt was settling herself down on the step beside her.

Mathilda floury white was smiling slightly for something that had probably not occurred as she undid her coat and loosened the blue woollen muffler under which Christina could see the gray voile of her high-necked blouse. Then because there are moments in our lives when faces are interchangeable, Christina asked, "And did you see anything?" wondering, even as she did, what it was Mathilda Doran got out of finding something she would never own.

Recovering breath Mathilda looked apprehensively back over her shoulder to make sure the hall door was closed, for Sophia didn't approve of her sitting on the steps, though she liked to and always did when, as now, she had the opportunity of company. Sophia herself would *stand* with the people in the house, but in an attempt to establish respect from her neighbors maintained an idea, which Mathilda had never understood, that standing wasn't the same thing as sitting and that if you sat people became free-making and thought themselves your equal which, of course, was ludicrous, Sophia said. But this morning Mathilda dared. Mathilda

145

could not resist. She had a lot to tell. Christina knew she would not ask much, but she would tell. And Christina was glad of this as she could not have answered. She did say the air had done Mathilda good. But Mathilda could not pause. She had to tell about the room in the house looking into the Park in Mountpleasant. A big room with a high ceiling and fresh papered walls. A fireplace of brass and gray marble. A room filled with sun and space. Space to move in. To breathe.

"And the rent?" Christina asked and suppressed breath unbeknownst to herself.

"Would be eight shillings a week." Mathilda remembered.

"It's expensive of course," she said, catching Christina's look.

"It's for nothing," Christina said. It would be just right for herself and Alfie Doyle. They would be made up with a room like that. Of course it would take a quare few quid to furnish it; twenty or thirty pounds, Christina supposed. Easy. But she would be away from the canal and the locks. And with only the two of them they could manage. But where would she get twenty or thirty pounds to lavish on furniture? A room in Ranelagh. A big clean room. And get out of this soured dark troubled kip. A lovely big room. She tried the door of the room and went in. There was the fireplace of marble and brass. And there were the windows. Curtains coy with pride hung from them. And in each window a potted fuchsia with white waxy sepals bent over the sappy spray of forget-me-not ferns. Home. My home, she said. She looked around for the familiar sight of furniture. And then for her own reflection in mirrors. In one gilt framed mirror and found it. And told it. But you'd need money. Fifty pounds! The loose seeds in the maraca were rattling again. Fifty pounds was a fortune. Only a fool would turn it down. Fifty pounds would buy a lot of luxuries. And take her to the altar. That much money would get him all the little luxuries his oul' wan said he couldn't go without. You could take the boat to England, you could get married, you could take that room and still have more money left over than you could count. With fifty pounds. Why fifty pounds? Why fifty?

Then, in a gust Christina knew why. She got up and shifted to Mathilda's other side.

146

"How long has that room been idle?" she asked.

"I don't know."

"Pity," Christina said, "Sophia won't take it. Anyway it might be too big for you and Sophia." But it would be just right for herself and Alfie. And it might go, for rooms didn't stay idle in Ranelagh, and she was suddenly impatient with Mathilda that she hadn't thought to ask how long the room had been vacant. "Poor Sophia," she said, "we should not be sitting here criticizing her."

"I'm not!" Mathilda looked nervously round her. In her agitation, she did not see the expression on Christina's face; for having relieved herself of her momentary resentment against Mathilda – Christina was turning to ways and means of getting the room. Her breath beat.

With money she could. Thought like water flowed and ran in rivulets, in devious directions, under her blouse and skirt and against her skin. It could have been water. She was looking at a world blurred by water. Money. Fistfuls. All she had to do was tell those two fellas what it was they wanted to know. If she knew. They said . . . Just tell, the little fella said, that's all, just say the word. If she knew the word. To get their hands on John Goss they were ready to fork out fifty pounds. How much had she and Alfie now? That room would go. They must have more than enough, for her hands were tired parting with money all these years. All those years of Fridays. Friday after Friday. Yet she was as close now to the altar as she had ever been. And not a damn bit closer! Her fingers traced her parted lips and came to rest on the square frozen white of her teeth. She'd get a bed for that room, a high bed with double mattresses, the class of mountainous high beds the dealers went in for, and a valance of fine calico. But when? Oh, God! When?

"Sophia has always done what she thought was best," Mathilda Doran spoke suddenly out of her hot protesting mouth. "And I was not criticizing her."

"Of course you weren't," Christina assured without turning her head.

And Mathilda tried, and failed, to remember what it was she had said to Christina Swords about Sophia. It was odd the way she could forget something said only a minute before these days. "Forget your head if it wasn't tied on to you," Sophia said about her, though she thought that was silly, of course she wouldn't. But she was forgetful, she had to admit. She was known to have gone for the milk and returned without it. And that was strange, for she would start out on her journey knowing exactly what it was she was going for, with the money in one hand and the jug in the other, and come back the way she had gone, and then Sophia would have to send her out all over again or go herself. Yet she could remember clearly, as if it was only yesterday, things that had happened years ago, surprising even Sophia with the accuracy of a memory that could conjure up the most minute details, details and events that even Sophia herself had long forgotten.

She could remember, for instance, Fanny Keogh vividly, and the school they had both gone to, and Fanny's brother Tom to whom she had been married for one whole day, and could recall standing at the altar with Tom Keogh and afterwards being led to his room and not to Fanny's as she expected to be. Tom was thick and red. He stared down out of his mystified blue eyes, which reminded her, she laughed, of the eyes of a young bull. She had married Tom Keogh only to be near Fanny. And Fanny knew it. And knowing it she had pushed her out of her room to which she had gone running. "In marrying you, my brother has committed a supreme act of kindness." And that was true, and she should've been grateful, only she wasn't a bit. What she was doing was laughing. At the farce. For that's what it was. "You can't leave my brother," Fanny said. But she could and she would. And she did. Still in her bridal white, her brittle body had gone through cold and ringing frost from one end of the village to the other – to Sophia; and Sophia had hushed her crying and put her to bed like a child and told her she need not go back, that she would take care of her. And Sophia did. And after – well, after, everything was astonishingly level and legal and unsurprising. Unconsummated, was the verdict. She was seventeen then, and Fanny Keogh was twenty.

It was Sophia who had forgotten the sale of the house that their father had left them, Sophia who looked amazed when she told her about the yellow and black posters that the house agent had plastered the palings with saying the house was going. And it was she who, whimsically superior and playing games that Sophia said should not be played after adolescence, spread out details about the family and the house in Fitzwilliam Square, with whom they had taken their first positions. But she couldn't remember the people or the house where they had last worked, and where they had stayed until Sophia decided the time had come when they could no longer give the kind of service demanded of them. Sophia remembered, and called the man who came to visit once a month and who always brought a cake and kept them supplied with coal all winter, Master Richard. She also called him Master Richard, but only because Sophia did, and he asked if she remembered Miss Nellie who had married Colonel Smyth and was now living in London. But she couldn't, and Sophia shook her head and the man they called Master Richard laughed.

"And don't go on about it," Christina said coming from the teem of thought and wanting to gloss over something that had strayed out of some place. For Alfie Doyle would marry her. She was positive. He had to. She knew that and so did he; and so did his mother in spite of what she'd said last night. She looked at Mathilda then looked away, thinking that she recognized her own troubled soul in the other's white face. "And it was a lovely room, was it?"

"Yes." Mathilda spoke with an air of surprise, as if it were too sudden to find herself again in the dream of actuality. She had forgotten the room, and now her gaze, placid and white, met Christina's, and carefully she began to fold her scarf neatly back under her coat, for Sophia did not like to see her looking untidy.

"And what was the number of that house?"

Mathilda remembered. "Fourteen," she said quietly. She felt tired. How white the sky was that day. For years now she had remembered the day. The wintertime day. The pale watered silk of the winter sky under which she had run. And behind her sound coming from a long way, her own feet or somebody else's. Behind or beside her.

"Wait, Mathilda!" called the woman's voice.

She stopped to look, through her tears that the frost had made, at a face she could not see. "I must go," she said formally and, when Christina looked up at her, "perhaps Sophia *will* take that room at the park."

"You wouldn't know," Christina said. 'Fourteen,' she was thinking. She got to her feet and pushing open the door for Mathilda. "Maybe. Maybe," she said as the woman went past her.

6

The night wind was slashing the seething dark when Janey Reilly, crouched in ambush on the top step, saw Christina Swords coming out the door clutching a coat flung around her. Like a trance child populated with demons, Janey in the half light slunk back and drew aside out of Christina's reach.

"Holy St Ann, send Chrissy a man!" Janey's demon voice asserted itself.

Christina thinking her unpeopled thoughts pulled her coat tighter, ignored the taunt and with head held high as though to keep her hair out of water, hurried down the steps on her way to Rock Street. Janey about to shout out again remembered something she had forgotten all day as she scoured the lanes and streets and negotiated unfamiliar labyrinths for Darky Kelly, the young fancy man her mother seemed to be in urgent need of. But now seeing Christina Swords go with awkward swimming movements towards the street she remembered what she had forgotten and grabbing at any excuse that would postpone the meeting with Harriet and the admission of her failure to find what she had been turned out for, she shrieked into the wind and darted back down the steps after Christina.

"Well?" Christina asked and frowned black at Janey coming

151

face to face with her. "If you think I didn't hear you just now you've another think coming."

"I didn't mean it but!" Janey was using her most candidly white-eyed expression.

"You never do." Christina made to push past Janey and the sudden chilling shudder of someone walking over her grave, but Janey reached and her hands closed like jaws on the arm before it was dragged violently away. "Well," Christina cried. "What do you want?"

Janey smiled. "Chrissy, do you remember the men looking for John Goss last night?"

"What about them?" Christina, ready to doubt whatever Janey said, drew back from her.

"Nothing. Except that I know where John Goss is," Janey replied innocently. She balanced herself on one foot and hopped as if she were beginning to play a game of 'Peggy', for something in the breath or in Christina's half-averted face told her she had her full attention and she was now on for the cat-and-mouse game which vexed saints and drove her brother Willie to wild distraction. A hop took her up close to Christina again. "And I'll tell you if you want to know," she said seeking evidence of the interest she sensed, and finding it in the too deliberate shake of the other's head and in the too easy twitch of the shoulders.

"I don't," Christina said. She waited a whole second, trying to appear casual. She looked down. "And now get out of my way."

"But I know! I could tell you." Janey cried thinking Christina was about to move on. But all Christina did was turn her body without moving her feet.

"I'm sure you could," she said. "You're as bright as seaweed." Christina's feigned indifference was flippant.

"Do you want to know where John Goss is or not?" Janey asked.

"I don't care one way or the other."

"Of course you don't." Janey grinned, but it was not a smile. Her eyes, those pale blue eyes, were loaded with rodent cunning and reminded Christina of the Jewmen who came round the houses selling cacks of clothes and religious pictures and of the speculative, mean stare of the forewoman in the laundry when

152

she knew you had the flag up or caught you having a drag of a butt in the lavatory.

"Just the same I know where he is," Janey said. And it was at this point that she saw a way of turning what she knew to her own immediate advantage and in the long run getting her own back on Christina Swords. Because Christina Swords would not be able to keep a thing like this to herself. Christina Swords would talk. She hated Christina Swords and despised her stupid pretense of not caring. She was just like her Ma, with her ravaged face and palsied hands, sending her out to look for young Darky Kelly and pretending by the way that she only wanted him because she had news to impart. But her Ma wasn't any cleverer than Chrissy Swords was, and she could read the pair of them a mile away.

"I know. You said. Where is he then?" Christina asked and suddenly into her mind the thought jumped that death came in forms other than the natural ones. She saw Janey sway. Against the night she was like a pale flower that blooms lividly on seashore foam on a black beach. She waited for her to speak. But Janey was exploiting silence now for all it was worth. In her own ears Christina's own mouth made soggy sounds. "Where is he?" she asked. And heard the snigger of a tremulous fern.

"What will you give me then?"

Christina Swords had become involved. In the dusk Janey showered spray.

"I might have known!" Christina reared her great furious head.

"Well what do I get for nothing? Besides information's always worth something."

"Depends who wants it." Christina answered.

"Those two men do. That's for sure. And fair exchange is no robbery."

"So go to them!"

"I don't know where they are," Janey said.

Christina opened her mouth as if to tell then closed it again.

Watching her, Janey wondered if she had made a mistake in thinking what she had to sell was worth anybody's buying but when Christina said, quietly, "Where is John Goss?" she knew well she hadn't.

153

Christina Swords wanted to know and in a tone that matched hers Janey asked, "How much will you give me then?" She waited, calm, uninviting through the silence that fell, pondering on what Christina would offer and on how much she could ask and just how much she could get.

Christina brought up her practical handbag in which she carried her betrayal money. "Twopence," she said.

Somewhere there were sounds of carbines of marching feet and a wild man or boy calling.

"You're codding! You have to be." And into the wind blowing sour around them and swelling and multiplying Janey flung a sour spit.

"How much then?" Christina stamped out the violence of compulsion that made her want to run from the child before her, swaying green-veiled in the street lamp behind luminous water-shadows in a new and strange motion of outlines, as if water was snaking up and flowing all about her or as if she, Christina, was seeing her through water. She blinked in an effort to clear sight, and was aware that the hand she rubbed accross her eyes was, for no reason, stone cold, while Janey continued to sway and float under the sea. The image steadied itself when Janey masking malice shook her head.

"*No*. You say."

It passed – the nausea – the sudden lather of deep misery – the inexplicable terror. She watched its going and around her lapped sounds that had been water-hushed before she spoke. "Sixpence then. And you will take it or leave it." Christina opened her bag. "And while I'm at it, I'll tell you something for nothing. If you don't stop devising dramas for yourself, you'll end up bad, or in an institution, or both, and it'll be the height of you."

"Is that so?" And where would Christina Swords end up? Janey smiled, because Janey thought she knew. She held out her hand then closed it to a tight fist on the sixpence Christina put into it.

"Well?"

"What?" Janey's gaze was wide and direct.

"Where is he?"

"Who?"

154

"Who do you think?" Christina bent menacingly. "John Goss!" she hissed. "Are you thick or what?"

She spoke from a height, and below her Janey swayed, shrugged off the hand on her arm to grapple with the cunning of things she was thinking. She would not ask too much because if she did she might put Christina off. She must on no account make it impossible for Christina Swords to hang herself. But she would go from sixpence to a shilling, and from a shilling it was no distance to one-and-six. She could see the shilling lying beside the sixpence. She could face them without losing the run of herself . . . and with another sixpence she'd have two bob. Two shillings. Christina Swords wouldn't have to plunder any nest egg to come up with a lousy two shillings. She looked at Christina, head bent, hair blowing like someone caught in the pangs of birth and fury, and remembered Harriet after delivering Willie cursing like a sailor as she rose up on her elbow in her bloody shift and looking about her in the bed as if she had lost something. "Oh for Christ's sake, for Christ's sake!" she kept crying like some fool of a kid who has stumbled into the beginning of a dust-up.

"Tell me," Christina said.

Janey laughed outright. "Tell you what?" She stared at Christina who didn't seem so big now. It was as if Christina Swords had shrunk to her own size during the bargaining, and was now, Janey knew, manageable.

"All right, you cross-born get! I'll give you another tanner and that's it!"

Janey watched and again her hand closed, this time on six coppers. Christina Swords was throwing her life away in pennies. "A thing like this is worth more than a lousy shilling!" Janey heaved her chest under the cotton of a frock which had been brand new out of the shop window in Camden Street yesterday. "Make it another bob and I'll tell you."

Christina did not protest as Janey half expected she might, and for a second she wondered if she should have tried for a half-crown or even three shillings! But that might have ruined what it was she was setting out to do. Might ruin everything. And when finally Christina did speak, Janey knew she had without risk reached the limit.

155

"All right." Christina without conscious knowledge and compelled against her will would go on now; and unknown to herself every word was weighed with care. "But I'm warning you, Janey Reilly, if you stretch me too far, I'll gut you!" She paused. "D'you hear me?" she snarled.

Janey drew back. "I hear you."

"You're an evil bitch!" Christina spluttered rage into Janey's white face.

"Ah, keep your hair on!" Janey tensed and readied herself to run if she had to, but running would not be necessary, she knew as she saw Christina begin to search for the shilling in her bag. This time it was a single shilling, and as Christina forced herself to part with it, Janey's cold gaze latched onto her face.

"There is no need to get yourself riz," she said as her hand closed on the money. "I'd have told you anyway." And she would have with or without the money.

For Christina Swords was a fool and unable to give herself warning. She met Christina's eyes, large, protruding and clear, and saw in them that mirrorless look of polished metals which report not so much the object as the movement of the object. And was reminded of cats' eyes and darkened windows reflecting a scene." John Goss is, since you must know, below in the basement with Jeremiah the Cats. That's where John Goss is." As Janey spoke she backed off and away towards the house. "And it would suit you better, Chrissy Swords, to put the bit in your belly and the screed on your back instead of devouring the heart out of yourself trying to get a man and chiselling kids, so it would."

Christina stood in the middle of the path erect and motionless, deaf to Janey's screams. Then she suddenly turned and went towards the street. "If it's waiting for Alfie Doyle to put the ring on your finger you are, you'll be left waiting," Janey screamed. She stopped, and when she went on the near hysteria had gone out of her voice. "Eh, Chrissy!" she called. Christina stopped and looked back. "Eh, Chrissy, c'mere," she cried. "Whatever became of Wa-Wa Legs, and Sam Keagan the Larkinite, and poor oul' Rashers off the railway who couldn't keep his trousers dry?" She paused when she saw Christina make as though to run back at her and laughed loud when she changed her mind, turned and walked on. "Poor Chrissy, thought you had your hands on a pension book there, didn't you? But he wasn't to be trapped by your bit of brass, your wages from the laundry or your Novenas to Esther's statue, was he, Chrissy? And where do you leave the oul' moff with the little cottage up in Gulistan?" Her voice rising to a scream was heightened with mock wonder as Chrissy drew further away. "And Soft Centers, with his cab-driving father, patent-leather shoes, spats, and bad stomach? Ah, Jasus, Chrissy, whatever became of Soft Centers? With his crawthumping and chapel going and trips to Lough Derg? Where are they, Christina Swords? Wax in the hands of every one of them. Where are they, Christina? Where are all the men who were going to march you to the altar and didn't?"

"We know where they are," she said quietly to herself, her eyes fixed on the money in her hand. "They were no fools," she said, laughing out of some hidden capacity, some lost subterranean humor and counting the money, she pushed open the door and headed for the stairs and Harriet, glad now of the despair that she and her failure to find her Ma's fancy man would bring.

157

FIVE

FRIDAY

1

A tune transformed into a kind of Arab wail
meandered through the dark, irritating the evening hush settling on
the house before it died on the stairs going down to the basement.
At the fire Jeremiah Hudson bent over the steam rising from the
saucepan of coddle he held over the red coals. And stretched out
on a paillasse on the floor in the dark of the little back room,
John Goss, with brows pleated and eyeballs straining, waited and
watched . . . Mickey Lynch hug the giant trunk of the oak that
stood between them and the plebeian dawn flattening the grass
as it keened across the scrub and slopes of the Phoenix Park.
"Ambushes, Jasus!" Mickey said, squinting bitter at the scourge
of wind and trying to bury his boyish face deeper into the warmth
of his upturned collar. "Why don't we shoot the bastards and be
done with it?"

"Because we want information and because we want them
alive," John replied. He withdrew his range of vision from the
rise of hill ahead, and looked back at the one they had blown up
and from that to the straight line of deciduous trees each side of
the road just before it. Behind the trees in a ditch Captain Cooney,
along with two others, crouched and waited for a signal from him.

"Jasus, if the poor oul' Dubliner isn't being stunned by over-
work he's being starved by unemployment," Mickey wiped his

159

eyes with the back of his hand and wished to Christ he'd never been thick enough to get talked into throwing his lot in with the Rebels. It was one thing fighting in the streets of the city, where a man could be seen building up a buoyant future for himself and his country, but another out here in the comfortless wilderness of grass, trees and skies. All right for bog-trotting culchies and knackers, but he was a big city man, he was a Dubliner. And what in the name of Jasus was them? He pointed with a rigid first finger at the hieratic dance of deer stretching, stiffening, repressing barks, prudently raising hoofs as they crossed the road and headed for the deeper depths of the woods – and his eyes following their flight caught sight of prey and froze speech and movement out of him.

"It's them!" John breaking his own tension spoke before Mickey could. The hill ahead was high and the body of the car was out of sight, but as he watched, the gray sedan came over the top and he turned and signalled frantically to Captain Cooney. With pounding heart he watched the car approach then pass, and from where he stood he could see the driver, the soldier on the seat beside him and the two others in the back.

Mickey recovered speech. "Fuck it! Four of them!" He had hardly spoken before the car dragging up dirt screamed to a halt and they were running towards it. The three young recruits quaking with fright and the officer were out and standing by the car when John and Mickey reached it. The recruits were very young. Seventeen – eighteen – nineteen years of age; their khaki uniforms were clean, well-pressed; their boots glittering. Caps came low over foreheads and shadowed strained frightened faces as they turned this way and that to scrutinize the men before them.

"The British only use the best." Captain Cooney had found his victim and clearing his throat and spitting continuously stood admiring the pistol he had taken from the officer, after he had thrown to the ground those taken from the soldiers.

"Take off your cap," Cooney scraped the side of the officer's face with the muzzle of the man's own revolver.

One of the soldiers, lobster-red and flaming with boyish passion, started for him but was held back by Jemmy Dillon's rifle. The

160

officer, utterly helpless, perplexed and abysmally ill at ease, brought down his hand to obey the pointless and petty command. Slowly he removed his cap. Without it his hair was fine, silky, it lifted into the air and fell onto his forehead. A good-looking man; he was older without his cap. Frail. The way his Da looked when he was asleep or when he thought nobody was watching. His face was tired, thin, gentle. He didn't look as if he had ever pointed the black barrel of a carbine at the belly of another man. A man easy to work or live with. Couldn't imagine him kicking your brains out because you hadn't learnt to march properly. Watching him John felt that if the Rebels explained what was happening on the streets of Dublin, and the necessity for it, the officer would understand. He might not agree that the means justified the end, but he'd understand. But nothing happened. He didn't move or speak: just stood, then for some reason he . . . it was a young smile; not the mindless, bloodless smirks he had seen on the faces of other Englishmen. Smiling that way he looked exactly the way his Da did when he was a kid and caught him hiding something away from him for Christmas. He wanted to smile back. Between him and the officer, something had forged a link. An unconscious appeal in the Englishman that some irrational emotion in him wanted to answer. Sudden fear and a speechless pity rose in him. He wanted to do something; tell the officer and the recruits to go. For suddenly none of it was real – him, or them. The officer smiling at him like that, and standing. John looked at Cooney and he knew with certain foresight, as with a prophetic instinct, that Cooney would not be taking the officer and the car and letting the recruits go.

Dirt-streaked and quivering he sprang forward. "We're taking him prisoner!"

"Like hell we are!"

He caught the glance Cooney flung O'Neill and Dillon and saw them hesitate and then he was slammed aside as the silence exploded and the recruits who had not spoken one single word, fell to the ground. He drew a tortured breath, momentarily drew back and then tried to jump Cooney but O'Neill and Dillon grabbed and held him.

Cooney's laugh sounded like the crack of a whip.

161

On the ground legs moved like drumsticks then stopped.

"If you intend shooting me," the officer said, "do so and have done with it."

There was a low mirthless slag of a laugh. And then with the infinite composure, the tremendous patience with which a man waits through half a lifetime for an event, Cooney moved forward. "I will," he said. And he spoke with an almost Buddhistic complacency rooted in some insane hatred he could neither suppress nor conceal.

"But that's murder!" His jaws stiff with sudden terror and soaked with a sticky sweat John yelled into the indifferent winds blowing steadily across grass and scrub, filling the grey light with single drops of rain and making, in intermittent rushes, a remote sad thunder in great trees.

"It's a legitimate act of war." Cooney, impassive as a bailiff bent on getting a debt paid, looked neither right nor left but straight ahead, his slit-eyed stare fixed on the officer's face. He raised the revolver and when John could see again the officer was lying face down and under him the knarled trailing roots of the tree were splashed with blood that stayed starkly still before it began to pour in greedy torrents between the cracks of the bark and spill over. Cooney swung his attention from the dead officer to the three soldiers still alive and slumped where they had fallen and from them he looked down to the man at his feet. He took in a sharp breath and making gutteral deep-throated noises began with maniac fury to kick the body of the officer, staggering in his raging efforts to use both feet at the same time. The body slid off the roots of the tree and turned over; a pile of purplish intestines formed a puddle under his bandolier.

"The fucker flies the Union Jack even when he's dead." Cooney stood not right on but very near the body on the ground.

Backing from the edge of terror and howling obscenities, John tearing himself free of the men holding him staggered on the ruins of limbs towards Cooney and lurching to grab stumbled and falling heard Cooney's shot over his head. He heard a salvo of shouts without understanding and as he pulled himself up Cooney swung the rifle square across his knees. He doubled over,

162

and on the ground beside him saw the blasted face of Jemmy Dillon . . .

Drawing away from the miasmic swamp of horror and from the specter of what came after, John's hand went with caution down to the splintered knee cap held together by strips of sheet and shooting savage pain at sporadic intervals.

At the fire Jeremiah gave the onions and bits of rashers bubbling in a mixture of water and milk a final stir and, scraping the sides of the saucepan, brought it to a simmer on the hob. "I bet your belly thinks your throat's cut," he said going over and opening wider the door to the room where John was lying and getting no answer left the door as it was and went back over to the table.

. . . Cooney's last blow had knocked the sight from John Goss's eyes, and when he came to see he was caught and held between Mickey and O'Neill and the nightmare had been peopled with Cooney belting into him a consciousness of what was happening to the English men. Over the smoulder of ashes and the charred endlessness of bones scattered across a knarled aboriginal landscape he screamed his own horror and heard in return Cooney's chanted roars carried on wild flames of fire onto which Cooney's teeth and the stumps of teeth clamped in grotesque delight. And later – much later while the wind moaned its primitive desolate grief and the stench of burnt flesh was still blinding vision and stuffing nostrils – Cooney told him he was under arrest, and with a drained sick heart and as if at some extravagant invention, or some recollection of the absurd, was only now fully appreciated for the first time, he had laughed . . . and felt as if *he* had been burned, as if the life-nerve in *him* had been cauterized.

And he had thought of the Rebellion as a Glorious Cause. Something like God's fist in lightning. A resurrection of justice, truth, honor. He had seen the Rebels with vine leaves in their hair and stars in their eyes. Caesars horned for victory by God Himself to blot out the evils of the world with their own blood. Proud and fearless as any of the heroes in Ireland's long and bitter history,

163

men whom God Himself had ordained should bring their country with victorious strength into the Freedom that down through the great processional of the enormous centuries she had been denied. His companions were of the stuff that made legends and when at last the day dawned and Ireland was no longer stained with the somber dyes of poverty, ignorance and death, the Rebel achievement would be glory, Glory all the way! For they would have fought like the warriors they were supposed, and like the great men he believed them, to be.

It was the satanic degenerate English with their human-slaughterings who committed the atrocities! The Irish were an honest upright people incapable of wrong, decent and God fearing, risking their very lives to hear Mass, and willingly slitting their own or another's throat rather than discommode a nun or a priest. The Rebels did not burn men alive! But the hydrocephalic infiltrators into their ranks did. The Cooneys did. He had heard how the Cooneys 'dealt' with those men who for one reason or another had turned from the Cause, but he hadn't believed – knowing that a surmise which creeps with caution from one mouth rages as fact from every other: he would listen, if at all, with the gossip's ear.

Nevertheless it was true, and the thing that had been puzzling about the men who had ended their search for him at Maisie Collins's hooley was suddenly clear. He had succeeded in escaping from the house in Thomas Street where Cooney had put him; but Cooney had told them where to find him; and now *he* was being 'dealt' with. But there was a piece of the puzzle he still didn't understand: who was it Cooney had told? Jeremiah said the men were English. That couldn't be so. But if it was? If Cooney had *allowed* him to escape from the house in Thomas Street? What would that mean? There was no shock in the turn of thought, only an intake of breath before he continued to review, in open order on the parade ground of his own conscience, the events leading up to this very moment.

He sat in silence.

"It was your howls of protest Sophia Doran heard." Jeremiah

broke the silence and pushed a bit of onion into his mouth with his fingers. "Since Sophia can't participate in events she spends what's left of her life reporting them."

"You should have called me."

"To what?" Jeremiah asked. "Bring you back to the fear and frenzy you've been hammered into by the ghosts of dead men."

"It doesn't matter," John said. Submerged in memories he looked back to the mute ghosts of the officer and the soldiers in the Park as they stood by the car facing Cooney. If only they had made a run for it instead of standing there expecting Cooney to adhere to rules. The English with their appalling faculty of self-deception – that essential requisite for a people wanting to master others. The despised and hated English who believed only what the eye could see, convinced that there was nothing more behind the physical squalor – the blind moral misery and the comic animal antics the Irish presented them with – refusing out of conceit or blank indifference to acknowledge the bleak and bitter hatred of them that lurked behind the fey Irish voice – the fine sarcasm, the wild excess of speech, feeling and gesture.

"You must eat," Jeremiah said for John had sat back his dark face set in brooding passionate intensity.

He shook his head. There was a taste of ashes in his mouth. On the mantelpiece the hands on the clock stood at six, and ahead of him the hours stretched until it should be time, and in the deeper dark, safe, to slip over the wall in the yard and make his way down to Liam Martin's room in Rock Street.

"What time was it when those men came on Wednesday night?" He asked suddenly.

Jeremiah raised his face, parchment-colored in the lamplight. "About ten," he said.

What time would they come tonight? John wondered. No way of knowing; and guessing his thoughts Jeremiah asked, "But if they didn't come last night or this morning, why should they come tonight?" His eyes were wide in question.

"I don't know," John answered. But he did, and about to tell Jeremiah why he was certain the search for him had not ended in Maisie Collins's room, decided against it.

165

"Will you be any safer with Liam Martin than you are here?" Jeremiah asked.

"I'm not safe anywhere," John said, and he didn't know that he would want to be. The death of the officer and the soldiers in the Park had killed him, left him disabled. But whatever happened to him now he didn't want it to happen here. He wanted to come to the end of his life where his Da wouldn't see. He leant across the table. "Tomorrow," he began, "tell my Da you saw me, but don't say where, just say everything's all right." There was a swift twisted flicker across his mouth.

"My Da will be fretting now he knows I'm on the run."

"Mollo was saying . . ."

The rest of the sentence froze in Jeremiah's throat as a great crash shook the house and a rush of heavy boots tore through the hall. Stiff with fright, John jerked himself upright sending the cat, who had sprung onto the corner of the table, scudding in roared terror as his chair crashed to the floor. Jeremiah, unable to move, slumped to the table, his lips murmuring sounds like the footsteps of mice.

"Christ!" John's exclamation toughly whispered spread with the noise over the house and he turned to face the door. Cooney. He thought suddenly of the blind window in the room behind him, and the iron bars prisoning the window behind Jeremiah and remembered all that he had heard with the gossip's ear: the field by the Dodder where the Cooneys brought from their hiding places and kangaroo courts informers and the ones they called 'outsiders' like himself and set them blindfolded against the wall; the cross that Wonder Boy Evans's mother had put in the field by the Dodder after the Cooneys had shot her son for a crime against Ireland, unspecified then and unspecified now.

He bent forward, but he could hear nothing. All had gone quiet after the crashing of the door. The silence was absolute. No sound except Jeremiah's mice-like murmuring, yet he knew that beyond the room the house was alive with men slinking with the stealth of rats up and down stairs, crawling to this door and that door, each with gun tensed, with a palm firm around the butt and a finger curved against the trigger. He stood in a great outer silence, immersed in a terrifying inner rumble. About to turn to Jeremiah

166

the door was smashed open and soldiers crashed their way into the room.

Jeremiah moaned, and John with fear-stark eyes snapped erect under the cold black mouth of the revolver dug into his cheek, while behind its globe the lamp's flame flared to smoke.

"Stand still! Don't move." The voice blasted his ears. A hand searched his body and tore and grabbed in vicious rape. For a moment his nostrils pinched white then flattened out like an animal's in fright. His lips drew back from his teeth while in his eyes every splinter of thought or sensation flashed like a streak of light across a pool. He eased out, looked into the broad, lined, tense face that almost touched his own, heard the clipped voice and thought, 'The English,' and remembered . . . the Rebels who had been brought to Portobello Barracks; the high wall that looked like a spread of lace from the hail of bullets that the firing squads had poured with such precision into the bodies of men that they went clean through and came out beyond, chipping the stones at different levels in straight white lines. He remembered the hanging tree at the bridge in Milltown from which the British strung the Rebels, leaving their bodies and what had been done to them behind as a warning and example. He remembered Cooney and the bristling beard wet with the spittle of hate, like grass in some secret hollow on the Canal from which the damp never goes. He remembered so much even as he tried to forget, to reduce thought to a single point, to concentrate on the thing that was happening now, to see it in the space between him and the men surrounding him, but it was no use. Cooney walked through his brain. His mind never got further than Cooney and came back from Cooney only to accept the fact that Cooney had seen to it, to acknowledge the fact that Cooney wanted it to happen this way, that Cooney had 'dealt' with him; that he should not escape from Cooney and not from the Cause and not from death. He looked at the officer. He was country-muscled and young. Younger than the officer Cooney had killed in the Park but like him, and also khaki-clad. He nodded his head, although he had not heard the question. But that didn't matter now. The officer would know the answer anyway, because Cooney had told him. He saw the officer stare at his silence and then forgot him.

167

A very quiet despair was in his heart, a weary peace that brooded too upon the room and the house, that flowed from Jeremiah's basement like a soft exploring wind up through its dark hall and stairs and crib of bones, soothing all things quietly with peace and weariness. The people in the rooms held their breaths or crept out onto landings to listen, or made their way to the street to gather whispering. The soldiers' coming had brought him peace and freedom, as if his limbs had been freed from a terrible weight. He felt suddenly the peace that comes with despair. The lost and stricken thing in him that he had never been able to share with anyone and which he would never find now had bitten into his heart. But in spite of it he had found himself. There was nothing more of himself to know. No more of himself could be given. What he was – he was: evasion and pretence could not add to this sum. With all his heart he was glad. He had come to the end of flight and pursuit. The prison walls of self closed entirely round him, walling him in completely by the esymplastic power of his imagination. He raised his head. He had learned by now to project mechanically before the world an acceptable counterfeit of himself which would for the time left to him protect him from all intrusion.

. . . And the air was filled with warm-throated wind notes. In a rapt dreaming intensity he saw the gentle face of the officer in the Park. Saw the hurt puzzled eyes; the mouth, full, sensual, extraordinarily mobile; the lower lip, scooped to pouting. Breath clouded his vision. The indescribable sweet cloying smell of death was fusing with his own. He went towards it until he reached that faraway point that was all the loneliness of death, and then forgot death.

At the table Jeremiah got to his feet. "He's only a boy," he said as the officer looked heavily at him. But Jeremiah was looking at John, at a face he had never seen before. He had not heard the crash of escaping life. He wondered why God allowed no man to die with his own face on. He stepped up in front of John with a quick sudden movement that was misunderstood and one of the soldiers brought his revolver crashing against the side of his head. The blow lifted Jeremiah clean off his feet and sent him crashing to the floor. He lay where he fell gurgling pain, and the officer looked down not at Jeremiah but at his cat which had reappeared, and bending down he stroked the animal's arched back, running his big powerful hand from head to erect tail before he straightened up again.

He glanced round the room, but deliberately avoided seeing Jeremiah. He gestured to the soldiers, then stepped aside to follow after.

In the hall, Ba Fay stood with Maisie Collins. Behind her own door, Sophia Doran waited with her ear pressed to it. On the steps the soldiers pushed through the rage of the crowd gathered and fought their way to the car drawn up at the kerb. And across the road, Christina Swords, hidden in the shadow of Maher's the bootmakers, drew her coat tighter round her as the car drove off. Then Christina left the hiding place from which she had been watching the house and the train of events set off by herself. It was time now to go; and cautiously keeping close to the buildings, she moved to the pub at the corner, deaf to the roar of the water in the locks, and turned into the Mall and towards the next bridge, which would bring her to Portobello Barracks and the money that would buy Alfie and the brass fireplace and the lace curtains which billowed, in her mind's eye, crisply starched, and through which she had watched John Goss go. They fluttered in a breeze no longer fearful, for who was to know? And lifting her face she felt an urge to laugh into the dark of the canal in front of her; for the fear which had kept her back had vanished, like John Goss and the city behind her lying under a canopy of red smoke.

169

2

"One thing positive: this fifty quid will do what no amount of Novenas could. It will take me to the altar, and up to that room in Mount Pleasant." In the mirror that had always been more door than mirror Christina Sword's reflection looked back at her. She examined coolly, dispassionately, the scrubbed face and the still damp hair just washed and smelling of carbolic soap. Lightly she gave a pat that was almost playful to the wound rope of hair which later on would stray but which now, while still wet, was a neat coil resting low on the back of her neck. With clumsy hands she began to rub Swansdown Cream over her nose and chin, blind in her excitement of the game begun again, to the wide expanse of cheeks and the heavy jawline which, generally, she had to avoid awareness of and which never failed to deflate. But tonight, dimming the mantel mirror-face with looking, there was no need to form the V with her hands at her chin and cut off the heavy side-face to create the illusion of beauty, for the difference in herself that she had awakened to on her way back from the Portobello Barracks had lasted throughout her preparations and was still strong as she readied herself for Alfie. She gazed at her high cheekbones and paused in her debate to wonder if she was too pale. Deciding that she was she dived into her handbag after the box of rouge and had to push aside the neat wad of bank notes to find it.

170

The notes were creased from having been counted so often. Now, when she handled them, they no longer crinkled. "For money such deeds are common to humans," she said. She dropped the money back into her bag and, in the glass, saw the red felt hat on the table and, beside it, the blue silk scarf that at her throat gave her eyes a depth of color they didn't have. How would she give the money to Alfie? I could slip it in his pocket when he isn't looking, or set it out before him. That's odd; that money's as mauled now as the last agony, but it was brand new when the British officer had thrown it to her just a couple of hours ago.

Another queer thing was the look on that officer's face as he threw it across the table; didn't seem a bit grateful, or thankful, or anything, just . . . Someone should tell him that, if we didn't have to account for them, there isn't a sin in the book we wouldn't commit, because judging from the expression on his English face his dealings with life are surely second-hand . . .

She fell silent and drawing back from the memory that followed, bent her face closer to the mirror, streaking her cheeks with the rouge and searching for the earlier imagined frailty and beauty. But the expression and the mood that had suggested beauty was gone, and in an effort to recapture it she laughed.

"Will you have it in your hand or in your eye, Mrs Murphy?" she said, lifting ironic brows, and waited for her own and the face in the mirror to come together again after the laugh, while her mind raced ahead to the vision-ized Alfie. I can just see him when I put that money before him! she thought, knowing a moment of desperation when his face failed to materialize, but it did, and she saw the lock of hair falling onto the forehead and the wet lower protruding lip onto which she fastened, because that was what she saw most clearly. Serious he'd be, as she held out the money to him. And intent he'd look, like an infant with the sun in its eyes walking slowly into the open for the first time. And when he asks me where I got it, I'll just smile – like this. I could, of course, tell him and the world the truth; tell him I've turned my back on the angels and given up reaching to the heavens to handle what isn't there. I could. But I won't. He's not the brightest and for all his trickery I don't think he's spry enough to trifle with the hangman. No; I'll tell him something he'll understand. I'll tell

171

him I had a Diddley; or that I was lucky at the fair. What I'd like to tell him is that my lips have thinned with waiting and that it's time he stirred himself into greater energy and put a ring on my finger. What I *will* tell him is about that room up in Mount Pleasant, and about the brass fireplace, and that black leather chair below in Black's window; and, maybe after, we could go up and see that room. Might even pay the first week's rent on it, tonight. You wouldn't know. Mrs Alfie Doyle: that's who she'd be.

Providing he didn't slip from her as miserably as a miscarried child. She looked at the one in the mirror. Herself and the one in the mirror sometimes seemed to live separate lives. She stopped searching and stared solemnly at her broad shoulders and her firm breasts jutting out and up under her best slip.

The very latest in shrouds. And gone gray from washings. Should have a new one to wear tonight; something fit for a doll; something with lace on it. Not that anyone will see it but, just the same, *I* see it. I know it's on me, and I know it's old. Should've bought a new one, or got a lend from Maisie Collins – except Maisie would've thought that a bit strange. People are not used to Chrissy Swords doing the extraordinary. Just the same, this only reminds me of all them things I'm finished with. That mob of lousers that never meant anything! All them pricks! Sometimes those fellas toll in my head like funeral bells; sometimes . . . You're raving, Chrissy Swords. The prospect before you is making you giddy. You're not even sensible. If you were, you would not have given it away – you'd've kept it tied up with yards of blue ribbon. If you had you'd be a virgin now and, when you went to Alfie, you'd be going as pure as the driven snow. What was it Maisie said the other day? "I let my right to bridal white go like summer." That's all very well when you've tits like targeted moons hitched to the sky, and when you're crushed with attentions. But I hadn't and I wasn't. And I didn't marry the fella. And when you don't it isn't at all the same thing.

What was the name of that first fella? Told me to call him Johnny Appleseed. But what was his real name? A six-foot-tall trickster with slow gray eyes and curly hair. A hard-muscled stallion, he was; all confidence and pliable stem. Flashing

172

aggression like an animal and, as he said himeslf, coming to passion easy and often with anything, anytime, anywhere – and without a screed of paper to prove the tales he told. As if he needed to! But, imagine not being able to remember that bastard's name! Johnny Appleseed. Christ I'm shivering. Someone going over my grave. Tell you what, Chris; you should've bought a good bottle of whiskey on your way in this evening. A drink is what you need; something to chase the ghosts away. Melt bones, the voices of ghosts do. A drink would've helped; would've ripened the pods and put color in your face.

Trouble is, not being able to, you lose the knack of spending; and, Christ only knows when I last sent two half-pennies astray. Never having it, it takes a person time to get used to it. That's a fact. Everything's a fact! This slip is a fact, so is this room and this house with its diseased sweat – flittered windows – jam rags and biddy bottles. These are all hard facts; so is that canal and them locks; and so are the men and women who go down into them, head first, every day of the week. And *it's* a fact that, after Sarah Goss enlightened me, I never did again. Except that once, and then I didn't; only wanted to, with . . . John Goss. But he wouldn't. Instead he ran off and left me lying there like the vomited evidence of a banquet. John Goss! John Jesus Maria Goss! Him and his wild talk of Druid moons and the murmured song of trees. Never was a doer of things, for all his talk and learning.

A dreamer under the fleeting solace of the drifting moon. One thing sure; that officer I talked to will wake him from his dreaming. Ask him some questions, is what he said he would do . . . That's all; just a few questions. Well, if that's the case he'll settle for half answers. People always do. Anyway what was I saying? Telling my stories to you has made me the liar I am. Lies to hide your mind's knaw, and take the agony out of your guts. Lies to stop you screaming your heart's dark and bewildering misery. Lying in my teeth to console and comfort you. Right now, you're looking at me as if . . . Are you waiting for something Chrissy? A burst of hiccups, maybe! Or for the past to relent a little? What are you searching for, Chrissy, when you stand and stare at me like that? A way to leave, and not to go?

173

Sometimes your face is as quick as conscience, and as clear as glass; did you know? Did you also know that, looking at you, I sometimes think I've not only lived my life for nothing, but I've told it for nothing. Did you also know that after Sarah Goss wised me up about wasting myself on every mongrel who came waltzing up the path ready to bestow on me the kind of favors that would land me in a bed up in Number One James Street I never did again? Would expect a thing like that to show, but it doesn't. Only you, yourself, know, and others – if you tell them.

Does Alfie believe me? His mother doesn't. She still thinks I'm an upright. Not that it matters what she thinks. She doesn't like me, and never has. But there's no love lost, because I can't stand her! I'll put up with that gut-greedy and fist-tightened oul' bitch if I have to; but only if I have to! I'm learning. I'm learning late, but I'm learning! And that's the important thing! People should be born knowing everything; the other way is not fair. We should be born old, and grow into children – and end up not in the grave, but back in the womb. Although, I don't know. Can you imagine having to streel the dowdy streets and roads of this lousy world looking for an oul' womb to crawl into? Jasus, a woman wouldn't be safe anywhere! You're childish, Chrissy Swords. Janey Reilly knows more than you do. But then that monster was born knowing. Funny thing; on the street today she was saying something and, for a minute, it was as if she was under water, or I was looking at *her* through water. I wonder if I talk to you too much? I always feel a fool when I've talked, even to the girls below in the laundry. Because in the heel of the hunt, who the hell cares what you think, or feel? Nobody. The trouble with me is, I've been torn to shreds by what I've had to keep hushed. Life! Jeremiah Hudson says life is nothing but an exercise in lacerations. I should think about that. Except that I've discovered that thinking about something you know nothing about doesn't help.

In the mantel-mirror Christina Swords saw the eyes of the other look out from their own pursuits and hurriedly drew her hands from her breasts and tossing her head fought back the thoughts that the gesture had raised to crowd before and behind her and, with swift grabs, began to gather up her things, coming back to put them on in front of the glass. The face inside the glass fumed

174

indistinctly on its surface: no one looking could have said who it was but Christina knew for certain it wasn't her. And if it wasn't who was it? And was someone somewhere howling in hoarse rain?

A boom of silence answered her; here, there, a marginal sound: gusts of wind in the chimney; mice in skirtings; the light scuffed feet of her who walks the stairs at all hours; and wind murmuring at doors conversing in sad lament on the ceiling blowing its damp sour breath into her face, breathing through the flecked decaying mantel-mirror in sighs of warnings or expectation of sorrow. In the glass images mingled, broke and turned into shadows of things in flight that shattered and crouched and didn't show except in footfalls overhead, lost and searching in the jungle of rooms for something that could never be found.

With ferocious contempt she swept aside the rancid wetness of shrivelled fear and stared hard at her eyes in the glass and saw them quicken in returning excitement forcing into herself an aloofness, a remoteness, a feeling that held her erect and pushed all that had gone before this very moment from her mind, making her feel clean and slender as if *her* flesh, too, had been blown away. And under her blouse and skirt she could feel her freshly scrubbed body move. Untouched even by her clothes, she was; and she would go, when she did go, as if it were down the chapel aisle she walked, clean and pure in mind and body, approaching Alfie and the night, whimpering against her window and down her chimney, with the same humility with which she would have gone to the high altar to receive the Body of Christ from the soft white hands of the priest.

She lowered her head and let her red felt hat gently onto it, solemnly crowning herself, and she felt its weight descend on her, forcing flat the side wings of her hair and, closing in on the mirror, smiled the wide smile of the self-abused at the indestructible glazed face of the glazed girl in the flecked mirror. Withdrawing, she reached out one hand for her bag and lowered the flame of the lamp with the other. Looking round then for something she couldn't see, she thought the room was gloomy and, in spite of her inner excitement, full of sighs and uneasy rustlings, as if men or ghosts were watching her from its outer darkness. It

175

was imagination. She turned back to the mirror for one last look – for one last embrace. And then in an effort to appease that other fury she began to mutter prayers that were directed at Him and at the shrouded statue of the Virgin on Esther Quinn's altar, ending only when she was outside her own door and on her way to Alfie's . . .

3

In her great bed that smelled of horses and leather and guns, Esther Quinn awake and troubled and looking amazed lay straight, almost rigid, staring with fixed intensity up at the ceiling. The vicious thing that had ripped through her was going now, leaving her feeling mean, sour and skinny and with an overpowering desire to bawl. Distantly she heard steps in the hall and then the closing of the door. Dimly she became conscious of the return of the house, senseless sounds, creaks, someone ear-wigging at doors, timbers settling under the spreading haunches of the damned – prostrate under the monstrous cocks of the betraying. Tonight she had come from sleep into pain, opening her eyes from the receding tide of her dreams, aware even in her sleep of the beginning tumult waiting to devour. Feeling with caution the already begun throb like the pulses of multitudes kneeling in some great and secret confessional crying between tongues, the terrible excommunication. But it came, as it always did, like an animal on all fours, all hunger and clamor, demanding the attention of her mind which she tried to divert by beseeching God to have a heart for fuck's sake. But God if He heard wasn't answering because it came regardless. Sly it was, like a blow aimed at someone else, quietly, lousily, mean, for it came into her at the pit of her belly and stayed like a cancer sucking strength

177

for one breathless second before it erupted in rage and exploded into kaleidoscopic flowers inside her brain, while its roots curled and closed in a rough fist round the firmer stem of her very guts. Sometimes she was on her guard when it came, and would watch and wait and even welcome the pain beginning, willing its terrible assault, delighting in the destructive subjection by which she proved Billy Boy Beausang's domination, glorying in his imagined granite strength. But tonight she had been caught unawares, and it was over before she knew what was happening, and when it was past she began to swear violently rejecting the return of sanity and the empty snarl of the cunt that had been cheated out of a good fuck.

I would have seen it coming if I hadn't fallen asleep, she thought lowering her gaze from the ceiling and easing her mind towards the search for the cause of her new misery. It was that dream, she said, and remembered the dream.

Esther dreamed that she was standing in a strange street looking for somebody, and through the air bits of burnt paper went black and flying in a grieving wind over the stiff bodies of horses stretched in death on the cobbles. The street was empty at first except for the horses and the grieving wind blowing and herself going through it to the house. A house she had never seen before – expansive, decaying with great big rooms, and she was standing in one that though set with all the belongings of others, was as bereft as the nest of a bird that will not return. Though deserted and empty now, she could tell from the way the air stirred itself against her face that it had recently been occupied. In fact, she half-remembered seeing the door shut to though it was only the handle that moved, turning clockwise as if a hand was controlling it on the other side and letting the lock slide into the socket with a soft sound. The room was as big as a dance hall when she began to move over the faded pale carpets to the windows that were curtained and shuttered. And when she tried to open the shutters she couldn't for laths had been nailed across them. Far from the shoaling tides, the room was a room she knew and when she came from the windows she looked up at the Italian-plastered ceiling for the meat hook she knew would be hanging out of the middle. The meat hook was there and so was the narrow iron bed on which

178

somebody had slept. The bed-clothes were still warm. She could feel the heat in them – and it was then the child had come into her dream. But from where? She couldn't remember leaving the room or the house or seeing the child come, she was just there, a little hurrying comedy jester pulling Esther to something unseen. She couldn't see the face of the child either, because the street was clouded with smoke, but she could feel the grip of her hand on her arm. Through streets screaming with gunfire they went and from every doorway people without faces called out as they passed and when they stopped running she was alone and the street was empty except for the man kneeling in the middle of it. She knew him even though she couldn't see his face and was watching him when the two soldiers appeared. She heard a fresh burst of shooting and saw the man stretched on the cobbles. Into the quiet she saw the child come back. Not an inch over a whiskey bottle and skinny, moseying along out of nowhere, down the long street deserted except for herself and the dead man in the middle. She tried to stop the child coming but couldn't, all she could do was stand and watch her relentless approach. "It's that man's cap," the child said as she came face to face with Esther and looked from her to the cap at her feet. She bent down and began to scrape up something off the ground into the cap. "I have John Goss," the child said standing up and covering the thing in the cap with straw. She walked away with the cap and the thing in it. Esther looked down at the face of the man at her feet. She saw the glitter of glass where eyes should be, and weeds upon the mouth, feeding on rains, canal flowers frothing from its ruin. She bent down to touch the face but just as she did so she came from sleep and from the dream and into the thing that happened to her.

She rolled over onto her back. Her imagined great sprawling body hurt. A dull exhausting hurt, and patches around her ribs and thighs ached as if she had been beaten. She hadn't. She was as strong as an ox and would live forever provided she didn't die of starvation. She was hungry . . . She was starving for Maisie Collins hadn't been able to give her anything at all this morning – and Sophia Doran had come at dinner hour bringing her a drop of soup with cabbage in it and, without actually saying so, had hinted that if the hunger and shortages beginning to trouble the city lasted, she couldn't promise to bring her anything at all tomorrow. It was all the fault of the Rebels, Sophia said; and Maisie, who was there when Sophia called, had for once in her life agreed with her.

Treading through the shallows of light, coming from each side of the red blind on the window, Esther turned her mind from the threat of the famine and from hunger that as yet was only a mild discomfort, to ruminate on the clairvoyant quality of her dreams. Always a sharp dreamer her Ma said . . .

Had to give her credit for that . . . big-hearted her Ma was, give you two half-pennies for a penny any day, oh, there'd been no love lost between herself and her Ma . . . and her Da thought she was asleep that night . . . She had heard him leaving her Ma's bed and his weight on the floor and the shifting of the table when he touched against it and the creak of the loose board just inside the door in the little room where she slept that you'd think that after all his fuckin' he'd have the nous to steer clear of . . . would've wakened the dead, let alone her Ma even if she was asleep, but she wasn't for she howled like a bitch fox just as her Da went in on her and went on howling, her Ma did, even after he got up and told her to shut her fucking mouth . . . his language was terrible, but the funny thing it was her her Ma blamed, not her Da, shocking things she called her, and her Da stood there listening and then he went out, and through the blows her Ma gave her she saw a light flare and knew her Da in the other room was lighting a fag . . . and smoking while her Ma dragged her out of the bed onto the floor, beating her with anything she could lay her hands on and all the time he went on smoking and smoking even when she called him to save her, and he didn't stop smoking till her Ma stopped lathering her, and when she did he said: If you've finished I want to get to sleep. Her Ma went then and she lay where her Ma left her, her arm broken, although she didn't know that till the next day. Then she didn't know it, and she stayed where she was on the floor and heard her Da and after a while knew her Ma was being warmed up by her Da's bigness and that he was putting a fistful of condensed power away without hindrance. Without protest. Without a fight. Nothing. Except the easy beginnings of a giving and a taking that would stiffen

180

her Ma's shammy-leather breasts and leave her face saintly and idiotic and rob the oul' eyes in her head of their focus.

After she got to her feet and found her clothes and gibbering and blubbering, her fingers dithering, she put them on and lay down on the bed till the light delivered her by waking her and she heard her Ma scrape out the grate and shove in sticks and paper. And after she put the drop of water on for tea she came in croaking her triumph and hatred through her teeth: "Go wan get out of my sight." Her Da was still in bed when she passed through the room, lying on his back waiting for the first cup of tea to be handed to him. He didn't look at her though she stopped at the table hoping he would; would tell her Ma that she was to stay but he didn't, just lay there one hand running over the hair between his breasts, the other under the bedclothes fondling his enormous jack, his exhausted balls. At the door her Ma stood with her hand on the handle and watched her go. In the street the wind in the raw red morning whipped the coat flung round her shoulders off her and unable to pick it up she stood there shivering . . . Billy Boy Beausang came and picked it up for her. When he touched her arm she screamed because it was broken and he told her and took her to the hospital and all through the nightmare of broken bone and torn flesh and plaster and bandages he smoothed her hair with the flat of his hand and when she came out of the hospital he was standing waiting where she had left him . . .

Esther closed her eyes and the people, scenes and places that had come to life of their own accord were shattered in an outbreak in the house of what might have been taken for murder by anyone not in the know; Esther was: she knew it was the howls of the damned. She opened her eyes and listened. A charred wind drifted through the open window plucking at the blind with a furious panting breath backed by the great passionate indifference of something that could have been the boom of cannons or the muffled sounds of summer thunder. The writhing of the blind on the window showed quick glimpses of the moon and shook loose a pattern of shapes and shadows rearing and falling on the wall of the fireplace. With breath balanced on a thread running thin Esther watched. The explosion in the hall had been the splintering of a door but the sounds coming at her now were wilder, human,

181

inhuman, Souls in trouble tearing themselves through the withering grin of the dead. She shuddered and swore as the house wept. The house was crying for all the abominations ever committed by man or woman. She settled deeper into the great polyp womb of her great bed, crouching away with a "Lord Jesus Christ, Son of God, have mercy on me!" Her eyelids quivering and searching with her mouth – like a child for a breast – the rumpled bedclothes for Billy Boy Beausang.

4

Christina Swords lurched away from the door and staggered to a halt against the mantelpiece. With one furious sweep she sent the articles littering it to the floor. She watched them fall, but refused to be gratified or to let up on the panic which had taken her back from the room in Rock Street to her own on the canal and held her now hump-backed in front of the mantel-mirror. Suddenly, she grabbed the lamp from the wall, and the light, from being restricted and austere, blazed at the self-portrait. She stared blind then returned the lamp to its nail on the wall.

He was gone.

Gone to Jesus.

In raiments of extremity.

In cardinal red and velvet.

Like the chisellers after being blinded and maimed on the streets of Dublin braving the British Army's bullets.

God forgot.

Alleluia!

In the room there was a dry crying like the wings of locusts, late come to their shedding.

Thought came and fled on sandshoes, the void filled with the inconsequential memory of the Salvation Army woman with the tambourine so consumed with passion for the cold wet miserable Jesus of Protestants that Christina the child watched unable to do other than watch – unable to drag herself away from the square-built albino woman with the terrible ghost-white hair – the navy skin shrivelled behind the desperate black mouth that poured forth torrents of saliva that crusted like stirabout on the stunned Sunday. She could see that face now with its over-large blind pink eyes, its square gun-metal cheeks and chin and the tough box-shaped body of a games mistress. See her ranting and roaring, her skirts heavy hemmed, flattening the ground where she walked; her Protestant God so ponderous in her mind she could have stamped out the world with him in seven days. Come to Jesus. Insanely gleeful. The terrible black mouth in the navy skinned face whipping itself into a frenzy that went pfft under the blow of Granny Swords's hickory. The devil had invaded Christina Swords while she was listening to the squared Salvationer, Granny Swords said, as she hawked her home and tied her to the foot of the bed, and now the devil must be whipped out. Spewed through the mouth, because that was how he had gone in and that was how he must come out. Open, wide open. And she had done as she was bid and without crying had born the blows of the hickory until Granny Swords could no longer raise her arm or the stick and had fallen to the floor. They had stayed that way for two whole days, herself and her Granny until Sheila O'Brien, missing them from the house, had come looking. But she'd got rid of the devil her Granny said while she scrubbed and scrubbed and scoured and scoured the spot on the floor onto which Christina had vomited him. And afterwards her Granny had drawn with chalk a white circle around the dark water mark on the floor, and the priest had come and blessed it and her.

Christina opened her mouth wide now just as she had done then and said, "Alfie's gone."

She ripped her red felt hat off and began to hack at the sickness in her. Shouting her protest against the room, the house, but mostly at the thing that squirmed in the dark recesses of the mind of the woman trapped in the coffin of the glass.

"She did this to me!" She was shrivelling. Twisting away, and with her hair streeling each side of her face she went with sudden

184

darts and stops around the room crying havoc as she pushed and smashed everything her hands touched. She went to the door, and flinging it open told the house. And the house heard her strong white teeth bite the dark – and with puritan misgivings the house heard her words chill and curve and twist their spines, but nobody came running to witness her descent, they listened and they heard and they waited on raised elbows or lay on their backs their feet upright till her mouth finished and the door was closed and she was back again standing at the bare mantelpiece.

"Alfie's gone." That was what Mrs Doyle said when, with her breath spiked with crubeens and cabbage, she opened the door to Christina's knock.

"Aye. Reverent and rubber-soled; and leaving me with nothing but hope of an early death as my sole provision against old age. He made seventy or eighty whole pounds on the sale of loot and he's gone with it, and Agnes Oats, to England. And all I can say is, while the money is a definite loss, I'm not a bit sorry to be rid of him. My only regret is he didn't take himself and his whore away sooner, 'cause now I'll get a rest from him and his trollops!"

Looking over her shoulder at Christina she had laughed then. And the laugh had stayed with Christina all the way up the street and into the room, was even now cupped in the fists with which she was beating herself. But she could hear beyond the laugh for its strength diminished as the room shrank, leaving her a stranded Gulliver amongst the wreckage engulfed in silence.

"Who told you?"

"His new mother-in-law! A dealer she is; stands outside the Bleeding Horse and if Agnes is anything like her Alfie Doyle will have his belly full! An' that he may! Jasus, when I think that for the first time in his life he gets his hands on a handful of money and doesn't pause long enough to ask if I've a mouth on me!"

Forcing a desperate calm into her voice, Christina said, "You're joking?"

"I'm given to joking!" Mrs Doyle was resenting the scene she began to expect.

She stood teapot in hand and with a jerk of her head she poured the tea with slow spouts into her cup.

185

"I know you don't like me," Christina said, "but that's no reason for your saying things like that."

"Like what?" Mrs Doyle put down the cup into the saucer with a clatter, angered by the truth of the statement.

"About Alfie and Agnes Oats. It isn't right."

"What is? But you had to be told, and I'm telling. After a life spent pampering to his every whim, he's gone and left me. He made all that money on the sale of the loot, and he's gone. Seventy or eighty whole bloody pounds! He got himself a wife and he's gone with her to England. There's only one way I can tell and that's it."

And she was glad. Glad to be able to say what she had said and what she was about to say to Christina Swords. True Mrs Doyle hadn't thought much of the woman who came to tell her about Alfie and her daughter, but she liked Christina even less, knowing or thinking she knew the place she would be relegated to if Alfie tied himself down to Christina. She wanted a daughter-in-law she could aim her tyranny at, but more than that she wanted whoever Alfie married to take her on as well, someone who would see to it that when her time came to leave the world she would have someone of her own to wet her lips and put the pennies on her eyes and see her buried decent and not thrown into a pit of quick lime up in the Union.

"He's gone," she said again, and Christina half crouching, half leaning, bent towards her, her lips twisted over the structure of teeth on which she was trying to shape words. "Alfie and me . . . were to be married. He wouldn't do something like this unless . . ."

"Unless what?"

Mrs Doyle glanced up and saw the panic in the big starkly naked eyes. She eased herself back on her chair away from Christina's big unmanageable body, sprawled across her and the table, and from the face twisted in quickening corruption.

"You put him up to it!" Christina accused.

"Me?"

"Yes, you, you piety-painted bitch!" Christina heaved herself erect as she rose to meet head on the thing she had from the first believed. And as her shadow crawled over the lamp the room

186

dimmed. "Ah, but you wouldn't. Even you couldn't . . ." Christina reached out a hand that begged understanding, but Mrs Doyle, alert, jumped to her feet and stepped back out of her reach.

"I did it, did I?" Her voice, as they faced each other across the table, was softly deceptive. "What did I do, Chrissy? Stopped you getting yourself a husband? Stopped you getting your hoor's hands on my poor defenceless son? Well, I've news for you Chrissy Swords. I didn't have to do anything at all. Didn't raise me hand or open me mouth, and if you hadn't been blind and bothered you'd have seen which way the winds were blowing years ago. You flung yourself at him. Hounded him night, noon and morning; trying to bribe him with shillings to make the pounds that would take you to the altar. It was the few lousy shillings you doled out to him on Friday nights that held him to you, Chrissy. For, Christ knows, it wasn't your beauty."

"I know I'm no take." Christina interrupted the flow of abuse. "I never imagined I was."

Mrs Doyle laughed. "Except in the glass! Jasus, *you* get outa the glass the same false comfort others find in drink!"

"But I'm not thick-minded, either! And Alfie . . . Alfie wanted me!"

From under the wide brim of her black straw hat Mrs Doyle croaked. "He wanted you so badly he got himself another." Without shifting her glance her hands found what was left of the crubeen and cabbage on her plate. Stone, she thought, and in a swift change of mood and temper she rested both hands on the table and bent towards Christina. "You're no child, Christina Swords. You're a grown woman and, Christ knows, you've been round long enough to realize things like this happen! You're making a coffin for yourself with your desperation. Well, you won't be able to view the world from any coffin, even a glass one; so you better pull yourself together and not let this bully you into oblivion."

Christina stumbled drunkenly against the table. "He was to marry me. He said . . ."

"Well, let's face it, Chrissy, it's not the first time you saw a future for yourself, or thought you had a man at the altar rails –

187

and it won't be the last if the truth be known. Besides . . ."

"It wasn't the same with the others. I never would have done it for them."

"Done what?" Mrs Doyle snapped.

But Christina had stopped, bent double, her hands clutching her practical bag against her belly as if to support some mortal wound.

"It was for him," she said. "Oh, Jesus, God! I did it for him!" She began to stagger round and round in crazed circles.

Like some class of animal, thought Mrs Doyle; and slyly edged towards the door, intending to call for help to get rid of Christina, who was venting despair with a volley of obscenities mingled with cries to God.

"I did it for Alfie. I got the money for him. It was for him." Her voice was suddenly sharp, suggesting a return to sanity and arresting Mrs Doyle's move towards the door.

"It was for him. We could get married and take that room. Fifty pounds!"

"Fifty pounds? You're carrying fifty pounds?"

Christina missed the ruthless speculation that shot into the eyes turned up to her.

"I sold that chap for him."

"What chap?"

Christina didn't answer.

Mrs Doyle supposed she hadn't heard. She moved in, "That's a lot of money to be carrying loose, Chrissy," she said quickly while behind her mouth and reassuring gesture thought turned slow. "Look, Chrissy, pay no heed to the things I said for, honest to Christ, I don't know whether I'm the fierce, the mean or the scapular-strung tonight, so I don't. For between you, me and the wall it's a bad day's work he's set his hand to, the same Alfie! But sit and I'll pour a cup of tea."

Erect and motionless Christina stood her eyes protruding and clear recording every minute action and expression of the woman before her. She allowed Mrs Doyle to lead her back to the table and then wrenched herself free.

"The bastard!" she whispered hoarsely. "The dirty, chiselling bastard! The curse of Almighty God on you and him!" She bent

188

enormous and polarized as if to head off some appalling catastrophe thundering towards her. "Do you hear me? I'm cursing you and your lovely son! I'm cursing you and that warped bastard you brought into the world!"

She backed and twisted and whipped past Mrs Doyle, dragged open the door and fled stumbling into space – into the darkness of the stairs, while behind her Mrs Doyle hurried to howl her bitter derisive laughter that helped a little to assuage the rage of being done out of something she had almost had her claws on...

Christina raised her head, her eyes went to the mirror and the face that wasn't hers, a strange withdrawn face behind which nothing was happening. A white dead face except for the glitter of metal on the wild grieving eyeballs. The face in the mirror was both detached and close. She could have touched it with quiet soothing hands. The pale skin, the indication of bones, the bare planes of cheeks. "He's gone." Her lips moved painfully deliberate over her bared teeth and slowly with a conscious attempt at control, for she would not now waste words or thoughts in an unguarded sprawl. "All them others meant fuck all!" She spoke eyeball to eyeball. "And he believed me – or said. But he didn't. Didn't believe the years before him. The years when fact made a balls of expectation. When fact corrected expectation. Starting the day Granny Swords died." Her physical removal, insupportable and irreparable. Dying having told her nothing, thinking the streets would. Leaving her alone at twelve to face the assault the streets and the rooms were. And the fellas with fists in their trouser pockets who didn't pause to read Birth Certificates. For two whole weeks after her Granny died she spoke to nobody because speech was terrible and her breath was hoarse. She moved nothing, disturbed nothing, afraid to disarrange anything in case Granny Swords might become confused and lose the sense of home. She went out in the morning and coming back to that room the last thing, the interminable night would begin. Listening to the sounds of the street coming from the dark yawns of gummy eyed tenements, the mutterings going on against life, the frantic call on St Jude and the Virgin, the absent help screamed for in times of trouble, from the rooms above and, from the rooms below the moaning hope and knaw of want and the sudden desperate cry that stiffened prayer. Listening to every near and distant murmur and for the footfalls to evolve from the cobbles, from the diminishing noise that would be Granny Swords coming home. Till one night, with an intolerable and conscious knowledge, fact corrected expectation and she knew for sure that she wasn't coming back and so the next day she lit out and stayed out for a month kipping anywhere she could, and with anyone who asked and then only went back when she had to. Nobody understood when she said she was lonely. Not even God. Were these the years that had taken Alfie from her? When what she was looking for was a man. A husband. Something, someone of her own. And before Alfie one man would have done as well as another, but now she knew it wasn't just any man she wanted, it was Alfie.

As an amputated leg cannot be disowned because it is experiencing a futurity of which the victim is its forebear, so Alfie was an amputation that Christina could not renounce. As the thigh longs, so her heart longed and looking now for what she was afraid to find, found it in her reconstruction of Mrs Doyle's screamed abuse. Then having found it shied from it but her thread of thought was a circle and brought her back against her will and picked it up again.

"It was the few shillings that held him to you, Chrissy Swords! For Jasus knows it wasn't your beauty!" Mrs Doyle's laugh pulsed into life and matched the streeling mockery of words flung with vengeance.

Christina reared up and clutching each side of the mantel-mirror she stared with desperate intensity at her face finding Mrs Doyle's mockery justified for what she saw there. It was not a pretty face. Only now and then in a rare mood had she imagined it to be. It was not an ugly face either. But now she saw it as he must have seen it, and cruelly and dispassionately she began to hack blaming the way she looked for the years of grievances that led up to this most bitter one. She stared at the hard bones of her jaws, covered by flesh stretched too thin. She saw and hated the revealing honesty of the shocking protruding eyeballs – the heavy brows and the teeth, large, white and prominent – like headstones under

190

a winter moon – and laughed; standing back from the critical eyes of the true untrue self in the mirror. She laughed, and continued to dissect herself finding faults and making wounds where before none existed.

She was no beauty, and her few shillings hadn't been enough to compensate for lack of it. She foamed misery as hate and rage, for which she could as yet find no outlet, coursed through her. She swept back a dark shadow from her face with her quite solid hand and then through the blurred speed of senses searched the room's scanty contents and not finding what she sought turned back to the mirror. Out of its rusted depths the sad face of the girl welled in circles of perpetual water, stirring with great gentleness the way water did in the canal, the eternal complement of skeleton and spawn.

She raised tentative fingers to touch the bones of her face and as she did so her eyes caught the lamp hanging on its nail. A sudden numbness of her whole body left her with an intensely clear vision. She reached and her hand closed on the globe of the lamp. Lifting it from its base she snapped its top off against the mantelpiece. There was the thin strike of glass and the lamp's flare. Slowly she took what was left of the globe in her hands and plunged it into her face.

The lamp's flame soared into a straight plume of black smoke as it streamed up and from rags of flesh, blood shot and spattered. She dropped what remained of the glass and then began very patiently and seriously to smear with her hands her own blood over the mirror's face. As she worked she bubbled at the mouth, mumbling, repudiating all that she was in herself – spreading, smearing, until there was nothing left of herself. In her eyes a light like the sun striking metal rims showed as she stumbled to the bed and flung herself on it to lie staring into the screamed night, lit by a lamp flickering.

191

SIX

SATURDAY

1

The priest came from the unreal splendour of the sun to brave the red-raddled gloom of the hall, raising his woman's hand in a gesture of blessing. Maisie Collins made a sly attempt to draw back into her room, but realized it was too late and came forward again.

"Morning, Father." Smoke-throated and lowering her glance she wished to Christ he hadn't caught her with her face not washed, nor her hair combed. Of course she should have known better than go unprepared and bollix-naked on a day like this. After all the house wasn't mourning the death of swans so it was only natural to expect the extraordinary.

"It's you, Mrs Collins." Father Robinson was unsure of himself and his reception.

"No, it's the scalpel and the Scriptures!" Maisie stifled the quip born of irritation at herself and dislike of the priest. For the sake of politeness she brought up a smile and balanced precariously the cup of tea in her hand intended for Christina Swords and with the other hand tried to pull her overall which as always suggested sex more than sorrow into the semblance of a suitable garment. "I wouldn't take bets on it, but," she said, aware that no answering smile broadened the priest's pale face. She wished to hell he'd shove off towards the stairs and the Gosses' room, and when he did neither she dismissed the effort she might have made at tidying herself. She saw him glance at the cup in her hand and deliberately ignored the inquiry.

God's uninhabited angels entering the dead and bringing no comfort wanted to know too bloody much and a lot the better you were for their asking! Maybe priests did piss the sheets and weep in their own way but you'd never know by looking.

"It isn't flying dandruff or floating kidneys that brings you round this morning, Father," she said.

Father Robinson dipped his silvered head and pink mouth while he mushed-mushed to himself as if it was a sorrow past he was mulling over and not one that was this very day taking place, and was still flower fresh and powerful. But then priests were like yesterday's few halfpence. Everything with them was past, or like Christmas not yet come. Up there on their mountains they knew bugger all about what was happening down in the valleys.

"Make you doubt if there was a God," Maisie said. "When you see Him allowing a chap like John Goss be lowered into his grave by informers."

It should not make you do any such thing, Father Robinson stayed silent, regarding her with his piercing eyes, knowing that if he waited long enough Mrs Collins would tell him all he ought to know before he saw Mr and Mrs Goss.

Maisie stared boldly back remembering the last time he had turned his inquisitor's squint on her, but she had been new to sin then. But she still hadn't given Ba Fay up like he told her she should, though like a coward in a corner she had actually considered doing so for one whole day. Jasus, and wouldn't she have been the right thick if she had, she thought, hugging to herself the thing she was now positive had happened to her.

"A terrible waste of a young life, it is," she said.

"I'm afraid it's a sad and corrupt age we live in," Father Robinson responded and knew even as he did so that he was saying the wrong thing again.

Maisie eyed him humorously. "They're saying he died for Ireland."

"For Ireland and for God," the priest said and hoped, while he wasn't sure what the words meant, that the addition of the Almighty would pacify and bring her attention back to him, for it had strayed to the open door, to the sight and tramp of British soldiers in British boots marching through Irish streets. An attractive woman Mrs Collins was with an abundance of brown hair scattered in gracious disorder on her almost naked shoulders and great spermy breasts.

She turned back to him. "If you have to have reasons for getting yourself hung, drawn and quartered, then I suppose God and Ireland are as good as any. And between the pair of them he ought to be well rewarded." She smiled bitter and waited for the protestations she was trying to goad him into making. But none came, and on a change of mood through which pity mingled with the warm assurance that had been hers since early morning, she gestured towards the basement.

"Taken from Jeremiah Hudson's room he was," she said.

"And Sarah and Jamesie?" The priest asked.

"Demented."

"When were they told?" Father Robinson asked and threw aside any idea he might have had at winning Maisie over, for with her natural intelligence she saw for what it was his attempt to sound concerned when all he was feeling was concern for his own inadequacy in the present situation.

"This morning," she said. Her eyes climbed to the polar white collar coiffing a pale fleshy face, alien in its unhampered serenity, in the passionate turbulence of the tenement. "About six. Didn't Mollo tell you?"

The priest's betrayals surfaced on tapering candles and on the darkening red of grieving busty Madonnas. He had not seen Mollo. Spared the disorder of that meeting by his housekeeper who knew better than to disturb the good man, as he ate his good breakfast, and whose job was saving the good Father from the disasters and dissolute lives of his parishioners which he was, in any case, powerless to alter.

195

"Yes. About six," Maisie continued, "I was in bed. The sleep had gone astray on me," she said, and from the sharp glance the priest threw her she guessed he knew who she was in bed with. Well, if he did he did: but she wasn't telling him. Any more than she would tell him what had kept her from her sleep most of the night, for she didn't want him going in there and draining what little of life was left in Christina Swords by throwing his useless shadow across her. "I was just lying there in that strange bad hour fending off the 'Hows', the 'Whys', and the 'Maybes', and thinking about John and the way you'd never see him without a book in his hand and about how quiet the house had suddenly become. For it had and for no reason and without warning – quieter than I'd ever known it. When some fella came, calling Sarah. Made my ti . . . hair stand on end. There was something about that man calling and calling, and for a long time nobody answering.

"I heard him coming further and further into the hall, and when he passed my door the whole room shook. I wanted to get up, but honest to Christ I hadn't the strength. Then I heard a door opening, and Sarah shouting, 'I'm up here, mister! I'm up here!' I could just see Sarah all trussed up in that old fashioned nightdress she wears: her hair hanging long and loose; her feet white and naked as she came to look over the banisters at the stranger on the stairs. And then I *heard* Sarah . . .

"Of course I should've known and I did the minute that fella opened his trottle that it was about John he'd come. There was something in that man's voice; and it wasn't the revelry of the season's fading. Anyway he was gone be the time I'd dragged myself, and a full bladder, up to Sarah and Jamesie. And Mollo was dressing herself to run over to you and Liam Martin. Poor Jamesie! Whatever about Sarah, poor Jamesie will never be able to live without his heart." Maisie paused and sighed. "Talk about never knowing what direction our ends are coming from! It was the first night Jamesie had been home this week. He won't need to go searching for his son John any more and neither will anybody else."

"And John?" The priest was unable to avoid the question.

"What's left of him is below in the Dead House in Saint

Vincent's hospital." Maisie's reply came quiet, thoughtful and calm.

Father Robinson let the full force of his gaze fall on her. Death no longer struck the mind with severity. He saw again the horrors in the streets he had had to walk through to get here. And the people in them: gusty, real, unreal, painted grotesques fiddling at life and playing at house with the red and purple maws of fiendish heads. Saw the cunning appearances and disappearances of nightmare and madness – while above them Death lay crouched on a mackerel sky and behind them, in lanes and streets and on roof-tops, men screaming up against tradition, like bats against window panes, were being shot, bayoneted, blown to bits or burned to cinders in the trapped furnace of their flimsy strongholds.

From the monstrous real unreal wilderness of many-storeyed houses plunging into the splitting flamed-jawed earth, he looked out at Maisie and recognized the gaum-like destructive Irish preoccupation with nothing in her brown eyes, and knew that she had withdrawn from him and the sounds of the ghoul-visaged streets, and he wondered if she and the rest of the people in the city of Dublin were even aware of anything other than their own shabby greedy and mean little needs. Did they not hear the thin stricken laughter above their heads? Did they not know that Irish men, women and children with unprepared minds and uprooted by insane fear and lewd torture were being brought dragging and squealing like animals to their slaughter by British soldier demons masked in human flesh?

Did they know? And he knew even as he asked himself the question that they did, and didn't care, and that all of death's importance and certainly of its cause had already vanished.

Only the fiend-voiced bullet wind blowing commemorated the dead.

"He was young to die!" Maisie said quietly. She lifted a work-roughened hand to clear her brow of her hair. "The British blew his brains out!" Her hand, holding the cup, shook and the tea, gone cold, splashed.

Half sensible, and still shaken from remembered terror, Father Robinson drew himself erect, bracing himself against

images that clawed wild through the tear-stained hall of the tenement, and Maisie saw his lips fold down as if, behind that pursed
mouth, his nice clean teeth had closed on something soft. She was
so sure he said, 'Sweet Jesus,' that aloud she finished the prayer,
"And have mercy on his soul." From long habit and old tutoring,
and without thinking, she added, "And all the poor suffering
souls in Purgatory." And together she and the priest made the
sign of the cross.

"Sarah and Jamesie are not waking him," she said. "He'll be
brought to the chapel tonight, and they'll bury him in Mt Jerome
after ten o'clock Mass tomorrow."

Father Robinson felt he should have known about these arrange-
ments, but he did not and he knew why not. Like his church his
housekeeper with her furtive cat-like cruelty and surface mild
placidity also kept her secrets. He made a mental note that he
would have to speak with her, but he knew that he would not.
Between him and his housekeeper silence bred like scum on a
pond.

"Sarah will be glad to see you," Maisie said.

In a transient resentment he wanted to ask: why? What was he
bringing that would make Sarah glad? Why did he go to them?
And why did they come to him? They came to him for the im-
memorial syllables that would smooth the way. Coming when they
were too far gone and already mauled and weeping. Coming to
him with their symbols – the gaudy prints of the Holy Child –
with the crowns, the snakes and the stars. Coming with their arid
acts of piety to gain salvation at his knees and bringing with them
their myths, their loves, their profaning bitter hates and all the
time expecting him to keep them hushed. And now this? That
boy who read books by the hundred. That boy laughing softly,
almost noiselessly, with his flickering exquisitely sensitive mouth,
his brooding black eyes.

Death, death! The Irish went towards the green corrupted hell-
face of malignant death like Lemmings with arms spread, head
down between them, eyes wide open and crying. His own eyes
brightened in his white face before something that resembled
sleep fell heavy on them.

Dear Christ, why don't they leave me alone!

He raised his fingers in blessing suddenly and murmuring an Ave Maria went towards the stairs taking them like a dung beetle rolling its burden uphill.

2

"I brought you a cup of tea, Chrissy." Maisie picked her way through the semi-dark and across the littered floor.

On the bed Christina lay under a blanket, her hand hiding her face turned to the wall. After a moment's hesitation Maisie mouth-pursingly thoughtful drew up a chair that had been knocked over and left the cup down on it beside the bed.

"John Goss is dead, Chrissy," she said, peering through the festered gloom for a sight of the face hidden from her. "Over in Thomas Street they found him." She paused waiting for some recognition of her presence and getting none. "Are you awake, Chrissy?" she asked, and was answered by a breath, a shifting of the shoulders and a hand that moved and closed to claw the bed-clothes. "The British, it was, thank God," Maisie said, "because whatever chance he had with them he'd have had none at all with our own.

"They took him out of Jeremiah's room last night, and shot him. They blew his brains out, so they did, the indecent murdering bastards! Are you listening, Chrissy? They blew his brains out and as an example to the rest of us left him where they killed him, stretched out like a dog on the dung-pooling cobbles of Thomas Street." Her voice rose in bitter indictment in the telling.

"Creeping Jesus is above with Sarah and Jamesie."

She turned from the bed to examine closer the desolation of the room. A slum room, but without a slum room's brightness. Here there was something degraded. A feeling of strife and bleak extremity and, in the swarming semi-dark, the yellowing calico smell of the mauled. She saw the bare mantelpiece and the hearth littered with its contents and then, with a terrible apprehension and sour fear, the wall and against it the mantel-mirror obliterated with congealed blood and about to exclaim on an intake of breath her shock and horror when a knock sounded quick on the door. The door opened before a second rap was given and Janey Reilly came with amazing speed and stealth into the room.

"Esther Quinn's looking for you." Janey explained her mission.

"And you knew where to find me?" Maisie exclaimed with rocking throatiness.

"I knocked on your door first, if you want to know, but you weren't there."

"So you put your ear to this one!"

"Esther said you were to hurry."

"I'm hurrying," Maisie said, for she had decided only this morning with that clear wonder by which children accept miracles, that the thing that had come to her was nothing if not the direct result of the prayers she had offered up at Esther's altar.

She glanced from Janey over to the bed. "Drink that tea while it's hot, Chrissy." With the back of her hand she wiped cold sweat from her brow and from the door she said, "If Chrissy wants anything come and tell me."

Janey squinted into the stony silence that followed the closing of the door, gathering into herself and yet rejecting the devastation that confronted her. She looked around as Maisie had done, but with less deliberation and none of Maisie's shock, her pale glance skimming coldly and lightly from the crushed glass and broken delf quickly as if there was nothing rare in the sight. She glanced over at the woman on the bed, pondering and suddenly for one bare moment oppressed by the sight of a world she despised and hated with a most bitter and alienate hate – that left her baffled before it turned to blind fury that threatened even to put from her mind what she had come to Christina's room for.

Bedded women gave you the sick, she thought, rebelling against the sight of Christina huddled amongst the wreckage of the room, the room that seemed to hold in its stricken misery all that she herself had been born into: the reeking mossiness of sluttish women, the sagging iron bed and the rough deal table covered with newspapers, the bit of twine stretched on nails each side of the fireplace and hung with the inevitable rags that never dried, the dead cinders in the great black maw of the grate and the ashes scattered on the cracked and broken slabs of the hearth. Her eyes, squinty and shockingly blue, moved swiftly from the bed and went to the blood smeared mantel-mirror, paused a cool instant, then travelled back again to the bed. Anger gripped her skinny body as she raised herself on her pencil-thin, bony-kneed legs and peered over the foot of the bed, anger that gave way to bitter resentment, ages old in its intensity, at the seething destructive misery grown-ups could create with their dark, degrading, vicious passions, at their absence of reticence and pride in the unappeased and unsatisfying sprawl of their wants, at the never-ending pain-ridden poverty-stricken adult world an unmerciful God had plunged her into, a gigantic rank-stenched uncontrollable void of singed animal and human flesh putrefying the air about and over stuffed trash bins, and in the diseased lice-ridden tenements, the ever-present sweet, sickly scent of fornication cloving the roof of the mouth and clothing, as with overalls, the white thighs and brazenly exposed indolent breasts of women swelling under the calloused hands of men, puffed-up backyard bantams, hoarse voiced and full of idiot laughter, giving what they had to, a thing that cost nothing and at the same time contriving by the mockery of leered sniggers to give the impression of bestowing favors.

"Wake up, Chrissy!" Janey cried roughly, although now all her strength had gone from her voice, rushing into her hands, small strong curling claws that closed on the cold black iron as she released her hate first against Christina on the bed, which she began to shake, and then against the smell of boiling cabbage that forever pervaded the house and of oil spilled, however carefully measured into lamps, that left corners dark from which prayers that were never answered were whispered and moaned

202

ignorantly and venomously to the Sacred Heart, the Little Flower and the Child of Prague, and the rain-soaked chapel man with great devouring strides and wet hairy hands held out in un-ashamed greed for pennies you couldn't afford, hands, the hands of the breakers of visions; the proposers of iniquities, hands like Hammy Collins's that, when off guard, found their way up your pinny to claw at your body; hatred against the unadorned, sweating, backyard imageless passion of the vulgar, the awkward heavy muscular louts who smashed your puny attempts at en-chantment; hatred against the drunken maniacal drawl of men and the strident rasping cries of women; against unclean flesh and the hacking coughs of the dead and the dying; against poverty and improvidence; against the lying empty pretentiousness of a world which tried to mask callous indifference and soothe what passed for conscience by sending with pastoral benignity a priest or so-called Sister of the Poor into the rat-infested and disease-ridden warrens with nothing more substantial than scapulars and bits of bone and gristle from the carcasses of saints with which you were expected to ward off hunger, want and disease.

Steeped catlike in the wickedness of near darkness, adrift in the brooding promise of pennies or maybe shillings or maybe even pounds, Janey edged away from the bed and around to stand beside it. "John Goss is dead, Chrissy." Her voice pitched to imitate a keen, her face a wizened old woman's. She paused and sniffed the air as if some nerve was sensing what the blind room was masking, and looked over her shoulder expecting to see behind her the thing only half-sensed. But there was nothing. No horned monster with sagging breasts and fierce red glaring eyes lurked in the room's concealing mangled shadow. Everything was as before. She leaned her weight onto her hands and pressed down on the side of the bed. "Chrissy?" she whispered. "The whole house is funeral faced and whispering!" She paused. "Are you listening? Sarah Goss is wanting to know who informed on her beautiful son, so she is." She peered down and after a moment her chest began to heave. The room was full of menace. There was something sinister in the absolute stillness of the woman on the bed. She wished suddenly that her brother Willie was with her. Willie with his old puzzled child's stare was remembered like a phantom. Willie wasn't much good on his own and didn't have her lust for darkness or battle. But the peering blind-eyed face and soft caressing voice, unlike any other voice she knew in either kind or quality, could always nuzzle her back when in spite of arrogance she stepped beyond the margin of safety. But Willie, the gentlest and saddest of boys, who sometimes fondled and even embraced her, wasn't there. Like God, Willie was away. With nerve centers twitching at the corners of her mouth, she dismissed Willie and went forward beyond the point where Willie's restraining voice, even in imagination, could reach her. But she had nothing to be frightened of! If Chrissy Swords knew what was good for her she'd think twice before she flared up into the panting darkness with that temper of hers.

In a voice she strove in vain to render steady she said, "High-sorrowful and sad Sarah Goss is, Chrissy, and if I were you I'd get to my feet and dress and wash meself. Not that it will matter but what you do because I intend telling Sarah Goss, so I do, and what's left of you after she hears what I've to tell soap and water won't help."

Under her weight the straw in the mattress gave way, and under the mattress the crossed flat laths, held together with wire and twine, cringed in rusty protest, but on the bed Christina Swords lay silent. Janey's voice, rough with threat, rose. "You better listen, Chrissy Swords, because I'm not loitering here all day, d'ya hear me?" She waited, but still the woman on the bed gave no sign that she was listening or even aware, and Janey, growing viciously impatient, began to nudge her with hard fists in the small of her back. "You better pay attention to me," she cried, and quickly then, "you better pay me off if you don't want to be torn limb from limb by Sarah Goss because that's just what she'll do if I tell her it was you that handed John over to the English.

"Are you listening?" Breathless now in the courage that was fast ebbing from her she leaned across and brought both arms down with all her force across the rise of the shoulders turned to her. Hate swarmed like poison through her blood. "Are you listening, Chrissy?" she screamed. "Are you listening?" She paused. "Will you be the one to fold the hands of death, Chrissy? Will you be the one to say the decent sad-sounding words? John

Goss is dead, Chrissy," she spoke gravely, unemotionally. "You killed him. You murdered John Goss."

Something roused in Christina then. An eyelid flickered, rolled back. With strange convulsive movements she raised herself up onto her elbow and drew across her face a black blood-sodden cloth. Her swift vision leaped to the child standing over her in the bed and something in her twisted aside, incredulous and afraid. As her mind groped out of fear and pain she looked with unblinking eyes at the child in the white pinny. Janey stared back and watched the hand holding the cloth fall down to the bedclothes. Her eyes travelled the miles again to Christina's face hacked with what looked like savage tribal marks through which her great protruding eyes, deadened with pain, stared. Beneath the glowing wounds the skin was already sallow with a dead ashen tinge; beneath the strong bone carving of face the skull had traced itself clearly. Overnight Christina Swords had withered beyond healing to a cadaverous sheeting of skin stretched on a too-broad frame. Under the elbow supporting her the pillow saturated with blood disappeared from Janey's sight as Christina lowered herself down onto her back.

"I can't stand here all day."

The voice bearing down on Christina hammered with enormous energy the pain and depletion and weariness inhabiting her. Her eyes which had been on the very point of closing opened and the lids streeled up just as Janey fighting a momentary cold nausea leaned forward to croak ghoulish satisfaction.

"You'll change your tune now, Chrissy Swords," she said, flicking with the pointed tip of her tongue, lips gone dry.

Discarding all caution she bent with cold indifference down to the face on the pillow and with eyeball to eyeball asked, "And which of the merrymakers did that to you, Chrissy?"

Getting no answer she drew herself up from the glazed eyes and hurried on. "Don't think, Chrissy, you're going to hansel my hand with a lousy two shillings this time, will you?" She paused. And then like one who has been mad and suddenly recovers reason, she said, "Christ! Your face . . . !" Touched for one brief moment with unaccustomed awe, she was distracted from her demands and her ferrety keen probings. Then she laughed. "Alfie Doyle made fast work of you before he . . ."

A movement on the bed silenced her, and her laugh hardened and was sucked back on a gasp that riveted her eyes on the face which, with one single move, had swung above hers. Her skinny body in its white-gophered pinny tensed, then shot stiff and un-yielding like a bullet across the legs raised to cradle her. She moaned once, a short sharp moan, and twisted in wild convulsion, but towards, instead of away from, the woman on top of her. Her hands sprang up and clawed in puny frenzy at the strong manlike ones closed around her skinny neck, and finally refused to claw, fluttered instead – the way leaves will to the remembered things of earth – as her body stiffened and then collapsed across Christina's legs.

Long after the voice had ceased to plague her, Christina's own stopped abruptly, and her hands rested from their pummelling of the soft thing in her lap. Her head lifted again on a cry that was the violence of memory. She pushed the burden she was not aware of into the jumble of bedclothes and rose up from the bed a stumbling precariously balanced cadaver in a room through which horror with a furious panting breath raged. Slowly from beneath the maddened fogs of her brain, comprehension gleamed in the dark canal of consciousness as she saw through the formless confusion from which she would not now be separated, the thing she was meaning to do. Inching her uncoordinating limbs after the rest of her body had gone forward she came to a halt, when memory, with breath, fled, deserting her to the noise that was water which trickled out of tufted grass, to fill and over-flow from rusted tins.

"Quit!"

Her fingers touched the bones of her head under her damp hair. They sooth the wounds. Lurching forward she began again her search for the handbag, which was where she had thrown it the night before. She picked it up and tearing it open flung aside its contents in an insane urgency before her hands found and closed at last on the roll of banknotes. Her breath beat. The walls of the room were bending outward under the pressure of the dreaded water. The room screamed. Unconscious of the additional effort she was making she staggered through the room over to the door, dragged it open and propped herself against its jamb.

Father Robinson was slow to get the sight of her, his eyes and ears clouded with the force of a misery against which he knew his bland platitudes had been useless, for Jamesie Goss had already retreated into that distance from which he did not intend to come out – and Sarah was grieving from a grief that only God and herself could understand and perhaps Jamesie . . . though he doubted it. But God was merciful even in His punishments, and He alone knew man's frailty, tempering the trials He tested us with and in His infinite mercy sparing us a knowledge not only of ourselves but of others, hiding our innermost thoughts and secrets which He alone had the strength to bear. For God so loved the world that He gave His only begotten Son . . . and Father Robinson prayed that Sarah Goss would keep to herself the anguish under which her soul labored because clearly no good could come of it if she ever decided to share it with her husband. And aware of his own failings, Father Robinson sighed for the talent God had not given him, his sigh ending on Christina's name as he caught sight of her.

So he came down the stairs. And it was *down*. Certain encounters took Father Robinson to the depths.

Christina made no obeisance, but spoke right away. "Hurry!" She beckoned impatiently and then led him quietly and decently into the room. It was only later, much later, he was to remember telling himself he must not shiver in the despair that engulfed as his gaze swept her first, then the room. He tried to shut his mind to what he saw but the signs of brutality were so marked that he could not keep disapproval out of his expression. He hoped Christina saw. But pain had stultified Christina and would anyway have left her indifferent even had she been aware, for all reverence had vanished. The priest was a means to an end in the act she was about to perform.

The man himself was superfluous.

She looked for the expression that had not yet evolved from the shadow of his hat.

208

"It's the money," she said humbly. She held out her hands. "I would like you to give it to Sarah Goss."

"Money? To give away, Christina?"

"Money," she said, or mumbled.

His eyes went from her to the bed and the bedclothes, concealing, though Christina had not tried to conceal, the body of Janey.

"For Sarah Goss!"

Father Robinson tore his gaze from the shambles of the room and brought it to rest in interrogation on the wreck that was Christina.

She held up her hands. "It's all here, every penny. I didn't break into it."

Father Robinson tried not to draw back but he did, and when he raised his face again his eyes were frozen with a knowledge from which his mind shied. He felt his hands being clutched and, too late, tried to withdraw them; but already his smooth hands were closing on the burden she had passed on to him and when he heard again she was saying, "*You* give it to her." He saw Christina hold her now-empty hands up, palms outward, before her and saw her turn on them a look of dubious dismay and sudden helplessness.

And he said, "Etsi incedam in valle tenebrosa, non timebo mala, tu mecum es, tu mecum es."

Outside the door Jeremiah Hudson's cat began to cry with astonishing shrillness.

"Dear merciful God! I will fear no Evil." Father Robinson's lips shaped the words, for when you have been listening for thirty years to the tormented whisperings of the confession box you know the extent and the might of man's wrongs; and he knew, looking out of the darkness of his own life, what it was Christina had done. He had known from the moment he laid eyes on her, but had tried not to know, unable and unwilling to come face to face with a situation he could not touch or to which he could apply the poultice of penance – an agony that not even the transference of the money could assuage, for even as he watched she began to cry her pain aloud, oblivious of his presence as she went from him to the table, from the table to the blacked out face of the mantel-mirror.

209

The priest's hand closed into a tight fist on the money and he longed as never before for the safe dark of the confession box and the iron grille that kept at a safe distance the God-forsaken, the monstrously alone, like Christina Swords, with their blind and tangled lives and blundering destiny that led them to him with suppliant hands and pleading eyes begging him to show them some entrance into or out of life, some secret undiscovered door that would admit them into death or fellowship – their mouths spitting and vomiting rot, and corruption that withered, struck sleep away, and *nailed* him – *him* who could only endure life after it had been shaped up into the stuff of dreams, life which he had to project into a future containing no Christinas and where no dark angels wept. Desperately he looked around him, straining every nerve in his plump body towards the paralysis of tension that should engulf him but did not and out of which would come rescue from the fear with which her confession that was not a confession was smothering him.

But nothing happened. Christina tangled in grave grass, and with flowers blowing about and between her, continued her struggle with darkness and death and dark angels hovering and through his still functional veins the blood kept its even flow and onto the putrid air of the room his breath fell causing not a ripple on the passive sense of familiar impotence cloying his face. Only his eyes quickened in the fleshy folds of their sockets, darting fearfully around the room for something onto which to fix his clamorous senses, but there was nothing. No symbols. No black Crucifix hung on the bug-riddled walls of this room, no nailed feet or upturned face worn to a fine silver by his lips, and over that face and encircling that brow no crown of thorns whose spikes he had blunted by the constant kiss of his lips and upon which his eyes would fasten and his mind stay in self-immolating meditation, while into his ears men poured the sagas of their unforgivable sins.

He drew back, for Christina Swords had come to stand in front of him and he knew that what she required of him he would be unable to give, for he could feel neither pity nor compassion, only a mute anger that she should heap the results of her greed and passion upon him, exposing in shameless abandon a despair he could not console.

210

"It will finish now, won't it?" she said.

Father Robinson worked his mouth to form a reply, knowing that this was the moment he should tell her to come to the chapel to let him hear her confession, but no words came.

He sighed relief, because she had not asked him to hear her confession in this room. But Christina was thinking only of release, the urgency of her questions emphasized by the gesture she made to touch. He drew back, as from a scalpel. "Now it will stop," she said quietly, but following him, catching at his arm for assurance.

Father Robinson tried not to run. He freed his arm and gave his answer in the platitudes he hadn't been able to utter to Jamesie or Sarah Goss, nor up to now to Christina.

"With God's help," he said, "but you must pray, we both must, for the salvation of your soul," and while he prayed she listened to the trickle of the water that had returned again after the brief pause and she knew that whatever he said would make no difference, for God was not prepared to defend or fight for or win the battle for Christina Swords's soul. God was away, and what the priest was saying was words, words that meant nothing, for God wouldn't hear them. He walked alone somewhere in darkness, some place where death and the dark angels hovered and where no one saw Him.

"And in His infinite mercy," the priest was saying. She saw him fix her with an unwavering scrutiny, searching for something but there was nothing and she continued to stare at him over her knuckles held to her mouth.

"Christ and His Holy Mother will help you."

As if she was dead, she thought. In one moment of absolute sanity she saw him and understood the fear she could see in him. Heard him shift around for words to resist her stare, her silence, and watched openly his sly attempts to edge back over to the door. Well, she Christina Swords would not detain him. Christina Swords would let him go and accept for what it was worth the blessing he gave with his free hand while he fumbled with the other for the handle of the door. But his blessing wasn't enough. She nodded her head giving him the permission he wasn't waiting for to withdraw.

"Run over to the hospital and have them dress those cuts."

211

It was the only sign he made that he had seen them.

He would say prayers for her. He was saying them now, great big prayers. But he hadn't given her any penance. And he wasn't going to. And it wouldn't have mattered if he had. And she wasn't going to ask him to, because no amount of saying . . . and that's what prayers was, just saying. Her penance she would find herself. And it would be of a doing, a big doing, a last and total doing, a total and undivided penance to God. And then . . .

"Go!"

She twisted her throat with a wild cry.

The door closed quickly on Father Robinson, who stood still in the hall, breathless with indecision. Just before he moved away he heard behind him a noise that stopped abruptly, and what he heard afterwards was the chanted anguish of a wounded beast.

4

Evening had streaked into the tension of night on the canal. Leaves, gathering in a coil, spiralled hissingly across the deserted expanse of cobbles scattered with horse shit, straw and paper. A big black tarry canal-boat loaded with a cargo of turf covered by a huge tarpaulin lay idle against the lock-gates and waited for the lock to fill up so that it might glide in and sink to a lower level. The sluice-gates were open, and the black water, churning foam, raged through into the vast pit of the lock, adding its energy to the water that had poured in before, and rising slowly to the level where the canal boat lay, waiting for the lock to fill. The horse that had dragged the boat to where it was stood and pissed hard, while the boy who led him watched. A sturdy paunch-eyed black-hatted man stood on the prow of the boat, gazing at the waters tumbling through the sluices of the lock, occasionally jetting a flying spit right into the black and white tumbling waters. A man on the boat, with a boat-hook in his hand, stared hard up at the skies. The black-hatted man hurried swiftly along the narrow gangway to the aft where he grasped the tiller, ready to guide the barge, for the lock was full. The young fellas loitering leaned against the great arm of the lock-gates and pushed the arm open through a gurgle of rippling water, then jumped onto the boat and crossed to the opposite bank to do the same with the

213

other arm. The man with the long handled boat-hook fixed it to a part of the gate, and began to pull and shove the barge forward past the open gates. When the boat had passed through, the gates were shut again, and sluices further down were opened to empty the lock and let the boat sink to a lower level. Down and down the boat went slowly; the men's legs disappearing first, then their waists, till only their faces could be seen peering over the stone parapet of the lock, the hatted man raising his face for a last look before his head and hat disappeared altogether.

When the boat was well down and trapped between the dripping walls of the lock the man with the boat-hook shoved the barge along out of the lock into the wider and further stretch of the canal ahead.

A boat going God knew where and leaving behind it poor Christians to die without moving hand, foot or finger to help them. No mistake about it but the Irish were the right pack of indifferent cowards. The Dublin slums at war with the British Empire; fighting all the vast power of a mighty army using a shagging sledge-hammer to crack nuts – and there on canal-boats Irishmen sailing away, with cowardly stealth, from the smoke still rising from the rank labyrinth of ruined streets, the firing squads and the unequal fight – away from the executions; the humming whine of motor engines coming along Rock Street at this very minute – braking British army lorries and searchlights pouring into the ruins of halls and the sealed dungeons of rooms and followed by the volley of battering blows on splintering doors, their crash mingling with the smashing of glass, the pulverizing of delf, the screams of women and children being dragged from their beds by ruthless ruffians – and then the wild terrible calling and dark shouts of men being punched in the stomach, the legs shot from under them and their kidneys and balls being beaten to a pulp with rifles and batons – and all the time, there on the canal, sturdy heifers of men sailed away on boats while on the bridge behind

214

them lousy savage-voiced gulls performed capers and somersaults like rowdy rough souls around an ornate catafalque. Jasus God! Was Ireland to remain forever historically England's greatest crime? Was there to be no end to England in Ireland? Was Ireland to remain for ever and ever a fertile testing ground for England's armies of vicious thugs, sadists and torturers, every single one of whom was conditioned and trained to institutionalized violence?

On the wrecked steps of the tenement those already assembled stood as close as answers to calls and watched the canal-boat drift away to where the ships go down to the sea and pass out, over the bar, to the rolling billows beyond – before they turned back to each other to wait, in the strangled splutter of gas light greening ghostly, for Jamesie and Sarah Goss to come. Risking a rifle shot or a hand grenade flung in passing from a British Army lorry they had waited, they didn't know how long, without caring, among the dark ruins of the houses, the lamp posts deformed from the play of children, the wind, the gulls, and the horse shit. And some of them could wait very much longer. Because it is sometimes like that: it is sometimes enjoyable just to wait. And wait . . .

"It's the sad poverty-stricken send-off he's getting and him a hero!"

A conventional piety had reappeared on Judy Madden's face.

"Maybe," Ba Fay said returning from that other plane from which he had reasoned aloud. "But there's one consolation, he'll never know it."

"I would've liked a wake," Judy said. "I feel deprived," she said and she did. She had imagined a wake, for John Goss. A grand one. She had visualized the wake and her own part in it as she hurried from house to house all that day braving the streets and the khaki British cut-throats; and somehow with expectations ahead the open hostility of the winged-capped servants and the frugality of her ladies at whose placid and obedient doors she battered hadn't mattered as much as it should have.

215

"A wake," she said. "And with no stretch on the limits of reason a grand one. After all Sarah and Jamesie Goss are not paupers and even if they were, couldn't they have got a lend? Like everybody else does in times like this? And John their only son. And he wasn't only a Republican, he was a hero into the bargain. I mean, it's only right that people should expect something out of the ordinary."

"Such as?" Martha Liller in a splodge of red and a sensuous sag tossed away what was left of her cigarette.

"A table of food and drink, and a good long coffin," Judy replied. "He'd've made a magnificent corpse, that fella; in a coffin of brassed oak and a flag over it."

"And yourself beside it drunk and telling the world?" Maisie said.

"Exactly!"

"But you hardly knew him?"

"That's beside the point," Judy exclaimed.

She had brought a bag of jelly-beans; she offered them around.

"Make believe comes as easy to me as the next one," she said. "What I don't know I could've invented. Besides it's unchristian to take that poor chap from the dead house straight to the chapel. That's doing it on the cheap, and taking short cuts on the route to Mount Jerome. He should've been taken home where everybody could see for themselves what happened."

"But we know what happened."

"*You* know what happened, *I* know what happened, but let's have some consideration for them that don't. It's them I'm thinking about. This is history. This isn't just getting yourself caught in so-called crossfire, or in the path of a stravaging bullet. This was for the Cause! This was . . ."

"You have your glue!"

Martha Liller had not even attempted to paint herself out. She turned on Judy her big kohl streaked eyes, and great big crimson mouth. Once or twice she licked her lips to make sure the enamel was intact.

"Do the Republicans give out medals?" Judy asked.

"Medals for what?" Martha couldn't spit it contemptuously

enough. "Medals for acting the fool? For getting yourself killed for nothing?"

"It wasn't for nothing."

"Wasn't it? Well, he's not going to his grave with any bantering grin of gain, or to a chorus of Alleluias; and what good was it? What's the use of John Goss being dead? What's different? The days of the week? This is Saturday. The English are still killing and wounding and roaming the darkened streets. Tomorrow morning you and the rest of Dublin will head for the first Mass and the short twelve, and Monday you'll make the rounds of what's left of your ladies. And next week or the one after, I'll be back on my beat – puffed and pearled and sumptuous – and hustling my poor neglected mount of Venus off on all four sides of the Green. So what's new? What's changed?"

Maisie was about to say "I have" but just then the hall door opened and into the purple night Sophia and Mathilda Doran came, embalmed in caution and hovering in breathless uncertainty for seconds they felt to be eternity.

"Ladies true and blue!" Martha Liller's bosomy waves confirmed.

"We couldn't not." Sophia's thinned-out smile was meant to be a visible expression of shared loss. Not indeed that she would have missed following what was left of John Goss from the dead house to the absurd mummery of the chapel. She had liked John Goss and had known a shrivelling sickness in her stomach for whatever it was that had exercised such an uncontrollable domination over him that it brought him at nineteen years of age to his death. Nevertheless she could not help but be gratified that her gesture was not only seen but appreciated.

"We are going to the chapel with you." Mathilda came from distressful confusion to tremulous smiles.

Sophia Doran being human was something Maisie Collins couldn't take, she turned her face and gave a subdued shout of greeting to Harriet Reilly, whom she was seeing for the first time in two days.

Unconsciously everyone looked past Harriet for her lover, Darky Kelly, but, obeying a social convention they would have

217

liked to think she had abandoned, she was alone, standing up bravely to the battery of calculating looks levelled at her.

"And where's the stallion?" Judy hissed, but Maisie was giving all her attention to Harriet. "Her ear-rings are gone," Judy muttered, but nobody heard for the absence of Harriet's gold ear-rings had been noticed by everybody at the same time except Mathilda Doran. "There's no wake," Judy announced, "just the chapel."

"And what would you wake?" Maisie asked roughly. "A bunch of bandages!"

"It's still going the longest way to a quick dismissal," Judy said.

"His poor head was blown off him," Maisie spoke to Harriet.

"As if," Judy said, "that explained the unchristian lack of a wake for him. And what about Jeremiah Hudson!" she asked quickly.

"Still beyant in the Meath," Harriet said. "They're keeping him in."

"The poor oul' bastard," Ba Fay said. "And he the only real patriot among us."

"Wasn't he the sly one but? I wouldn't have guessed in a million years he was a Republican," Martha Liller said.

"And it wouldn't do me a bit of good, Martha, if I was to tell you he wasn't yesterday, but he is today," Harriet replied.

"But who knew?" Ba asked.

"Nobody, or so he imagined," Harriet said.

"That was a mistake," Judy said.

Harriet nodded. "Sure! It was a mistake for Jeremiah begging his killers for leniency. It was a mistake for Jeremiah to open his door to him! It was all a mistake! Jeremiah says it was a mistake he wasn't killed instead of John Goss."

Harriet's glance rose and swept briefly the front of the house, past the darkened window of Christina Swords's room and the lighted window of the Gosses' and above that the blinded dark of Esther Quinn's, and lowered itself again for behind the darkening bricks and the dark and lighted windows was her own room, holding in its lamp-glow her children, and him, all of her own life. Watching her, Maisie thought Harriet Reilly's throat made a dark sound.

218

"Jasus what's keeping them?" Ba Fay stepped out from the door, leaned his head back and looked up at the house. When he lowered his face again everyone looked at him. He shook his head, and Maisie, just about to tell Harriet about the child she knew for certain she was carrying, was stopped by the swift opening of the door behind her.

But it was only Willie Reilly and breathing patience the mourners settled back into their splodged red, borrowed black and looted blue for a further wait, everyone but Harriet who looked down at her son: at his screwed white little face almost hidden behind the metal-framed cracked glasses. The light glanced off his teeth and his glasses. He struggled past Sophia Doran and twisted at an angle round Maisie as he caught sight of his mother, then smiled an answering shy one at Harriet.

"Me Da is looking for Janey," he said. "Says he'll demolish her when she comes in."

"Where is she?" Harriet's arms reached out from the warm of her shawl as he came and stood in front of her and almost mechanically drew him to her, her hands cupping his head and her fingers beginning their customary search through his hair.

"She didn't come in all day," he said. His face still smiling was turned up to Harriet and patiently he let her have her way.

"I saw Janey in with Chrissy this morning," Maisie said. She looked down at Willie, "Have you asked Chrissy?"

"He asked me," Sophia Doran said. "And I heard him knocking on Christina's door, but she hasn't been home all day."

"Is she up with Esther?" Harriet asked.

"No. I was in with Esther before I put my hat on," Maisie said and in answer to the question in the faces turned towards her she said, "Yes, she's still in bed."

"Isn't Janey the right little bitch to walk off like that and leave this child and that man without a bit to eat or a sup to drink all day?" Harriet cried.

"You can't put an old head on young shoulders," Sophia Doran stared her dislike and impatience at all so-called mothers who took off with their fancy men and left their lawful wedded husbands and children to the waves of the world for days at a time.

219

Rattled at the accusation in the levelled glance that not even the wide brim of Sophia's black plumed hat could hide – and by what she imagined the others were thinking, and by the unaccountable sense of unease and foreboding that had descended upon her, Harriet said, "When she does come in that door tonight, I'll break every bone in her body."

A silence fell and into the hush Sophia, with vindictive pleasure, quietly asked, "Will you be there too, Mrs Reilly?"

Harriet rounded on her just as the hall door was drawn back and Sarah Goss came out with Jamesie, and behind them Liam and Mollo, and Willie Reilly's mouth closed for the answer from his mother that hadn't come. In the hurried pulling together of coats and shawls, Willie stood forgotten. He moved his hands in a little half-made gesture that went unseen by everyone except Jamesie Goss, who stared and went on staring at him out of sockets for eyes. Jamesie's stare made him afraid and he drew closer to Harriet. "I'm going to bury my beautiful child," he heard Sarah Goss say to his mother, her voice bearing down on him, sounding wounded and wolfish, and he thought he had heard before exactly the same words spoken in exactly the same dark way. He felt his mother draw in her breath as if to speak, then expel it on a gasp as she shook her head free of her shawl, and against her, for one second, Sarah Goss sagged, then with a frenzied shift she drew away, and the others were forming themselves into twos and threes and following her.

"Ma." He spoke to the tall line of Harriet's shawled back.

Harriet turned back to him. To the curious wishbone look: frail but resilient. In an attempt to ease conscience and wipe away the loneliness surrounding him, she pressed a penny into his hands. Those who fail always give. "See if Janey's below in the lane, or in with Chrissy Swords," Harriet said, and now she wanted to stay with him, but already Maisie was shouting to her to hurry up and, bending, she kissed him roughly and told him to be a good boy and hurried away.

He watched her catch up with them, his eyes behind his cracked glasses growing drier, brittler, then he turned back into the hall. He knew the uselessness of it but because he wanted to complete some act that she had actually set him, he knocked on Chrissy

Swords's door. There was no response and, becoming afraid of the sudden quiet and the dark of the hall, he hurried away, his hurry breaking into a frantic run as he touched the stairs.

Willie Reilly's feeble scratching on the door reached with the speed and power of a man's fist through the cold drip of silence and brought Christina Swords up from below the dark surface which the necessity for keeping herself still and concealed had finally sunk her, and now, slowly, as an animal will drag itself from the incomprehensible pangs of birth, she drew herself up from the slimy depths of the floor and stood reeling and uprooted in the evil green-stormed nightmare of the room. She did not know what had roused her, and was not even aware that anything had, sensing in her dream-choked head only the swamp of quiet to which her demons had at last abandoned her, and the immense tangle of what looked like seaweed and through which nothing was distinguishable, not even the thing on the bed over which she hung for one second before she groaned and turned her head away.

Filtered through ferns and the roots of water plants floating, she had heard the sounds that had gone through the rib and cage and bones of the house all through the long day, warring loud and lusty, unlike the preposterous slither of the water-snakes imprisoned in the labyrinth of her brain, a squirming sloughing of snakeskin that was meant to be heard by her and the haired ears of grinning devils. But with the noises of the house gone, the others were, too, and the sudden realization that they were struck deep and held her breathless in case breath itself disturbed to life again the thing that she knew lay in wait. She listened. In the grave damp chill of the house: no doors were opened. With native slyness she grew receptive, admitting the sight creeping back into her eyes already glazed and fixed for the rest of time: and as stirring senses eased out from under the grip of her will, she shuddered in violent recoil from the smiler with the knife beckoning her towards full remembrance and relentless consciousness.

With a brain within a brain she remembered the priest, the child's voice calling, the more authoritative woman's voice offering tea and the blasts of muttered anger when she wouldn't open the door. Cunning they were in their wizardry with their baits of tea and drops of hot soup made from the ratty carcass and bones of rabbits. Coming to her the stranger in the house and the stranger in her with unbent face. As if she didn't hear, know and see what lay behind the door of silence and their 'Are you there Chrissy's?' when all the time what they wanted was to lay their great big trunks of hands on her, but were they lightminded or drunk? To imagine she couldn't see through the quiet shell of her flesh what it was they were after?

But she was alone now in the room with only the high red-raddled walls to give back their grave-damp chill. There was nothing inside or outside the room but the living silence of the house: no doors were opened. Arbors of green spider silk shrouded all. Then the house shook and drawing up her still curiously solid body she began to gulp in great draughts of the room's quiet, seeing clearly the thing she was meaning to do. The thing she must do. She had a moment of great wonder – the magnificent wonder with which we discover the simple and unspeakable things that lie buried and known, but unconfessed, in us. Then a strange thing happened. The room was filled with a dark murmuring of boughs that came from green and shifting pines: from the veins of fleshy water plants and from the trunks of trees sown in watery rocky crevices. In the sough of wind the trees made it was as if something great and extraordinary was being explained.

"Yes," she said. Her hands searched.

223

"Yes," she said, but her hands could not find.

From the very center of her forehead a single crimson pinhead of blood formed and bubbled.

The room swelled and loosened.

The sound of the water was far away as though between her and it mountains towered. And yet, and since lucidity isn't necessarily a perpetual ailment, she realized instantly that this wasn't so, and that between her and it there were only two doors and then none, for her mind brushing past several old coats, hanging stiffly from nails on the back of the door, went to meet it, and it came through the speckled shade of surrounding trees decently and well-mannered, knowing its place, recognizing and respecting her horror, forgotten now, and no longer certain of its welcome. And it stayed on the threshold – the lapping water of inland seas – and searched with gray eye sockets the room's darkness hived with flesh and pain – and she saw it find her and look at her with scorn, with pity, with tenderness and with tears for something that lay in her, something that could not be seen at first glance; something the face of the woman that dwelt within her had never shown. But the eye within the eye, the brain within the brain, the woman within the woman, were alone now, strangers in the one room in the one house in the one street – and one of them moved but sideways and forwards like a crab whose shallows have been disturbed – and began then to follow the murmur that had begun to recede because now she had become afraid of the forms that slid, dropped and vanished.

Her eyes venous burned on her face which still wore its rags of flesh. Its fever fluctuated. The violet welts and crimson wounds glowed. The cat-forms slid. The night cold drew a wild cry from her lips. Wells of pain bubbled. Then heedless she went where the suave pouring of the water led: afloat in her stockinged feet tumbling down the steps and across the curfew-deserted street her hair streaming, her arms pinned to her sides, the tattered blood-stained skirt and flittered blouse pressed tight against the exulting length of her great limbs by the savage pressure of the crying wind.

From the bridge the roar of the water was tremendous now, raging in its own might, its own untrammelled power, thrashing in a maddened frenzy of torrents below the wet granite walls of

224

the locks, the black water rising to lip the rim with white foamed tongues of promised ease.

It had been there all this time.

Why had she never been told?

Halfway up the bridge she began to run towards the watery inferno – towards the penance and the sentence she had with her own voice given herself: towards the big doing, going towards her expiation with fury when a twisted foot on the cobbles threatened to send her sprawling to her knees instead. On and on she went, from a stagger to a run, she went round the curved wall of the bridge filled with a feeling of power she had never known before. At the black-tarred arm of the lock-gate she stopped, pressing the backs of her legs against it while she sucked in impotence at air saturated with fine stinging moisture.

A cloud rushed out of the moon's way and its light fell on her face, exposing with stunning and merciless clarity the mutilation of the senses whose death could be seen in the caverned eyes, the big naked eyes flowing with sudden dark and secret beauty. It may have been only the wind lifting the flittered banners of her blouse. Either way you couldn't be certain, for with a shudder she moved on and plunging towards her chastisement went head bent forward.

The splash was unseen, the howl of terror unheard, for the moon had dimmed behind what could have been the flame-tipped flush of roses of increasing crimson across the sky and the howl was drowned by the crackling of the city's fires, which in turn was silenced by the ghostly throbbing of great guns.

SEVEN

SUNDAY

1

In the stark swarming realities of noon no sound came from the machine guns or the trench mortars or the eighteen-pounders, and only occasionally could the swift evil spit of rifle fire be heard. In the ash-toned streets the Republican flag of hopeful green flew over isolated buildings; but the Rebellion had not ceased, nor was it true that one hundred German submarines freed from battles elsewhere and dispatched to Ireland's aid were anchored in the Liffey. And the rumor that England had been invaded in twelve different quarters and her fleet totally destroyed was also untrue, as was the legend that huge death-mocking German armies had landed on the Galway coast and that Spain had declared war on England on Ireland's behalf and the American Navy, stretching great benevolent hands across the sea, was rushing to her aid. What was true was that the Volunteers with fabulous and solitary wonder were surrendering all over the charred and still smoldering city, lurching with their bodiless phantoms and visionary fanaticism out of trenches and barricades in the wake of haunt-eyed leaders, trying desperately to recover what they had been part of, watched by hostile and murderous crowds who only days before in strewn and meaningless Irish largesse had applauded the Rebels' lonely adventure with death, but now queued in bitter antagonism and cringing apathy,

227

indifferent to the sight and sound of the surrender of guns and men in their greed for bread, glory no longer the deity it had been.

By five o'clock the flash and sparkle had gone slithering with disillusioned maturity out of the day, hurried on its way groaning and dry mouthed by a solitary gun that exploded once and was silent, as Republican flags were hauled down from buildings, their going unseen by the small band of snipers who suffocated by smoke and unyielding idealism still fought from rooftops, like lost dark angels hurtling their charges against the spires and ramparts of eternity – ignorant of the trickle that was turning into a flood of surrenders by their comrades in the streets below, and of the raids begun on the grand houses of the chosen who ruled above the rest from their menaced empires in the great Georgian squares of the city.

On the canal, hived evening life awoke in sharp broken fragments. In the blue dusk of twilight a soft wind pressed the boughs of trees. And above them thick clouds that for days had mitered the sulphurous ruins of a town and nation seething in the yeasty ferment of war had been torn asunder and through the deep ragged vault of the sky stars proud and splendid showed bright and unwinking. In houses still drugged with sleep and death people began to shift themselves. The bare feet of women moistly thawed and softened began to pound bare boards. In fetid bed warmth naked men ploughed slowly up out of milky boiling creeks like straining animals into the dark to search the darkness of their lives and the slow passage of the world for women on whose doors they had never knocked.

In the middle of the road Nan Oxer, who sang 'Star of the Sea' in the chapel's choir in the morning and played Chopin Nocturnes in the evening on the canal's one and only piano (and who couldn't bear to leave a chord), stood looking as if she had lost her way or was searching for something strange and passing. Past her a rabble rout of children who had escaped the pain, the horror, and the tarnished minstrelsy streel of death went full of life and business with jam jars and white caned nets to fish the canal.

228

Through the shadowed deepened dusk at the roots of trees whores dislocated and comic greeted their own and each other's survival with ironical obsequiousness, mocking and jeering at the world and each other in sisterly alliance. Through them and the manipulating shadows of trees and water and the lusty shouts of children, Billy Boy Beausang came looking anxious before he darted across the open stretch of black cobbles and ducked into the hall of Number Twelve.

I just hope to Christ she d-d-d-doesn't yap, he thought. He had a dark hungry face covered thickly with dark young hair. His face was delicate and fierce with black scowling eyes. He liked the hidden. The deep womb, the dark flower. The brooding dark of rain-sodden nights. He liked his women silent. Liked to see them in dark dens stir. He walked with quick stealth across the hall and up the stairs and rapped gently on the door, and opened it quietly, groping his way through the hot devouring red dusk to the bed in which Esther Quinn lay. She muttered as if drugged as he touched her, turned towards him, and sleepily awakened, reached and drew him down to her with heavied braceleted arms.

Esther was the yielding and sensual Jewess.

In her room below Maisie Collins lay quietly on her back in the shaded blue dusk listening to the deep and powerful lunged breathing of the sleeping man beside her. Outside in the blue light, there was a brisk stirring of life. A great thunder of flanked wheels and slowly climbing the rise of the bridge she could hear the heavy ringing clangor of shod hoofs. After the enormous silence, life was waking. Into it on the street outside a man hurled dark savage curses and then burst into hoarse unstrung hysterical weeping. In the Gosses' rooms above there was a faint clatter of cups and plates and voices. Wondering whose, Maisie marvelled at the resilience of humanity which could be shocked into insensibility one minute and, while still stunned, begin to drag itself upwards and continue again all the terrible agony of effort. It was monstrous and brutal that human beings should have to and be expected to. She thought of Jamesie Goss and his granite death-tinged face this morning and of the lost son that no one had been able to save for him. Of the ugliness of the ritual of mourning that must be observed: of the cemetery and the black feverish devouring eyes of Sarah Goss on Jamesie's face: of the swarming neighbors with their whispering and feeding with that obscene Irish hunger for death and the grim vision of always someone else's struggle and stark naked terror. And while her mind groped about and fumbled like a child at a million different little and big things her mind's eye swept clear and sharp over the day's events in and outside the house and lit on her meeting with Liam Martin and Mollo Goss in the hall this evening just before herself and Ba took to their bed.

From the faint cloying odor of tears of weeping ferns, incense, cheap fresh and withered flowers and the drawn-out sprawl of hard grief they had come and then gone over to the priest to put up the banns. Even with the ghost of grief in her eyes there was in the face of Mollo Goss a radiance in the strong clear cut of her features that in the past week Maisie had never thought to see again. But the cold detached eyes of the stranger miss nothing and looking at Liam Martin and seeking beyond the borders for what over years of listening and talking she had come to know was there she couldn't help thinking that only in fairy tales did men die cleanly.

Through Ba's bull-lunged laughter she had heard bits of what Liam Martin was saying and hadn't believed a word of it. No, Liam Martin hadn't lost his fixed vision of adventures into new lands. He was marrying Mollo Goss and staying in what she had heard him call 'this barren spiritual wilderness – this hostile and murderous entrenchment against all new life' – only because Dublin and Ireland was where Mollo wanted to be and because right now she meant more to him than his vision of America, on which he had set his sight ever since he discovered it was possible for a man to choose his own life. Well a man could draw in his range of vision. And be none the worse for doing so she had heard him say in answer to Ba's 'But what about America?' And no doubt it had sounded right then in his own ears, and even a little heroic to blather about the country's needs, about the struggle ahead for the country's survival, about one's own place in it; and she was sure he believed the things he was saying but he couldn't go on believing. He couldn't go on lying to himself. And when the blinding and maiming stopped? What then? What after? What now?

A face that wasn't Liam Martin's quartered like the moon across heaven. Harriet Reilly came swaying back and forth gravely and with alcoholic dignity. It was how Maisie had seen her this morning at the funeral. Had she found Janey? And what had them spendthrifts of energy the police said? And while she was at it what strain of wild unbridled romanticism had led Christina Swords astray? Eye hadn't been clapped on her. What strange happening had taken that woman so far from the shoaling tides? Later when she roused herself she would try Chrissy's door again and see if there was anything she wanted. Right now bed was the best place. The house felt thin and sere. She thought about the house and the people in the house and about what they would say when they knew about her. What miracle would they come up with? Harriet would say it was the three licks of the blessed salt. And Martha Liller, Ba's last erection. But it was neither.

Her full and sappy self was the direct result of years and years of prayers at Esther's altar. Nothing but. She was reminded of something and couldn't think what and then did. It was a tree. She had first seen it through a northerly wind and a flippant brightness. A giant old mulberry, split, patched and splintered, in the garden of a house she had worked in. It creaked barren and brittle in winter wind. Looking, you'd think it would never amount to much. Never come to life. But it did. Year after year in the spring it drew itself up then bent under a great load of fruit and heavy blossom. Growing young again. Overnight dark red mulberries glowed like blobs of blood and shook and clung to frail little stems. They fell bursting on the loamy wet earth when the wind blew. When the wind blew the garden was filled with the sounds of dropping and splashing.

Sleepless, straight, alert, her part of the sheet molded over her body she listened to the dropping; listened to the soft thick splash of ripe fruit. The sound spread on an undulant tremor that flowed through her great white body; her hips and her round heavy

231

breasts. Something new was cleaving making its own way. Staggering on through her flesh. The dark of the room was hived with flesh and mystery. The man beside her had flung and scattered. And loosened she had received like the stained moist earth under the mulberry tree. His seed. He drenched her with it. And it had flowed thick like white wax or milk from a breast. It had gone through her like blood through veins. Under the sheet her limbs and the heavy curve of her breasts moved. But how? When? After all this time. 'Balance on that and don't move'. But when? What night? Memory was ransacked and spaded and rolled back like flesh. Counting all the nights. Take it. Don't. The thick pour. The stream of white wax streaming. Full now she would fatten and plump. Growing young again. Till the blossoms dropping. The coal in the fire tossed sparks. There was a momentary rain of red cinders onto the hearth.

She turned her head on the pillow and with sharp wetted hunger thrust her right hand scratching down under the sheet to the dense hair-thicket between the man's powerful thighs. Her breath came quickly, her full tongue licked across her mouth. Gradually her fingers began to hoe gently round the thick root of the vine – until under them muscles twisted slow and veins protesting invitations swelled and throbbed and staggered up. Herself and the man began to moan softly. Between her hands she held his heavy clustered grapes . . .

Far off, she listened to the ghost of her own breath or voice.

"Now!"

She extended her arms as though for balance, the man threw the sheet back cleanly, swung in an orbit to a mounting position while beneath him she stretched her legs apart in a wide sweep and extended the great undulating mooned landscape of her body upward. She saw his dark boned structure, the broad muscled shoulders, the red glow of his tits in the undergrowth of hair on the full-breasted chest and for one moment in savage beast lust – the sculpturally and enormously heavied vine just before he buried it. It would find no barriers. Around the man's furnace-heated unmerciful thrust her arms and then her legs wrapped loose for what she knew would be a prolonged siege. Until the loaded

232

dewy richness of the man's thick white wax soaked the parched earth like rain falling. Until . . .

Into the broad column of the man's throat the woman sank her strong white teeth.

2

Streams of enormous silence slid in ghostly loneliness through the bones of the house and crept in like a sly dream to finger the stillness that had descended on the room after Mollo and Liam's going. It swamped with a thousand forgotten acts and moments the gray deserted shell of Jamesie Goss, who lay on his back on the bed, covered by his wife's black shawl, and filled with grief the already grieving burning eyes of Sarah, who sat, in an agony of repentance and guilty abasement, on a chair by the long window staring with tormented eyes into the deep indolent blue of the night. A deep haunted pain-ridden Irish city twilight through which nothing moved, for even the clouds mitering the Dublin mountains in the distance had stayed their amble across the face of the vaulted heavens and hung suspended like an arrested gesture, in photographic abeyance over the just-heard voices and briefly glimpsed figures that for a moment in their passing were touched by the topmost branches of the aisled trees standing in patriarchal dignity on the edge of the canal's banks. Underneath the trees at the grass and waters' edge, a little boy with an empty jam jar and a fishing net in his right hand paused in his hunt, forgetting his pursuit of a solitary pinkeen for the breathless moment of discovery, as he edged farther and farther out into the weeds for another and yet another look at the thing which had surfaced unbeknownst to him near the far bank, something which, as yet, was indistinguishable, but would in another minute send him shouting his horror over the bridge for the lock-keeper who – without rousing himself to undue haste for what was, after all, a commonplace – would fetch the sinister long handled hook which he kept for such occasions outside his door.

The commotion once begun would go unheard by Sarah, the shouts silenced by the effort she was making and would, for what was left of her life, go on making to understand the inexplicable absence of an emotion which she knew she should have felt and did not at the death of her son. Her despair, when she had learned of his death, she had forgotten. Forgotten, too, were her unreal whimpers of wonder and wild disbelieving this morning as she watched black strangers lower her son into that (never for one moment imagined) place, his grave. Now what she remembered was that after the first screaming shock, when the stranger on the stairs had gone and Mollo had left her and Jamesie alone while she went for the priest and Liam Martin, she had known a deep secret sense of relief. That was all.

The sensation, when she became aware of it, had downed her. Horror for herself had swarmed like poison through her blood. A raging hatred from which it seemed she must never recover; for she had loved her children; this she reiterated over and over to herself, stupefying by the assault of her emotions her intelligence and blinding her to the answer which lay on her lap and which her clasping, unclasping hands fingered like her rosary beads. It wasn't nature not to love your children, not to want to repossess the flesh to which she had given life, and the unnatural terrified her, and yet it was true that with all the love she should have had for them, and did have, in the final summation she loved Jamesie more.

On the bed he turned his head and his eyes strayed round the new empty desolation of the room, then came to rest on her. She felt their weight and turned from the window and her thoughts.

"You mustn't fret yourself," he said, his voice strangling in his throat.

He had said the same thing earlier, only then she had been

covering him with her shawl and while she stood looking down on his ravaged face and eyes which mirrored his son's, before they had gone rheumy with sorrow, she had been tempted to tell him the cause of her torment, knowing even as she thought of doing so that she wouldn't, not now, Lord, not ever. He would not have understood, and she could not have explained how she felt about him and the children and the years when the children were enough – and so they had been, for as long as she knew they needed her. While theirs had lasted, her own need had been forgotten, remembered again only when they were both grown, and by then it *was* too late. She couldn't remember now when she had been first aware that it *was* too late, aware of the tie that existed between Jamesie and John; or when it was she first felt, and what it was that had made her feel, like a trespasser when she ventured too close to the fortress they had built up around themselves. She imagined there must have been a first moment of awareness, but if there was the memory had escaped her utterly. She recalled only her turning to Jamesie, expecting to find with him her remembered place, and discovering too late that he had found in his son the deeper more binding emotions which she, in her remissness, had neglected to give him all those years. It was then she began to hate her son. Hating the lost stricken thing in him that he would never find. Hating his dark brooding face, his deep absorption in a dream, his lean hungry look, the air of anarchy and arrogance in the sudden proud stiffening of the chin, the dark outraged mouth and the level gaze that told nothing. The secret life – the interior world he shared with no one but Jamesie and which she could never touch and never understand, and into which he sank year after year – choked her with fury. As did the strange cataract of tenderness that bloomed like some dark flower between them. Sometimes, frantic with some swift tangle of nerves, or rebelling with biting vitality against the grimy smudges of their lives she would attack him viciously. Seeing his dark face brooding over a book or some vision she would tear the book from his hands and in a sweltering and inchoate fury fling it into the fire or out the window – ripping him apart with her cruel savage tongue – screaming her poisonous hatred in a torrent of venom, finding a scalding but purging release in her savage

236

attack upon him and at the same time crucifying herself with a gallows-black guilt which no amount of chapel-going or knee-bending at Esther's altar could rid her of. And always down the long horde of the lost bright years of her life blaming him for his and her own sickening defilement and holding him responsible for the loss of a love that only Mollo, with her deeper intuition and from her position of enforced detachment, knew she had never possessed.

But she had, Christ knows she had! loved John in spite of it, and yet and yet, there was this terrible gap, this appalling absence. She could not feel the sorrow that she felt she ought to feel for John. The sorrow she labored under was for Jamesie. It was Jamesie she wanted to help and couldn't, him above all she longed to console: the trumpeted thought was almost audible as she watched him throw back the shawl with a clawed hand and raise himself off the bed.

"Why don't you stay and rest yourself?" she said somewhat timidly.

"Stop coddling me," he spoke over the head of the ghost playing tricks with his bootlaces; and Sarah knew it, knew his bewitched and listening face was turned again to the hidden world.

"The place feels queer and empty," he said, his eyes beginning again their search for that strange bright loneliness that would not return. When they reached the curtain in the doorway of the little room they rested, and she knew he was seeing the empty bed which tomorrow she would take down and hide away somewhere.

As if unsure of the tenancy of his own body he made his way slowly, more slowly than ever over to the chair beside her. Easing his long spent sparse frame onto it, he turned his face to the light. "Are you happy about Mollo and Liam?" Sarah asked, her eyes on his hands lying on his knees upward and open as if he had just let go of something.

He nodded without looking at her.

"Liam's a good man and will make a good husband," she said hopefully, deliberately striving to move one step, then another, away from the watch at the chapel last night, away from

237

the barbarism of that raw open ditch this morning, but unable (or unwilling) to inject into the question and comment the energy required to dispel the sounds of the gathering of ghosts.

"When children start going, they go fast," she said.

"Everything is going. Everything changes and passes away. Tomorrow we will be gone and . . ." he stopped.

"They were children for such a little while," Sarah said quietly.

And now they were gone, thought crippled, prowled over the lost years, the forgotten days, the unremembered hours. First his lovely lost son! Jamesie's mind protested against remembering how it was God had taken his child, his son, his lost and virgin flesh, from him, clawing desperately past the place at which his mind hesitated and rushing on after the elusive memory that was all he had of Mollo, all he would ever have of Mollo, for somehow she had always been so much Sarah's, and now she would be Liam's. But for a moment he clutched at the elusiveness of his own making, then he released his grip on her, as he so often had when she and John were children on the canal and he was unable to keep up with them, when like fawns they vanished into the long grass, vanished, returned, vanished calling back to him to come and find them. John never waited to be found but would come with cat-speed tumbling out of his hiding place as if he dared not risk it and panting with shining excitement would appear beside Jamesie, tugging the leg of his trousers and shouting, "I'm here, my Da. I'm here"; and he, in turn, pretending neither to hear nor feel nor see the lost child face would wait for something which was no part of the game but which he knew would come, he would step back then and regard John with feigned surprise before stooping down suddenly and gathering up into his arms the slender wiry strength of his body, his fine small-boned resiliency, and hearing against his face the breathless murmured child-sayings. In an agony of love he would stand crushing him, stroking him and kissing his child's tawny flesh. He would be filled with granite strength then, and drunk with the mad surge of love for the child in his arms, a wild powerful love through which his heart and soul soared, making him a match for giants or gods, obliterating completely the fretful humiliating failures, the unfinished enterprises, the lost

238

dead lusts, the unfound door and the mourned deaths of the dreams. He was deathless James John Maria Goss then, and in his arms and against his heart he held his son, his unchanging Him. And in the grass, fretting him back to earth, Mollo kneeling complaining, "Nobody ever finds me".

My son! My son! My child! Come back! Come back!

Against his closed lids the cry beat with the flapping wings of frantic birds and he paused breathless as he willed the extinction of his own heart, but it pulsed and throbbed over the wish in stubborn perseverance, and he opened his eyes to find Sarah staring at him.

"What is it?" he asked gently, feeling the force of her moon-bright eyes.

"Nothing."

For if he did not know that he had just now cried aloud, she would not tell him . . . no more than she would ever tell him about last night, when he had sat up in bed to cast his arms forth in agony, in bewilderment. He had cried all night long, softly and fitfully in his sleep, like a child, and she could only lie there, not able to touch him in any way, not able to reach into that long night of dream deaths and save him, not able to do anything but listen. And listening, she had not heard Mollo get up out of her bed in the next room and come to the doorway until she was there and heard her whisper: "Da's crying!" She hadn't answered, but gestured the girl back to bed while she had gone on listening . . . listening . . . and all the time, Jamesie had cried.

And there she was all that long haunted night, loving him yet not able to help him. And as she sat there more quietly now, swarming pity rose in her – not for herself alone, but for herself and Jamesie, and for the waste, the confusion, the groping accident of life. She thought of the loneliness of love. Because that in some mysterious way was what it was: a world of loneliness after the island of isolation which you had created out of nothing more lasting than the passions of your own flesh . . . with no more substance than that of which dreams are made and on which you managed to live and draw breath adrift from the world like a child's kite in the air, only half aware of the things going on around you, but independent and unconcerned for didn't day dawn and night fall and always in between was the loved and the loving?

And then, plants in the black wintered earth, children grew up ... the process nurtured by you and them sprouting thoughts and demands like the green shoots of the plant ... and the geranium-pot tight little world in which you held them collapsed under the relentless hammer blows of year being added to year, and the fabric of the island unwound in the unravelling waves of clashing emotions, and when the waters did at last recede you were alone. Stranded and destitute among the débris of your own making ... and they were gone the way Mollo would go and the way John was already gone ... the way now that Jamesie was gone, and the love you had borne them kept you apart. And yet the chaos in which human life often ended, in which hers was ending now, wasn't all your own making ... and Sarah, who had never given more heed than she felt necessary to the teachings of her church, clutched now at half-remembered Faith. For how often in reply to a mildly voiced complaint had Father Robinson shut her up by reminding her that 'Everything is God's Will', and our trials and tribulations part of the plan, ending his admonishments with the comforting phrase that we are not alone!

But we are alone. She was alone, monstrously alone, caught between the window of sky and the moon bright ghost silence of her life and nothing to help her across the soaring ranges of her despair at losing Jamesie and at not being able to grieve more than she did for the death of John. She *was* alone, terribly alone, a limb hacked from a body, and God was nowhere in sight, and her eyes closed on a great burst of longing, not for Him but for the life, the crowded world of loving in which she had drawn breath ... past, past, for now it was all yesterday and tomorrow ...

Sarah sat heavily on her chair, her face bent sideways. She was weeping, her face contorted by the comical and ugly grimace that is far more terrible than any quiet beatitude of sorrow. She wept not for Jamesie or for herself, or even for the boy whom idiot chance had thrust in the way of British soldiers' bullets –

but for all who had lived, were living, or would live fanning with the might of their prayers the useless altar flames, suppliant with their hopes to an unwitting spirit, launching the deep-hungering missiles of their belief against remote eternity, hoping for grace, guidance, and delivery upon the spinning and forgotten bier of this earth.

"If only I'd known," she began presently, "if only I'd known how and where it would end —"

She turned her face away.

And Jamesie, stricken and bewildered and unable to help her, got to his feet and stood watching, listening to his name trailing off into the black shock of her bent head, remote and aloof, held from her by his own stunned sorrow and by the wind-grieved ghost at his side. The dark lost face gleamed like a sudden and impalpable fawn within the thickets of memory. He turned away and his hands went in a clumsy familiar gesture to the cap of his white head, fighting off Sarah's misery and the ghosts and the paralysis of restraint with violent blows of his fists. For a moment the blood quickened in his veins, filling him with a strength that was false, but was enough, and for the first time a full consciousness of her bore down upon him, and he moved and knelt beside her, gripping her hands, rough from a lifetime of work and healing, in his, and muttering incoherently he buried them against his mouth.

But he was cheating Sarah, lying in his teeth, cheating her with words spun from his own terrible inadequacy to grant her the fufilment which in the evening of her day she had every right to expect, doing nothing more than mumble lies with which he hoped to stifle her sad and bitter lament. He had heard her cry before, but he had heard her laugh, too, laughing when, Christ knows! she had little to laugh about . . . laughing when he was without a job, and at his and the children's needs, her laugh hiding the shattering efforts she was making to supply them, making light and little of his desperate failures, minimizing by her attitude, sprung from her love for him, their importance, so that for him, too, the waste lost its power . . . spending herself in overwhelming generosity on him and the children she'd borne him . . . wanting but never asking, that they in

241

turn should give her what was most certainly her due. And he had cheated her for all those years . . . robbing and denying her the only thing for which she had ever in their life together asked him. And bowing to the inexorable tides of necessity he must and would continue to cheat her, for now what Sarah wanted was no longer his to give and he —

With the very quiet despair of a man who knows the forged chain cannot be unlinked, the threaded design unwound, the done undone, he turned his head away from the great mask of her grief and the eyes shining through it with an unnameable lust, a terrible and indecent hunger. In a sudden rush of bitterness he got to his feet and raised his head and let his gaze stray to the window and beyond it to the huge immensity of the sky through which his mind's eye hurried, seeking and finding the new raw ditch in the raw clumped earth which now held all there had ever been of himself outside himself. A wild, strange cry was torn from his stonily clamped mouth.

Slowly the coffin was lowered on two ropes held by four men into the grave.

A handful of dirt fell.

"I am the resurrection and the life —"

He watched until the first shovel of dirt was thrown into the grave. He saw the new raw grave, the sere long grasses, noted how quickly the flung mourning flowers had wilted. Then he looked up at the high cold terror of the stars. His love. His lost dark stranger. It would make the grass greener and the flowers sweeter, that love he had never given Sarah. It would plump the worms which even now would have found and begun to feed. And beside him, Sarah, withered and grown old from his denial, clutching his pauperous self to her as if his robbery of her had never happened, begging a thing from him who for so long had been destitute of it. Did she know? And if she didn't need she ever?

Her crying had stopped and now the terrible silence came between them once again. He felt her eyes and turning to peer down at her he saw the answer. Smiling tremulously she got to her feet. "I'll make a cup of tea," she said. Her words, he thought, were light and lightly spoken, and they both knew why, but

242

she was sparing him even now, not wanting him to hear the bitter song of all her life, not wanting him to know that she knew or even that she had missed the love he had been unable to give her all those years, not wanting to burden him, or rather to shell that was all that was left of him, saving him a knowledge that she knew would lacerate.

Behind him he heard her drag herself above the waste land of the past, above the dusty racket of their lives and, busying herself with little things, knew she was readying herself to go on. There would be no forgetting, no forgiving, no denying, no explaining, no hating. He heard her stir the fire to life, and wait on her knees beside it until the flames grew into vigorous life before she placed the kettle above them. But something was missing. No echo of her lingered in the corners of the room the way it used to, vibrating with sturdy vitality that made people say Sarah Goss could be heard a mile away. They would not be able to say that any more, for Sarah had changed. His eyes were blind with tears for what he felt and wanted to say and now never would. Everything was passing. Nothing stayed the same but people pretended it did . . . they had to, had to settle for something less than the dream.

The Dublin mountains were blooming in the dusk.

Only the mountains in their moon bright silence refused to surrender to the dark menace and savage chaos of human life.

My son! My love! My child! Come back! Come back!

At the table Sarah heard and waited. But no word came to her, no word could come; he was crying and kept crying again and again, "My son! My love! My son!" And looking. Frozen in the moonlight Jamesie Goss was combing the night with the blind searchlight of his heart for the dark flickering grin on the face of the lost ghost for whom his heart would still be weeping when they found his eyes cold.

"Poor man! Poor man!"

At the table Sarah, rigid and still, whispered huskily, faintly.

In the sky the stars which had paused in their majestic pro-
cessionals across the vaulted heavens to witness in the death-
flared dusk the final convulsive death throes of the week-old
Revolution moved on . . . and on the canal they bundled the
thing they had taken from the dark sullen waters into a horse-
drawn cab . . . and in the hall Maisie Collins hesitated, for she
had knocked once on the door and got no answer. "I'll give her
one more go," she said, but didn't. Instead she turned the brass
handle on the door of Christina Swords's room and went in.